HIS LAST BREATH

DI KAREN HEATH CRIME SERIES

JAY NADAL

Published by 282publishing.com

For Barbara.

Thank you for your unconditional support and kindness.

PREFACE

Question… After they have chopped off my head, will I still be able to hear, at least for a moment, the sound of my blood gushing from my neck? That would be the best pleasure to end all pleasure, don't you think?

The strange thing is, I've always had a desire to inflict pain on others and to have others inflict pain on me. A strange symbiotic relationship. The desire to inflict pain, that is all that's uppermost in my mind from the moment I wake.

One side of me says, I'd like to talk to him, date him, lose myself in him. The other side of me says, I wonder what his head would look like on a spike or on the top shelf of my fridge?

Some may say I'm a psychopath, a loony, or just fucking unhinged. But I prefer the term creative. If you could read my mind, I'm sure you'd be traumatised for life, because it's a dark place, a one-way ticket to hell.

When this monster entered my brain, I will never know, but it's here to stay. How does one cure themselves? I've not found the answer, and maybe I don't want to find it. I can't stop it, the monster goes on, and hurts me and society. Maybe you can stop this. I can't.

If you see me walking down the street, cross the road, please cross the road for your own safety, or you might not see tomorrow morning.

1

"I'm missing a date with a chicken chow mein and a bottle of cold beer for this." Karen sighed as she stepped out of the car. The last week had seen temperatures soar in London. As Karen walked into a wall of dry heat that drained all her energy, the cool air conditioning of Jade's car appealed as the first beads of sweat broke on her forehead. Her blouse, though fine and sheer, clung to her back like a wet blanket. She made her way towards the cordon, lamenting her unattractive and soggy appearance.

It amazed her how everything in London slowed to a snail's pace when the city basked in extreme temperatures. Conversations stalled, people walked slowly, and the pace of life felt as if it ground to a halt. The soupy air forced every breath from the lungs, making them feel laboured. Recent weather forecasts had warned about a layer of smog that hung above the capital, casting a grey hue that pinned the heat in and tightened the chest.

Karen struggled in this weather even though it created a

pleasant change from the long, damp winters. She woke up sweaty, went to bed sweaty, and got out of the shower sweaty. The oppressive and ever-present heat lasted every day. Without respite. Without end. An eternal, horrible blast furnace. As she glanced around, even the trees appeared defeated. Leaves that should be firm and upward tilting drooped, flaccid as old lettuce.

Jade threw her jacket on to the back seat of her car and wrapped her bobbed hair around her ears to cool herself.

She glanced out over Virginia Road, a typical cramped suburban street. To one side stood a row of terraced housing, and to the other a housing association block of flats. Karen smiled to herself as she noticed that the block was called Mandela House. The presence of several police cars, two white scientific services vans and several unmarked cars added to the cramped feel of the road. A row of cars parked on either side meant tight access, and cars were getting stuck at each end of the road. Karen noticed that police officers were at each end of the street allowing the road to be cordoned off.

Onlookers walked past slowly, and residents positioned themselves by their windows, peering through the net curtains, as their evening entertainment played live to them.

When the call had come in from a distraught resident, Karen had been wrapping up for the evening and completing some case file reviews for her officers. She'd had her evening all planned out, stopping off at the local Chinese takeaway in Epping before heading home to settle down with her meal. She doubted if she would be in the mood for food after this.

Karen and Jade signed in with the scene guard before they

donned Tyvek coveralls, masks, green nitrile gloves and blue overshoes before entering the property. Protocol required all officers entering any crime scene to wear the appropriate protective clothing in order to reduce the risk of any skin cells, hair or clothing fibres contaminating the scene, and help protect officers from the risk of exposure to biological substances, dirt and liquid splashes.

The two officers exchanged glances as they walked into the house. The extra layer of clothing added to the misery and discomfort they felt.

"Jesus fucking Christ, I'm bloody melting in this."

"Just think of an ice-cold Magnum, boss," Jade teased. "Or an igloo in Antarctica. With penguins."

"I don't think a *box* of Magnums would help at the moment."

It appeared to be a compact house from the front, but a Tardis from within. There were some stairs to Karen's right. To her left was a long hallway with doors leading off to the lounge, dining room, study and a kitchen towards the far end. The light from outside faded the further she looked down the hallway. From initial inspection, the rooms appeared to be well proportioned. Karen took a few moments to look around the lounge from the doorway. A grey corner sofa suite took up a large proportion of the room, a large television hung from the wall, and the floors had been sympathetically stripped back to their natural wood. Some plants sat on the windowsill, and black-and-white prints of the coastline and shells dotted the walls.

Everything seemed to be in its proper place with no signs of disturbance, and none had been reported. She made her way into the kitchen. It was filled with modern appliances, mainly Neff, but she noticed an expensive Smeg retro fridge. It had been the exact one she had considered for her own apartment and knew from her own research that it cost one thousand six hundred pounds.

"It's this way, boss," Jade chipped in as she stood at the bottom of the stairs, having taken a brief update from one of the uniformed officers.

"Have we got a name for the vic?"

"Yes, ma'am. Adam Manners. Aged thirty-four."

As they both climb the stairs, the heat intensified in the narrow walkway until they turned and reached the top landing. Karen made her way towards the front of the house before she stopped in the doorway of what she imagined to be the master bedroom. Two forensic officers in matching outfits to her own examined the area.

Mason Brophy, the crime scene manager stood off to the side, and stepped away from his two officers to join Karen at the doorway. "This is a nasty one. We are advanced in our examination of the scene, so you can take a closer look when you want to."

"What have you done so far?"

"The usual. Cordons are in place; the scene has been preserved and a risk assessment undertaken because we found evidence of toxic fumes. We needed to make sure it was safe enough before going in. Anyway, we've documented and photographed most of the crime scene. You'll find most of the evidence recovered in my van, and the exhibits officer will stick it on the system for us. We've still to remove the tape across the victim's mouth and the cable ties. There's a good chance we might lift some prints or DNA off them."

Karen nodded her approval. "Thanks, Mason. Meticulous as ever; appreciate it."

"Whoever did this was mad as a meat axe," Mason added.

Karen smiled. Mason's accent always amused her. Even though he'd been in the UK for fourteen years, he'd never lost his Kiwi twang.

The tall, gangly figure of Christopher Wainwright, the pathologist, sat crouched by the body, making notes, and looking up at the body, and nodding to himself. The stench of death reached her nostrils. All officers got used to the putrid smell, but never accepted it. She took a step back into the cramped hallway and bumped into Jade.

The sun poured in through the bedroom windows and heated the room to an unbearable temperature, each window acting as a magnifying glass. Unfortunately for them it had also sped up the decomposition process.

Karen took a deep breath to compose herself before making her way back into the bedroom, followed by Jade. She stopped at the foot of the bed and examined the victim. He was a naked white male, each wrist tied to a bedpost with white cable ties, and his mouth sealed with silver duct tape. Her eyes were drawn to the man's groin and what appeared to be extensive scarring and burns around his genitals. The wounds were still fresh, red and blistered. The skin had melted and formed a gnarly, sticky mess.

Karen scanned the room, noticing the presence of a few houseflies. She'd seen enough of them at crime scenes to know what damage they caused to the evidence left behind.

A quick check of the windows confirmed that one louvre had been left ajar. It amazed her how houseflies could sniff out dead flesh and gases released by a body. She had no doubt that left undiscovered for a few more days, the body would have been in the advanced stages of decomposition.

There appeared to be little evidence of any other trauma to the body. There were no signs of an altercation, and nothing had been disturbed.

Wainwright was in the middle of rambling to himself in a hushed tone when he twisted over his shoulder to see Karen and Jade.

"Ah, ladies. Good to see you. Sadly, the setting leaves much to be desired, but it's an interesting case."

"Aren't they always interesting?" Karen asked. She blew out her cheeks causing her mask to inflate for a few seconds. "What have you found so far?"

Wainwright stood and took a few steps back to stand along-side the women, his tall frame towering over them. He took a few moments to compose his thoughts as he stared at the body. "Well this poor chap has experienced severe burns to the groin region."

Karen tutted. "Well, that's obvious, Wainwright. Tell me something we don't know…"

"You can be so impatient sometimes, Karen."

"As much as I enjoy your dulcet tones, we do have a crime scene, and the first twenty-four hours are vital. So as much as I would love to stand and chat, I'm melting in this thing, and don't want to hang around," she said, tugging at her suit.

Wainwright nodded and laughed; he was never one to be riled by Karen.

"At the moment I can't confirm the cause of death. I can't see any evidence of any injuries sustained that may have led to his death. Other than the horrific burns to his groin, I can't see much else. There's some dried residue on his thighs, and around his mouth. But that's all I have to go on at the moment. I will know more once I've conducted the PM first thing in the morning."

"Time of death?"

"Within the last forty-eight hours. More likely less than that. The heat doesn't help. That sped things up a tad. I'd say this was the initial stage which is the first one to two days. Bloating hasn't begun which happens after forty-eight hours and within the first week. I've examined the body's orifices, and I found evidence of eggs in the nostrils and ears, and some on the wound area. These eggs often hatch within twenty-four hours to release a larva or maggot."

Karen nodded and digested the information, grateful for Wainwright's insights. She thanked him and confirmed that she would attend the post-mortem tomorrow morning. Turning towards Jade, they stepped back out into the hallway. "Who found the victim?"

"His wife, Jackie Manners. She had been away on a business trip in Edinburgh and returned to discover his body. Poor woman."

"And where is she now?"

"They have taken her to hospital suffering from shock. Shall I appoint a FLO?"

"Yes, please. Arrange for someone to meet her at the hospital. We need to make sure we get a full statement from her if she's up to it."

Jade made her way down the stairs to arrange for officers to attend the hospital, leaving Karen to take in the scene. With no visible cut marks, stab wounds, gunshot wounds or strangulation marks, it left Karen considering the cause of death. When she had attended murder scenes before, there had often been tell-tale signs that confirmed the likely cause of death. In her experience, most of her cases had focused around strangulation, fatal wounds inflicted with a sharp instrument or blunt force trauma. On first inspection, none were apparent. It left her with a burning question which would determine the path of her investigation.

What happened to Adam Manners?

2

At the mortuary, Jade reversed her car into an available slot alongside Wainwright's. She had stopped off along the way to pick up Karen, and they had taken a detour to pick up some coffee en route. Jade had offered to buy them breakfast, but Karen had dismissed the idea knowing just how uncomfortable post-mortems made her feel.

According to Wainwright, the post-mortem would begin at nine a.m. sharp, so they'd arrived about thirty minutes later, giving him ample time to begin his preliminary observations. After being let in by a mortuary technician, they had been given gowns and masks before being shown into the main examination room.

Pushing through the doors, the tones of classical music that wafted around the cold and clinical space greeted them. The heavy and nauseating smell of disinfectant and air freshener swirled through the atmosphere and wriggled its way through the microscopic pores in their face masks. The air conditioning unit above them pumped cooled air into the room, sending a shiver racing down Karen's spine. Wainwright hummed along whilst examining the cadaver, he bobbed his head in time with the music, and seemed lost in his own little world.

The design of mortuary examination rooms created a minimalistic aesthetic with tiled floors that matched the white-tiled walls. Three stainless steel tables in a row lined the centre of the room. Each one had a slight dip towards the foot end which led to a hole in the table from which bodily fluids could drain into a sink attachment. A small silver hose and nozzle was attached to the sink. A bank of fridge doors filled one wall, the other three had shiny steel work surfaces and a few sinks which allowed the mortuary team to conduct more detailed examinations of organs.

"We're not interrupting anything are we?" Karen asked, as both her and Jade stood to the opposite side of Wainwright.

He let out a small laugh from behind his face visor.

"Sorry, I didn't see you come in. Karen, if you want to do this properly, then you need to ensure you're on time. I could have discovered something significant, and you wouldn't have been here to inform."

Karen folded her arms. "And did you find something important?"

"What? No. Not on this occasion."

"So, Wainwright, you're blowing hot wind for nothing? Huh?"

Jade remained silent as she watched the two of them wind each other up.

The humour released some of the tension. To the outside

world, a mortuary was a sombre place where those who met the end of their lives came before their final place of rest. But to Wainwright and his staff, it was a place of work. They respected those brought here, but it didn't stop them from sharing experiences most employees would have in organisations up and down the country. They talked about what they did last night, what they had for dinner, holiday plans going forward, hangovers and relationships.

Wainwright took a step back and cast his eye up and down the cadaver as if admiring an abstract piece of art.

For a moment Karen and Jade joined him. The body of Adam Manners lay on a cold steel examination table. A rubber brick that Wainwright referred to as a "head block" sat under the shoulders of the cadaver, hyperflexing the neck making the spine arch backwards whilst stretching and pushing the chest upward making it easier to perform incisions. The front of his torso had been cut in the shape of a Y, beginning just beneath his collarbone, before joining at the sternum and down to his pubic region.

Having seen many of Wainwright's post-mortems, Karen knew he followed a four-step process every time, including inspecting the body's exterior; examining the internal organs' position and appearance; dissecting and examining the internal organs; and the laboratory analysis of tissue, fluids and other specimens.

They had removed the front part of the ribs and breastbone in one piece, exposing most of the organs. Karen placed a hand over her mouth. Despite witnessing these numerous times, she couldn't get past the point of thinking that the innards looked like a stewing pot from a cannibalistic tribe in the Amazon rainforest.

Wainwright glanced at the body. "Well, it's not a pretty sight."

"Bloody hell, you're not joking. He's a right mess," Karen replied.

"Adam Manners was five feet eight, of average height, weight and build. An external examination of his body revealed no distinguishing marks, such as birthmarks or moles." Wainwright reached for one hand. The pale fleshy limb hung loosely. "There are ligature marks and soft surface abrasion around both wrists which we would expect having found the body with both wrists secured with cable ties. At the scene I wasn't sure, but I can confirm that the victim struggled. There's evidence of the skin being broken in places with deep tissue damage."

"He must have been in some excruciating pain…"

Wainwright nodded in response.

"We've scraped his fingernails so that any material beneath may be examined for traces of skin or blood, possibly that of an attacker. His pubic hair was combed for traces of skin and we swabbed the area around the sexual organs." Wainwright's commentary stopped as he focused on the man's groin region. "He experienced significant tissue damage and burns to the groin. So yes, if he was conscious when this was inflicted, I'm certain the pain would have been indescribable."

"Any thoughts on the substance used?" Jade interjected.

Wainwright grimaced. "Hard to say. We've taken samples of tissue for analysis, but my guess is something toxic or caustic. Probably acid based. Other than that, I can't be certain."

"Sex game gone wrong, and then the victim killed?" Jade proffered. "It wouldn't be the first time."

Karen shook her head. "Well, there was a sexual element involved in the beginning, being naked, gagged and tied up, and possibly dried bodily fluids. But things took a turn. That's fucking torture," she added, pointing towards the disfigured groin. "I can't think of anyone in their right mind who'd say, I know, let's throw some acid on my cock."

Jade scrunched her face as a vivid picture formed in her mind.

Karen walked around the table, pausing every few seconds to look at the cadaver from different angles. "Could he have died from those injuries?"

Wainwright's forehead creased, his eyes darkening. "There are no discernible wounds or marks, so I checked the deceased's eyes. If suffocation or smothering has taken place then the eyes would have been bloodshot, with some bruising around the nose and mouth. But there's none. I've collected trace evidence such as hairs and fibres from around the nose and mouth just to be sure."

Karen stared at the corpse and swallowed. "Are you sure?"

"At the moment I can't confirm the cause of death until further analysis, so far my results are inconclusive. There's no trauma to the head, and we'll examine the brain when we remove the skull."

Frustration crawled up Karen's spine. She hoped there would be enough evidence to get the investigation off on a strong footing. "Wainwright, give me something. Anything. There must be something you've found?"

"Well, there's residue on the thighs, possible dried semen. We've taken samples, and then there's this…" Wainwright took a thin metal probe.

Karen leant in closer to see the exact spot where Wainwright held his probe on the cadaver's arm. "Puncture wound? Needle?"

"Looks like it to me," Wainwright replied.

"Drugs?"

He shook his head. "I'm uncertain. It's a single puncture wound, not typical for an addict. You'd expect track marks up and down his arm, perhaps some behind his knees. But it's a single mark. The bloods will confirm any evidence of substances."

Karen wondered if the needle mark could be significant as the case progressed. The shrill, high-pitched sound of the high-speed oscillating saw interrupted her thoughts. She joined Jade at the foot of the table away from the grisly action as Wainwright's technician used the saw to expose the brain. He had parted the hair and made an incision behind the ears and across the base of the scalp. The front part of the scalp had been reflected over the face and the back part over the nape, exposing the skull.

A few minutes later, and the skull cap was separated from the rest of the skull with a chisel. It allowed Wainwright to examine the meninges, a covering of the brain, and the inside of the skull for signs of infection, swelling, injury or deterioration.

Wainwright peered inside. "Brain looks intact, no visible injuries or trauma."

He moved back towards the torso and proceeded to tie off

the major vessels at the base of the neck, before severing the oesophagus and trachea just above the thyroid cartilage.

Karen watched in bewilderment as Wainwright moved around the cavity with speed and precision. He pinched off the aorta above the diaphragm and cut it and then removed the heart and lungs together. Each organ was examined, weighed and documented on a large whiteboard behind them. There wasn't much left of the victim once Wainwright had removed everything other than a bloodied cavity.

"Damn..."

"What?" Karen piped up. She exchanged a glance with Jade.

"I still can't identify anything that would suggest or contribute to the cause of death. Blood loss was minimal, and there are no penetrative wounds."

Karen blew out her cheeks and paced the room as Wainwright continued his examination. "So, time of death?"

"My initial estimation still stands, Karen. His body was cold and stiff when I first arrived. With a rectal temperature reading and factoring in the heat in the room and eggs in his ears and nose, I'd estimate that he died between eight and sixteen hours prior to his discovery."

Karen and Jade left Wainwright to complete the examination, with the promise that he'd call through if any further evidence came to light.

3

Death and pain fascinate me. Intrigue me. What does it take for someone to feel pain so extreme that they would much rather die than live? Satisfying that curiosity compels me forward, sending every nerve ending firing with a perverse pleasure. Do people have a breaking point? That question burns in the front of my mind. It seems it always has.

I started out pranking people because I loved the reaction. A jab of the compass tip in the arm, a hidden drawing pin on a chair, and daring people to put their finger in the naked flame of the Bunsen burner at school. The more they hurt, the greater the surge of satisfaction that rips through me. I always search for the weakest, those who live their lives in isolation, who are defenceless and don't have people to stand up for them. They prove to be the easiest targets.

My mind drifts back to those fun days at school. With my innocent expression, very few knew that evil hid behind my smile, just waiting to show itself. Many found me friendly, but my smile represents a diabolical selfishness that I alone savour.

I read something once that unkind people excuse their rude, venal and even cruel behaviour because the recipients deserve it. But I don't see myself as unkind, simply curious, adventurous and artistic. I express the free-thinking side of myself. I drive it by compulsion and just one question that precedes everything I do, "What if?"

We didn't have much growing up. I played up for the other kids and they took pity on me. They called me a charity shop reject, with ill-fitting clothes, that were often a little too short, and out of fashion. I knew nothing new, unless I stole it. Oxfam was the go-to place for my mum, and that didn't help me. Some kids saw me coming out of the Oxfam on the High Street and word soon spread around school. So, I guess it brought me more attention than I wanted.

Kids can be so bitchy. Hair pulling, sticking chewing gum in my hair, taking the loo roll out of every cubicle so I ended up shitting myself and running home. After enduring endless taunting and mean-spiritedness, I declared them the evil shits, not me. I hid the bruises well. It soon became hard to recall which ones I received at home and which I received from school.

Mum said I needed to appreciate stuff more, and would leave me outside every day at weekends, especially during the cold and wet winter months. She insisted it would make me value what I had, not focus on what I lacked.

But I guess at some point, though I can't remember exactly when, the tide turned, and something changed. It felt like something snapped in me. My tolerance levels became non-existent. The novelty of sticking compass points into myself or other kids evaporated, it no longer excited me, and left a dulled response in its wake. I tried to create the same feeling in other ways. It started with pinching myself, not gently or in a playful way, but using pliers I found in a small toolbox beneath the stairs. The cold steel on my arm tickled my skin, and I would pinch and twist until pain rocketed through me, watering my eyes.

It wasn't long before they confiscated those pliers from me at school as other kids grassed on me. A call to my parents only worsened the situation, and to this day I still feel the stinging pain across my cheek from my mum. Bitch.

Sally Marchant. Another superbitch. The bully in the year; the most popular kid in the year. She was the envy of every other kid. She smoked, which was cool, drunk booze like it were Ribena and got fingered in the boys' loo long before any other girl in the year.

She took an instant dislike to me and I ended up being the butt of her bullying and teasing. She touched my arm and then screamed, "lurgy" before running off to the loo to wash her hands. The others fell about the place in fits of giggles, poking and jabbing each other. But when that random trigger snapped within my soul, that was when I first experienced death.

Sally Marchant had taken things too far. *Today she must die.* The words resonated deep within my mind, spinning uncontrollably. My mind drifted back in time and I saw her standing there. Pointing. Laughing. Telling me I was filthy, germ-ridden and that no man would ever come near me. According to Sally, I had more chance of pulling a blind man with a dog than being liked by anyone. She told the other girls that I'd end up with a crusty fanny that not even a crowbar could open.

Between classes one day she cornered me alone at the top of the stairs. With no one to witness her misdeeds, she pushed and pulled me around, ripped at my hair, slapped me around the face and spat at me.

Poor Sally fell down a long flight of stairs, her screams drowned out by the school fire alarm after I smashed the glass with the heel of my hand and pressed the button. She fell a long way, twenty-nine steps to be precise. I counted each one as I walked down after her. Each thud and each crack of a bone left her even more contorted the further she fell, culminating in catastrophic head injuries as she bounced like a ping-pong ball down the concrete steps and landed on the cold wooden floor at the bottom.

I thought I'd panic and run, scared someone would find us, but I stood there. A mixture of bewilderment and fear replaced with a curious sense of excitement at what little old feeble me had done whirled through my body, jockeying for position. I watched as a red, thick liquid trickled from her mouth and ear. She looked towards the ceiling; her eyes fixed in a wide stare. Her mouth moved like a goldfish sucking air. Then everything went still as she let out a last gasp. That was my first experience of death, and I was hooked on it from that point onwards.

One taste of that euphoria, and now I can't stop.

4

Coffee, coffee, coffee. Karen banged the word around in her head, using it as her morning mantra. She'd skipped breakfast ahead of the visit to the mortuary. Experience had taught her to err on the side of caution as post-mortems had caught her out in the past when she'd been just a trainee detective constable. She'd never forgotten barfing over the shoes of her then DI. The look on the woman's face had been burnt in Karen's mind ever since.

Now she'd grin to herself each time a junior officer rushed for the nearest exit. Only those with a cast-iron stomach braved a breakfast ahead of a post-mortem.

Today had been no different. Though back at the office, hunger still didn't figure on her mind, and the only thing she craved was her fourth cup of black, strong coffee. The short break behind her desk had given her the opportunity to catch up on emails and check on the latest reports added to the HOLMES2 database.

The last few months had been a challenge for Karen, fighting hard to establish herself back in the team. Having reached a successful conclusion in the last case and bringing the killer of two local high-profile criminals, Dean Macholl and Jack Taylor, to justice she felt some credibility restored to her reputation. But it didn't stop the occasional look from other officers. Memories faded slowly in the force, and that was clear on the faces of those around her.

Despite rescuing a girl from a potential grooming situation and breaking the backbone of a local gang that terrorised an estate, the memories of the past still overshadowed her successes. Paranoia and self-doubt ran through her veins, but she was a fighter, and refused to buckle to those weaknesses.

Checking her watch, Karen realised she was running late for the impromptu briefing that she had organised. She pushed back in her chair and sipped the last dregs of the coffee before grabbing her phone and notepad.

Nervous energy pulsed through the room as she took her position at the front beside the whiteboard. She cast her gaze around the assembled group of officers. Jade, Steve and Brad pulled up chairs closest to her. The rest of the officers, which numbered over twenty, either swivelled in their chairs or perched on desks. There were a few new faces amongst the crowd, as other officers had been reassigned to her team for this case. Flexibility was the key when working in MIT, workloads could change in an instant, and the teams needed to be fluid, reassigning resources where needed the most.

Karen noticed Skelton take up his usual position at the back of the room. His eyes scanned the back of the heads of those gathered, before he levelled his gaze with Karen and gave her a single nod to proceed. That single action was enough to rile Karen. Despite being the SIO, Skelton always charged Karen with overseeing investigations and conducting the briefings. Lording it over her at the back of the room, Skelton appeared to be waiting for her to screw up again. Either way, she really didn't give a toss.

"Okay team, sorry for the late start, my fault. But thanks for attending. We have a new case, the victim, Adam Manners, aged thirty-four, a marketing executive. He was found dead yesterday evening by his wife who had returned from a business trip to Edinburgh."

"Not the homecoming she expected," came a voice from amongst the crowd.

Karen nodded in acknowledgement as she turned to face the incident board. Pictures of Adam Manners were pinned to the board, showing the position he was found in on the bed. Those pictures were tame compared to the close-up shots that the forensic team had taken of the deep burns to his groin.

"This is our victim. As you can see, he sustained significant injuries to his groin, and judging from the abrasions to his wrist, he put up a bit of a struggle."

Karen noticed one or two of the male officers, scrunching their faces and crossing their legs as they examined the photo. They exchanged silent looks of horror.

"Some of you here can probably understand that a kick in the nuts can put you on the floor, and you're unlikely to get up for a while. We can only imagine what he would have gone through if he'd been conscious."

"The injuries to his groin were secondary?" a female officer asked.

"According to the pathologist, yes. Wainwright suggested that had Adam been awake and conscious, then we would have witnessed much deeper lacerations to his wrists as he fought the excruciating pain of whatever had been doused on him. It is our understanding that he was unconscious, if not dead already prior to having received these injuries."

There was a collective of understanding nods from those gathered.

"The post-mortem results will be with us soon, but the early indications suggest an inconclusive cause of death. They're conducting further analysis to see whether he perhaps had a heart attack through shock, or if there's something else."

"Any further thoughts on the puncture wound, boss?" Jade chipped in.

"Good point, Jade." Karen used the tip of her pen to circle the spot on the victim's arm where Wainwright had identified the puncture wound. "Wainwright discovered a single random puncture mark on his arm. Nothing suggests the victim was a substance user, but toxicology reports will hopefully confirm that for us one way or another."

"Were any drugs found at the scene?"

Karen turned towards the officer sitting to her right who had asked the question. "An initial search of the scene uncovered nothing. The search is still being conducted as we speak, so that may change."

"What about something like autoerotic asphyxiation,

bearing in mind he was strung out like a turkey. There has to be a sexual element to this," the officer continued.

"Agreed. There might be some sexual behaviour involved, but then we end up with this," Karen said, pointing back towards the picture of the victim's groin. "This makes little sense. We know some sexual practices involve extreme pain, humiliation and degradation, but this one is right out of the ballpark. I don't think any of those things apply in this case. This is something different."

"We need to discover what perhaps started off as a sex game, turned to murder?" Steve speculated.

Silence enveloped the room, as each officer processed their own thoughts.

"Have we got a statement from his wife?"

"Not yet, Jade. Unfortunately, she was too traumatised yesterday, and I'm not surprised. Coming home to find your husband bound to a bed and naked is bad enough, but to find out that he had been brutally assaulted and died is enough to leave anyone devastated."

"So, where do we go from here?" Jade asked.

"Well, you and I will pay her a visit to see if we can get a statement from her. In the meantime, we need to do the usual. We need to access his bank, medical and phone records. Have a look through social media accounts and see if we can find anything that may link him to another woman."

"Or man…" Jade added.

Karen agreed with that suggestion. Until they knew more

about his life, they couldn't rule out whether he had been murdered by a man or woman.

"Jade, can I leave it with you to organise door-to-door enquiries? Look for any signs of domestic CCTV installations along the road and secure any footage from the last twenty-four to thirty-six hours."

Jade scribbled a few points down in her notebook and confirmed with a nod.

Karen picked up her notes and instructed the team to get started as she made her way back to her office. She dropped her phone and notepad on her desk and then stretched her arms up into the air to relieve the tension in her back. Suddenly aware of a presence behind her, a slow shiver crept up her spine. She spun on her heel to see Skelton lingering in the doorway, the slightest of smug grins on his face.

"Sir?" Karen straightened her blouse and retreated towards her desk and settled herself in. An uncomfortable silence hung between them, as Karen waited for Skelton to say something. But he appeared to be in no hurry. She couldn't be certain what he was thinking, but knowing him, it was nothing good.

Skelton stuffed his hands in his pockets and waited.

5

"Boss, boss… are you listening?"

Karen had been deep in thought as she sat in the passenger seat of Jade's car. Jade had been talking for the last few minutes, but Karen hadn't heard a single word. Her mind drifted back, still smarting over Skelton's comments.

"Sorry, Jade. What did you say? I was side-tracked."

"Yeah, I gathered that. What's up?"

"Oh, nothing. I've just got a lot on my mind at the moment. Too much to do, and not enough time. Sorry, what were you saying?"

Jade smiled and laughed. She kept both hands on the steering wheel as she made her way through Dalston. "I always thought Dalston was a shithole, and it probably once was. But from what I've seen so far, it seems a swish place."

For the first time in their journey, Karen took notice of the roads. She noticed a mixture of terraced housing, intermingled with dark brick elegant-looking detached properties, that sat behind tree-lined pavements. It had a feel of what the old East End of London looked like fifty years ago, and nothing much had changed since then. The only difference was that it had become gentrified.

"I think you're right. Some of these houses are easily pushing one million plus." Karen imagined the gloom of the dark Victorian nights, and people walking beneath the dim glow of street lamps. She wondered what it would have been like to live during those times, and how life had changed.

Karen returned to her thoughts, as Jade's commentary faded into the distance. Skelton had pissed her off, standing there with his smug grin as he questioned her about the case. He'd spouted the same bullshit he'd said to her after Jack Taylor had been murdered. And despite proving herself, Skelton still questioned her capabilities. Whether he meant it or pushed merely to get a rise out of her, she wasn't sure. But his thinly veiled threats about her mental health, and being too caught up in the past, irritated the hell out of her.

Whatever his game, Karen was determined not to fall victim to it. She'd been keeping a close eye on Skelton for the past few weeks. She had monitored his movements. And had even tried occasionally to follow him, but he had an uncanny knack of losing her. Even those attempts had cast doubt in her mind. *Has he cottoned on to me following him?* It left her at a loss as to her next move. Karen still needed answers about the hijack, but she had made little progress in uncovering anything of interest.

After continuing their drive in silence, Jade pulled up

outside a small, but grand-looking double-fronted detached house. It carried much of the similarity in style to the properties they had passed. As they made their way up the small path, towards the front door, Karen looked down at the ornate black-and-white tiling that made up the path. It beat a concrete path in her opinion, and she admired how some historic features of the property had been kept.

A woman who identified herself as Catherine Wilson, a family liaison officer, answered the door. The officer showed Jade and Karen through to the lounge where they came face to face with a slim woman, dressed in a casual blouse, smart jeans, and brown loafers.

Karen and Jade held out their warrant cards before introducing themselves. “Jackie Manners?”

The woman shook her head apologetically and held her hand up to her chest. “Oh, God no, I’m Angela her friend. I thought it was best that she stayed with me.” Angela stood to one side for Karen to see another woman sat on the sofa behind her.

“I’m Jackie.” She stood and shook hands with both Karen and Jade. Jackie had brown shoulder-length hair, and black wide-rimmed glasses that framed her round face. She wore a thin vest T-shirt, and a pair of cut-off denim shorts. Plenty of heat still lingered in the air, as the temperature topped thirty degrees today. Jackie sat down, and the two officers sat on a sofa facing her.

Jade took out her notepad, as Karen took the lead.

“First, we’re sorry for your loss. We know that our visit comes at a very difficult time, but we need to ask you some questions as a matter of urgency.”

Whilst Karen spoke, Jackie stared at the floor and wrung her hands in a tight ball. She didn't raise her eyes to meet Karen's and offered nothing more than a small nod.

"Can you tell me about Adam?" Karen asked.

"Like what?" Jackie asked softly.

"Perhaps we can start with the type of person he was?"

Jackie sniffed and wiped her nose with the back of her hand. "He was just your average guy. He worked hard; Adam was a marketing executive at IQ Communications Consultants. He often brought work home with him, but he loved his job."

Karen scanned her face for any change in expression. "Any recent change in his behaviour?"

Jackie shook her head.

"Okay. Had he been in a disagreement, or an argument with anyone?"

"No. No. He wasn't that kind of person. He was so laid-back and enjoyed life. Adam would sit down and watch football on a Sunday afternoon like most blokes. We'd make time to go for lunch on Saturdays to one of the local bistros or pubs."

"And you'd been in Edinburgh, on business?"

Jackie didn't reply to begin with. She hadn't raised her head to any of the questions asked of her. Karen saw tears collecting on the end of her nose and dripping to the floor.

Karen's heart squeezed with empathy. "Jackie? I know this is difficult for you, but we need to get as much information as possible, so we can start to build a picture as to the events leading up to his death."

"Yes. I go to Edinburgh once a month. We have an office in London, and I work for a telecoms company. I'm one of their senior account managers. We have another office and call centre in Edinburgh. I spend my time between the two locations. I've just spent two days up there, and when I returned home…" Jackie's voice trailed off.

Karen exchanged a glance with Jade, before approaching the subject that proved delicate at the best of times. "Jackie, I will ask you a question now, and it may appear insensitive, but I don't think I have a choice. Did you at any point suspect that Adam was seeing anyone else?"

The question tore through Jackie like a sharp sword. Her shoulders twitched, and she clenched her hands tighter. For the first time in the interview, she raised her bloodshot and watery eyes and levelled them with Karen.

"No."

In Karen's opinion, the answer was less than convincing.

"Listen, Jackie, I need you to be honest with me."

There was a pause that lasted a few minutes. Karen sent the FLO to make some tea.

"We didn't have the perfect marriage. Like most couples we had our trials. We've had a few marriage difficulties in the past. I… I was unfaithful to him once. It only happened once," Jackie spluttered. "It was a fucking stupid mistake, a drunken mistake with a colleague. And ever since then, there's been a doubt in both of our minds as to each other's loyalty."

"And why did you doubt his loyalty?" Karen enquired.

"Because after what I did, he cheated on me several times. We argued about it. He kept saying that if it was okay for me to fuck someone else behind his back, then it was okay for him to do the same."

Jackie pursed her lips tight, and stared up towards the ceiling, desperate to hold back the tide of tears that threatened to engulf her. Pain and anguish etched her features.

"How did that leave you feeling?"

"I don't know. I think at the time I was lost for words. I couldn't comprehend how I was feeling. But we both tried to make it work. We promised each other that it wouldn't happen again. We tried to do more at weekends, and in weekend breaks away, anything to heal our marriage. That's why we started to put Saturdays aside just for us. I think that's what we needed, more us time."

"And he didn't mention anyone else's name? Any names that seemed to pop up?"

"No, nothing."

"WHAT DO YOU THINK, BOSS?" Jade asked, unlocking the car and opening her door as wide as she could to let out the wave of heat that seemed to smother her.

Karen did the same, in no hurry to get in. She took off her jacket and folded it before placing it on the back seat. "She seemed plausible enough. Visibly hurt. The grieving widow in shock. Just check out the details of where she was staying, and where she was working whilst up in Edinburgh."

Jade made a note. “Jackie said that Adam had cheated a few times after she had played away. It’s always possible that there was some jealousy over his wandering?”

“There’s jealousy Jade, and then there’s twisted as fuck. I’m not convinced that she could have inflicted that level of injuries. But for completeness we need to check out her movements and send someone back later to do a buccal swab on her.”

“We could have done that whilst we were in there boss.”

“Have you got a swab kit on you? Because I haven’t got one.”

Jade smiled and shrugged.

“Oh, and Jade. When it’s just you and me, please don’t call me boss. I hate it. Just call me Karen.”

“But… you’re the guv. It feels odd calling you by your first name.”

“Listen, Jade, you and I have known each other for a long time, and we get on better than just colleagues. So please ditch the boss, it’s Karen.”

“Okay, boss… err… I mean Karen.” She laughed.

6

As they made their way back towards Virginia Road, Karen mentioned that they would need to contact IQ Communications Consultants to find out more about Adam Manners. In the meantime, they had just enough time to visit the crime scene once more before heading home for the evening.

The road was much quieter than it had been twenty-four hours earlier. A solitary police officer stood guard at the front door of the property as Karen and Jade approached. With parking being so limited in the street, Jade had parked some distance away, and they covered the remaining distance on foot. In the dry and humid heat, they both just hankered for a nice air-conditioned room.

The scene guard acknowledged Karen with a "ma'am" before informing Karen that crime scene investigators had finished up for today but would be returning tomorrow to scour the back garden now the house search had been completed.

It was cooler and less oppressive as Karen and Jade walked into the lounge. The cool wooden floors helped to keep the temperature down. Now that the house was empty, the rooms had a spacious feel to them. They were clean, and contemporary. There were only a few items of furniture, and each one of them looked expensive in Karen's opinion.

Karen gazed at the picture postcard prints hanging on the wall she had noticed on her first visit. Each one depicted a different coastline or shell. It had the feel of a house that belonged to trendy urbanites who preferred minimal fuss and clean lines. White laminated cupboards lined one wall, and Karen took a moment to inspect the contents of each drawer before moving on.

"Have you noticed what's missing, Karen?" Jade asked.

"No. Not yet anyway. But I guess I'm about to find out."

"Well, one thing I noticed yesterday, and it's still clear today. There are no pictures of the happy couple. None of them together, or alone. I thought there might be some in the bedroom, but from the brief time that I spent in there, I found nothing. I checked both bedside cabinets." Jade held her arms out by her side and spun round three hundred and sixty degrees. "Most houses would have some photographs of their occupants in the lounge. And there's nothing here. You might even find a few in the hallway, but there's nothing. Don't you find it strange?"

Karen agreed. "But if you look around, it doesn't look like the type of house that has a homey feel. It's sparse, even clinical to an extent."

"Maybe they weren't into material things?" Jade assumed.

"I doubt it. They've got a sixteen hundred quid fridge in the kitchen. Not your run-of-the-mill Zanussi."

After rummaging through the kitchen, they made their way upstairs, starting their search in the bathroom, looking for any prescribed medicines, before moving to the smaller bedrooms. The smallest bedroom was nothing more than a box room. But in estate agents' spiel, they would always class it as the third bedroom, only suitable for an infant or toddler. They had converted it into an office, with a wrap-around glass desk, and two large computer screens suspended above the desk. Karen left Jade to search through the folders and files, as she made her way towards a large bedroom.

The forensic team had removed the bedding and mattress, leaving just a base in place. She could still see the corpse of Adam Manners stretched out in what she could only describe as a crucifix position. Her eyes remained glued to the place she had last seen him, before she broke her stare and moved around the bedroom. Her feet sunk into the lush deep grey carpet pile. It had a luxurious and soft feel.

What were you doing, Adam?

The work surfaces of the dressing table and door handles of the cupboards carried a fine layer of grey metallic dust, remnants of the fingertip search by the forensic team.

Karen tried to imagine Adam's final moments, and how much of it he knew of. She wondered how the killer had made their final preparations, and at what point did they strike?

What did the person look like?

What did they bring with them?

And how were they able to put you into such a compromising position?

To do that, he must have known them, and trusted them. That, or he got off on the risk of the unknown.

She moved over towards the base of the bed and looked through the bedside cabinet. The first drawer she searched through had a few magazines and a book. This was Adam's side, because the second drawer was stuffed full of cables, batteries, several pairs of sunglasses, an assortment of keys, scissors and receipts dating back more than a year from Tesco, Costa Coffee and Esso petrol stations. This was a man drawer. It made her smile, as her mind recalled a Michael McIntyre sketch about how a husband's worldly possessions would always be stuffed in just one drawer in the bedroom, his wife having all the remaining drawers.

The bedside cabinet on the other side was Jackie's. Trendy ladies' magazines, nail files and varnishes were amongst just a few of the things she rifled through.

Karen stood and looked around the room again. Nothing in here would look out of place in any couple's bedroom. She even looked through the wardrobes and examined all the clothes and shoeboxes. The minimalist theme from downstairs carried on in their wardrobes. Most wardrobes that she had come across were stuffed full of clothes, and every conceivable space had been utilised. But the cupboards in this bedroom had plenty of room.

She joined Jade in the box room, only to find that Jade had drawn a blank as well. There was nothing in the house that suggested anything untoward. There were no secret mobile phones, or hidden cards. Their search had drawn a blank.

Karen hoped that the forensic team would have had more luck.

As she and Jade walked back to their car, Karen checked in with Steve who was covering the late shift. She told him to call her if anything significant developed during the night and to contact IQ Communications Consultants.

STEPPING off the train at Epping, Karen breathed a sigh of relief, as the fresher, more cooling breeze of Essex replaced the suffocating, hot air of London. She stopped off at the Chinese restaurant and picked up a takeaway, the one she had been wanting the night before and made her way back to her apartment.

Epping was much quieter than London. It was a small town, which sprung to life on a Monday when the market was on. On her days off, Karen enjoyed the opportunity of blending into her surroundings and mingling amongst the crowds.

She would often pick up nice home-made cakes, and fresh cuts of meat, knowing that the money was going to local producers rather than the big national supermarket chains. There weren't many markets that she knew of these days. But the one in Epping had been running for more than eight hundred years, and ran the whole length of the High Street, with more than fifty stalls all vying for business.

Without the market, the town always stayed quiet, just the way she liked it.

Manky wrapped himself around Karen's ankles within seconds of her opening the door. His thick coat tickled her skin, his constant meows following her down the hallway as she kicked off her shoes and headed for the kitchen. The cool floor tiles soothed her burning hot soles as she pulled a bottle of beer out of the fridge, popped the cap, and took a long slow gulp. She let out a sigh of relief as she felt the cold beer trickle down her throat and hit her empty stomach. A wave of relaxation spread across her body. She closed her eyes and tilted her head back, savouring the taste of the beer. Karen pulled herself away from that moment of nirvana, her eyes widening upon the realisation she had just necked three-quarters of a bottle of beer in one go.

She finished the rest, before giving in to Manky's demands who stood ready by his food bowl waiting for his dinner.

Having heated her food, and spoilt herself with another bottle of beer, she crashed on the sofa, Manky joining her just a few moments later. He sat beside her purring contentedly as she tucked into her sweet and sour chicken and special fried rice. It was a simple pleasure, but one she loved. She'd hardly eaten all day, and her stomach growled in protest.

Karen enjoyed the peace and tranquillity of being away from London. It felt like another world being out here. The odd siren from a passing ambulance or police car interrupted her silence as she watched an old episode of *Friends*. She had the volume on mute and enjoyed just trying to figure out what they were saying.

The day had been long and frustrating by the time Karen collapsed in bed just after midnight. Cases like this sucked up time. Even with the resources that she had available to her, she never really felt that they could devote all their attention to the case in the way she would like to. That, coupled with the fact that she was making slow progress with her own investigation on the side, frustrated her further.

Karen stared at the ceiling, her body willing her to sleep, her thoughts stabbing at her brain. The images she had witnessed danced before her, ensuring that sleep would prove elusive tonight. Her mind darted back over the last twenty-four hours, and though she'd been busy, she knew the next few days would be busier. Whoever had killed Adam Manners, hadn't just killed him, they had left a message. What that message meant, she wasn't sure. But something told her that she was about to find out.

7

I'm not a morning person. It takes a lot to wake me up. I much prefer the night-times, where I can blend into the shadows, or mix amongst the drunken crowds, many of which would never remember my face again.

But I always take my place by the kitchen window whilst I work my way through several cups of coffee. It gives me the opportunity to contemplate life. But then again, I don't really understand its meaning. For me, it's been a solitary existence. I've never been able to hold down a stable relationship. And the prospect of a stable relationship terrifies me. Maybe I don't want one, or maybe it's because I fear what I might end up doing.

I've had a few relationships in the past, if you can call them that. I've never been in one where I can be myself, because I always worry about the damage I might cause to my partner. If I look hard enough, maybe I can find someone just like me. But there's a side to me that I can't control. It loves the risk, the thrill of the chase and the excitement.

And when I'm like that, there's nothing or nobody that can control me, not even myself. It's like I have an out-of-body experience, where I'm doing things on autopilot.

Despite the dark shadowy corners inside me that harbour evil, many other parts define the human experience just like everyone else. I love sex, just like millions of others. But I have this habit of taking it too far. I especially enjoy being in control, and on top. I'm not your normal vanilla person but love the extremes. I think most men would run a mile if they could see what lurks in my cupboards and drawers. Handcuffs, whips, nipple clamps, surgical instruments and anything else that can induce pain, even if it isn't originally designed for sex. And it's not just about giving, because I get just as much from receiving. It amuses me when I look at the terror in a man's eyes when I tell him to hurt me. They then slap my arse, and I then insist, "no, really fucking hurt me."

After my coffee, I set off for work as normal, but today I take one of my detours through the cemetery. I stop at my dad's grave. It's untidy and unkempt, just like he was. I stand there with my hands in my pockets, feeling no love towards him, no sadness towards him.

He could have been a better dad and husband and kept mum. But she couldn't put up with his roving eye much longer. She worked all the hours, doing two jobs, one in the local supermarket, and the other, an evening shift in the launderette. It gave my dad plenty of time to fuck about and sit at home drinking beer. He'd get her running around after him and take her body whether or not she wanted it. Even though he kept me in my room and made me read after school, I could still hear him with one fancy woman after another.

He drove Mum to drink.

He drove her to not believe in herself and not like herself.

I remember the time that I saw her body piled in a crumpled heap on the kitchen floor. Her face was black and blue, her bottom lip swollen to twice the size and bleeding. He really lost it that time. For once in her life, she refused his advances, and in a fit of rage, he stripped her naked and tried to rape her. I could hear her screams from upstairs as they fought in the kitchen. Smashing plates and cups, crying, guttural screams, and aggression, pure aggression. I drew on all my courage and sneaked downstairs and nudged open the door to the lounge. Peering around the corner I could see into the kitchen.

Only an eerie silence met my prying eyes.

I couldn't see Dad, but I could see Mum's legs on the floor. She wasn't moving, suffering from one of the worst beatings ever.

But she took it, and life carried on.

I stare at the grave, summoning the will not to desecrate it. *I looked after Mum after you fucked off. Correction, after she finally plucked up the courage to tell you to fuck off. I nursed her through her breast cancer and the dark days until that cruel disease took her. It should have been you by her side, not me. I never got the chance to live my life because you lived your life with your dick.*

After losing my internal war and spitting on his grave, I make my way to work.

Yes, I'm the weirdo who works in a charity shop. I guess I have come full circle. Now I'm seeing the lonely, the poor and the well-meaning pass in and out of the shop. I'm the one in the back working on my own just the way I like it. I sift through the bags of clothes that get dumped on our doorstep every day. And what disgusts me is how so many of the clothes are dirty and stained. Men's trousers can be so disgusting. Do they not consider washing them before donating them?

My job is to make something good from cast-offs. My manager always wonders why so many clothes given to the charity are torn around the groin area, especially men's jeans and men's suit trousers. I act dumb, and shrug in ignorance. Little does she know what I get up to with my pair of scissors.

With one eye on the front door, and the other on my work, I can see everyone who comes and goes. And anyone who comes in and gives me the eye ends up fair game. With a glint in my eye, and with my manager asking customers if they'd like to contribute financially, it's easy to get names and addresses. And the sad fuckers who eye me up are the ones who often pay the price. I can think of at least three customers who never saw the light of day again after their lurid gazes swept my body.

Dirty bastards.

Enough of your thinking, time to open up the next black bin liner of shit, outdated, ill-fitting cast-offs.

8

Karen threw back the covers with a heavy sigh, any chance of a decent night's sleep dashed by her racing mind. Glancing at the time on her phone that read not long after one a.m., she strode back into her dining room, flicking on the main light, her eyes stinging in response.

She pulled her laptop from her rucksack, and fired it up, the bright light from the screen causing her to scrunch up her eyes. She tapped away at the keyboard and entered her username and password, and whilst the laptop loaded up, she retrieved a notepad and pen. Karen wasn't sure what she was looking for, but she thought it made sense to do something useful.

Karen made a few pages of notes, gorging herself on information. The more engrossed she became, the further she hunched over her laptop, as documents, statements and pictures of exhibits flashed before her eyes.

Eventually she sank back into her chair and sighed. The

time in the bottom right-hand corner of the screen now read three forty-seven a.m. She drew two long lines underneath her notes before logging off.

KAREN HID her bloodshot eyes behind dark sunglasses as she made her way towards the station. The sun hung high in the sky, and the few white wispy clouds did little to shield her eyes against the morning glare. A warmth permeated the air already, and Karen knew it was going to be another hot one.

She was desperate for a coffee to wake up but opted for a cold bottle of water from the small kiosk shop at the station. She noticed that the Tube was quieter than it had been for the past few weeks. With it being late July, schools had broken up, and families had jetted off on holiday. There was less hustle and bustle, and just the diehard city workers joined her on her journey into work.

Karen always noticed how her heartbeat quickened, and her eyes would furtively dart up and down the carriage as people entered and exited the carriages the closer she got to London. The whole pace of life seemed to quicken as each station whizzed by. When she boarded at Epping, a sense of calmness and serenity continued right through until Leytonstone, and from there onwards, the pace of life seemed to pick up, people moved quicker, conversations were louder, different dialects hit her from all sides and congestion on the trains increased.

Karen arrived earlier than many of the others. It gave her the opportunity to go over the details on the incident board and examine the photographs of the deceased. It was never pleasant to examine someone's life through a series of still images. She had stood in this position before, many times, with far more grotesque images. Severed heads, missing limbs and twisted bodies haunted her.

The same questions ran through her mind. What had led Adam Manners to find himself in that situation? And at what point had he turned from a willing participant to a victim? And the burning question remained. Did he know the person who'd killed him, and if so, how well?

It was still early in the investigation, and Karen was sure as the case shaped up, new information and evidence would start to come together.

Finishing the last of the Danish pastry, Karen rubbed her stomach. "God, I feel fat." Every year she talked herself into joining a gym but hated the thought of exercise as much as she hated the thought of looking like a sweaty out of shape blob. There was a perfectly good sports centre just up the road from her apartment, so there was no excuse not to try, but she always managed to find one. Hers being, she was too busy.

Returning to her office, Karen sent out a groupwide email to her team instructing them to push ahead with witness statements. She was just about to pick up the phone to call Wainwright, when Jade popped her head around the corner.

"Morning, Karen." She smiled. There was a lightness in her tone, that reflected her upbeat personality.

"Morning, Jade. Did you have a good evening?"

"No, just a quiet one. I was shattered after yesterday, maybe it was the heat. But I struggled to get to sleep. Even with all my windows open, and sleeping on top of my duvet, I still couldn't. And by the looks of it, you couldn't either?"

Karen laughed. "Is it that obvious?"

"Well, you look as bad as I feel."

"I'm getting too old for this."

Jade rolled her eyes. "What's on the agenda for today?"

"There's an email sitting in the inbox for everyone. We need to make sure we're on top of all the witness statements. I can't find any on there, so check that for me. Oh, and also, I was just about to call Wainwright for an update on the PM. It's been twenty-four hours and the initial report isn't here, I've checked the database. He's usually quick, but he's bloody dragging his heels on this one. We seriously haven't got time for that; can you chase it up for me?" Karen replied, a hint of strain in her voice.

Jade nodded. "Okay, leave it with me. Sorry. I'll make sure the team get on to it."

Karen leant back in a chair and blew out her cheeks. "No, it should be me who's sorry. I'm just ratty this morning. I got about two hours' sleep, and I feel like shit. I didn't mean to come across ungrateful."

Jade shook her head. "It's fine. We all get days like that. I'll get on to it now."

"The problem is the day has only started," Karen replied yawning, as Jade left the room.

"Right pull yourself together, Karen, and get your shit sorted," Karen muttered to herself. With few people around, Karen logged online. The hijack on herself and her fellow officers a year ago was never far from her thoughts, and until she cleared this up in her own mind, she was always going to find it hard to focus. It was like her mind was being torn in two. She wanted to put the past behind, but the events of that day followed her around like a heavy cloud.

Maybe she was overthinking things. But this felt different. Like a blot on her career, just one event, just one day, from which her whole career was being judged. Skelton used it as an opportunity to undermine her fragile confidence, and she herself used it as a point of self-criticism daily. One way or another Karen needed to let this go but wouldn't until she had exhausted every opportunity to discover who had been behind this, and ultimately, who may have betrayed her.

Karen searched the files and records, examining the case details once again. This time around focusing on the eyewitness reports and making a note of their names as she heard footsteps approaching and the sound of voices. She glanced over the top of the monitor to see a few other members of the team arrive. Karen tracked them, waiting until they were settled before she continued.

She scrunched her eyes and pursed her lips. Omar Rashid was one eyewitness that drew her in. She had cross-referenced his name against some officer's notes, but couldn't find details on the system, and more worryingly, couldn't find his witness statement. She checked his name again. Perhaps she had misspelled it. But going back over the old case notes again confirmed the correct name. Perplexed, she ran a hand through her hair.

"Guv," Steve's voice snapped her head up.

"Jesus, you made me jump."

"Sorry, I should have knocked," Steve replied.

"Don't be daft. I was concentrating so much I didn't know you were there. What's up?"

He ambled into the room. "I've got an appointment with IQ Communications Consultants. Do you want to come? Or shall I take one of the others?"

"No, I'll come. I could do with the fresh air. Give me five minutes just to finish this off, and I'll meet you downstairs?"

Steve agreed and disappeared.

Karen widened her eyes and took in a deep breath, annoyed she'd nearly been caught. She was thankful that it wasn't Skelton who'd interrupted her.

Karen wrote Omar Rashid's address on a piece of paper and stuffed it in the back pocket of her trousers before logging off and grabbing her handbag. It could wait.

9

The journey to IQ Communication Consultants took Karen and Steve across London to the heart of the commercial district, the time in the Tube intolerable. The heat of the day before hadn't dissipated, and they had endured the hot, stuffy and claustrophobic atmosphere inside the oppressive carriage, breathing the dry and suffocating air.

At ground level, Karen sucked in a breath, noting only marginally better air quality, but no let-up in the heatwave that gripped the south-east. They skirted around the back of Liverpool Street station and through the Broadgate Circle. Investment bankers, forex traders and analysts from the firms that made up the Broadgate Circle surrounded them and Karen noticed a difference in the view. There was a sense of wealth and power as she noticed small huddles of people discussing business and the volatility of the markets whilst they sipped on their double espresso shots. She could spot an investment banker from a mile away, they all wore chino jeans, and expensive Oxford weave flyaway collar shirts. They finished their appearance with polished Church's brogues.

The hustle and bustle of the Circle faded into the background as they turned into Sun Street. Modernistic buildings stood shoulder to shoulder; reflective green glass hid the faces of the workers behind them.

IQ were located on the third floor of a six-storey building which had an impressive glass archway as an entrance. After signing in at reception, a security guard steered them towards the lifts.

Stepping from the lift, they were in front of a large low-level reception desk, adorned with a glass top, and three immaculate receptionists sitting behind it, talking into the headpieces. Artistic pieces, and creative images, no doubt from previous projects lined the corridor as far as Karen could see.

"How the other half live," Karen whispered as they made their way towards the desk.

"That's the difference between working in the public and private sector. The Met would blow their entire budget if we had offices like this," Steve replied.

One receptionist ended her call and greeted both of the officers with a courteous smile. "Hello, may I help you?" she said in a jovial voice.

"We're here in connection with Adam Manners," Karen said as they both presented their warrant cards.

The smile faded from the receptionist's face at the mere mention of the name. The other two receptionists, though on calls, looked over with concern and sorrow etched in their features.

"One moment please." The receptionist tapped around a keypad and waited for her line to connect. "David, I have two police officers in reception." The receptionist fell silent as she listened to the reply. "Someone will be with you in a moment, so please take a seat over there."

Karen and Steve stepped away and settled into a plush retro-looking leather couch. A few minutes later a short, overweight man strode up the corridor and made his way towards them. He offered them the smallest of smiles as he extended his hand in Karen's direction.

"I'm David DeGlanville, managing partner. Please, would you come through?"

DeGlanville led them back up the corridor, and towards his office, a big glass-fronted affair, with expensive-looking furniture. He offered them both a seat, before stepping around to his side of the desk and settling himself into his large and comfortable leather chair.

Steve took out his pen and notepad, and Karen placed her handbag down by her feet.

"We're here in connection with the death of one of your employees, Adam Manners. I understand my colleague here, DC Nugent, spoke with you briefly yesterday," Karen explained.

DeGlanville offered a small smile in Steve's direction. "Yes, he did. The firm is deeply shocked by Adam's death. In fact, several of our staff who were close with Adam have found it difficult to come to terms with the news."

"Yes, I can imagine," Karen said, nodding. Although she wasn't certain that it *upset all members of staff*, as she heard the distant ripple of laughter from somewhere within an adjoining office.

"What can you tell us about Adam? We are trying to build a picture of him as a person, and his life."

DeGlanville rested his elbows on the table and formed a steeple with his fingers. "Adam is… was a marketing executive. I'd say he had been here for about three years. He was a solid worker. He had a good eye for creative detail and had the knack of taking a blue-sky concept and translating it into marketing messages that were very good."

"And how did he get on with your clients?" Karen asked.

"Very well. He was part of the team that worked on just one or two key accounts. And from what I can gather, there were no complaints. As I said, he got on with everyone."

He hadn't said that, but Karen continued anyway. "What about other members of staff?"

DeGlanville frowned. "I'm sorry, what do you mean?"

"How did he get on with other members of your organisation?"

The man shrugged. "Again, no complaints. He was well liked. He didn't go out on all the socials, but he certainly made an appearance at most of them. Though I hadn't seen it myself, someone mentioned that he was a flirt with some women in the firm. Nothing bad, I might add."

Karen continued questioning him, but DeGlanville could not shed any further light or give them anything of significance. According to him, Adam had not had any disagreements or run-ins with other members of staff, nor had there been any indication of anything untoward or upsetting in his personal life.

Having drawn a blank, they had offered their thanks and left, informing DeGlanville to call them if anything else sprung to mind.

After Karen turned down Steve's offer of catching some brunch in the salubrious surroundings of the Broadgate Circle, he returned to work. A part of her wanted to stay and soak up the atmosphere, but she had other places she needed to be.

Thirty-five minutes later she was in Camden and staring down the road where the events a year ago changed her life. Around her people hurried from one place to another. Cars and lorries trundled along the road, crawling through streets not designed to carry that amount of traffic. Their exhaust fumes only added to the heat and the choking sensation that smothered her with every breath. Her body was going into sensory overload as her limbs tingled, and her brain raced in the most unhelpful way. After all this time, the reality of being back here still felt alien.

The sweat trickled down her back, free-flowing like condensation on a windowpane. It beaded on her forehead, and she wiped it away with the back of her hand. Karen turned into a side road and walked a few minutes before she found the shop. Stop and Go off-licence was owned by Omar Rashid. Peering in through the window, a man behind the counter flicked through the pages of a newspaper. She hadn't met him before and had only been made aware of him as a key witness after the incident.

He greeted her with a hint of suspicion as he narrowed his eyes. And offered nothing by way of help as she strode towards the counter.

Karen pulled out her warrant card. "Omar Rashid?"

The man glanced at the identification, his eyes twitching as he focused. His lips tightened into a thin line. He nodded once to confirm.

"I'm Detective Inspector Heath. I'm just following up on an old case file relating to a serious incident that happened just down the road about a year ago. From the records, I understand that you witnessed two police cars being attacked, and a woman being abducted by some masked men. Is that correct?"

Rashid remained poker-faced and shook his head. "No… no, I saw nothing. I have nothing to say."

The speed of his reply, and hesitation that tinged his words annoyed Karen. He knew something.

Karen moved closer. "That's strange, because in our police records, you appear to give a very detailed account of what you saw."

"Listen. I know nothing. I'm not looking for any trouble. Please, I have a business to run. I'm busy."

Karen looked around the empty shop and raised a brow. "Busy? Or are you hiding something? Perhaps you're not willing to cooperate?"

The man raised his hands to pacify her. "Please, you must be mistaken. I was mistaken. I saw nothing."

Rashid averted his gaze from her to the street and back again. "Please – you must go."

Karen pressed harder, but he stayed adamant he couldn't remember much of the event, and it seemed too shady in his mind. He kept reiterating that it happened over a year ago, and that he'd been mistaken in what he had seen.

"You realise that failing to cooperate with a police investigation is a criminal offence?" Karen was clutching at straws and fast running out of options.

Rashid exploded. "Please. Go away. I have nothing I can help you with. Get out of my shop, now!"

Karen folded her arms across her chest, more confused than before. She had scanned his statement before it had disappeared from the system. It was rock solid. His descriptions, the sequence of events, and where he was standing at the time of the hijack were clear.

"Please understand, Mr Rashid. I'm trying to identify some very dangerous criminals, people who would not hesitate to hurt, maim or kill. It's imperative that we find out who they are before they hurt others." Karen sighed and stared at the floor for a moment. "If you change your mind, here's my card, so please contact me," she said, sliding her business card across the counter.

Rashid didn't take his eyes off her and didn't touch the card as he watched her leave the shop. Karen stood outside and glanced up and down the road, frustrated and annoyed. He'd given a crystal-clear statement before, and now it seemed a blur. Someone had got to him.

Either way, Karen steeled her spine, determined to find those responsible.

10

"Fuck, Fuck!" The only words that could slip from Karen's lips were curses as she stared at her computer screen, her brows creased and her face tense. She had wandered the streets for thirty minutes after leaving the off-licence trying to make some sense of the situation. Part of her wanted to rush back in, grab Rashid by the neck and throttle the living daylights out of him to surrender the truth. Despite knowing it would have been career suicide to do so, her sense of justice egged her on to demand answers.

Staring at the case file for over an hour, she felt even more conflicted. She needed to be one hundred per cent certain that her eyes weren't deceiving her. Karen had been right in the first instance; Omar Rashid's witness statement had disappeared. She felt frustrated and annoyed. Her mind *wasn't* playing tricks on her. His statement didn't exist. In fact, since the last time of checking, no reference to him existed in the case file. Someone, or something had removed all reference to the man. She felt a swell of anger rising, her chest contracting as she struggled to breathe and remain calm.

Am I on a wild goose chase that has no end?

Someone was monitoring her movements on the system and staying one step ahead of her.

But who?

She tugged on her bottom lip, biting it between her teeth. If she announced that the case file had been altered, and vital witness statements removed, senior management would know that she had been reviewing an investigation that had nothing to do with her.

Karen tapped her fingertips on the desk whilst considering her next move. Her eyes darted between the screen and the corridor outside her office. Using official police time to investigate something for her own agenda was taboo. Her mind tracked back through the events of that fateful day, and the repercussions that followed. Karen's eyes widened as her mind latched on to another nugget of information. Keying in the details in the search bar, she searched through the results that the system threw up for her.

Taxi driver, taxi driver... where are you?

Karen remembered a taxi driver that had stopped to help. She couldn't remember his name but looked for any reference to taxis until uncovering the information. Marvin Harris, aged fifty-seven years old, a black cab driver. She found his address and contact details on the system and then punched his number into her phone and waited a few moments for the line to connect.

It didn't connect. The number didn't exist.

Karen scrunched her face and gritted her teeth whilst trying the number again, pleading for the line to connect. She let out a sigh of disappointment when it didn't connect. Not wishing to give up, she dialled his home number. Again, hitting a dead end when a recorded message replied by saying, "it has not been possible to connect your call; please try later."

Cold fear spread through her like an Arctic chill.

How can this be happening?

Returning to the database, she pulled off the registration number of his taxi and searched for that.

Karen froze, her mind unable to comprehend the information that stared her right in the face. Police had found the taxi burnt out three months ago in Southend. She tried to dispel her fears, assuming joyriders had stolen the taxi. But black cabs were never stolen. This was too much of a coincidence. Her desire to find the truth kept her searching for the next few minutes until it felt like the computer screen had reached out and slapped her.

She took a double take at the screen reading through the misper report. Marvin Harris had been reported missing by his brother three months ago. There had been no sightings or contact with him since.

Karen ran a hand through her hair, her thoughts in free fall.

What the hell is going on?

Karen printed off Marvin's statement and headed for the incident room to retrieve the warm sheets of paper from the printer before anyone else saw them. She would look at them later.

11

Karen slid the papers into her notebook before weaving her way through the desks towards the front of the incident room. She glanced from desk to desk. Some officers were on the phone, their conversations drifting around the room. Others waded through mounds of paper, and a few busily tapped away on their keyboards, which were ancient in comparison to the sleek, modern wireless keyboards of today. These resembled those plug-in kinds from the last century, keys the size of tombstones and a trailing wire that disappeared through a hole in the desk.

Karen glanced at the group and inhaled. "Okay team, whilst I'm here, let's get a quick update. Those not on the phone can relate anything of significance back to those who are busy."

A few of the officers rose from their desks and made their way towards the front. A few leant against the windowsills, others pulled up vacant chairs and dropped themselves into them.

"Has anyone got any updates on the outcome of the post-mortem? I checked earlier, and there was nothing on the database. Anyone?"

Jade waved her pen in the air. "It's delayed, guv. I called Wainwright first thing this morning. He is running an additional tox analysis. Something was bugging him, though he couldn't be certain what it was. But he said it was in relation to the puncture wound that he found on the body."

"Could he give you a timescale?"

Jade shrugged a shoulder. "I'm afraid not. He said he was sending it away for further analysis, so to a certain degree, it was out of his hands."

Karen asked Jade to keep on at him, and to chase him again first thing in the morning.

"Anything in the background searches?"

An officer towards the back of the room piped up. "We haven't found any unusual transactions with his bank. He had a limited social media presence. From the looks of it, he was on LinkedIn and Facebook. I'm focusing on LinkedIn. This is where I found most of his contacts, and they were other business professionals."

"How many are we looking at?"

The officer glanced at his notes. "He had two hundred and ninety-eight contacts on LinkedIn."

"And on Facebook?"

"Seventy-three, ma'am."

"Does anything stand out?"

"Most of the pictures and posts on his Facebook account

are to do with his cycling club, and what looks like a few socials from work. But that's about it."

Karen turned towards the members of her team closest to her, perched on desks and slumped in chairs. "Work with the rest of the team, and I know it's a bitch of a job, but we need to make sure that we get in touch with every single one of his contacts. We need to know what their connection with Adam was, and whether they had spoken to him, or seen him recently. And finally, if he had had any run-ins with anyone."

Steve, Brad and Jade nodded in agreement, whilst they made a few notes based on Karen's thoughts.

By now Karen had over thirty officers hanging on her every word as more officers joined the briefing. Support staff, including data inputters and compilers hovered towards the back of the incident room keen to not miss out on any information that might steer the direction of their work.

Karen stressed the importance of crossing off every single contact, no matter how tedious the work would be. It was imperative to find anyone with an axe to grind.

A junior detective to the right of Karen raised her hand to catch Karen's attention. "Are we only looking at females, bearing in mind it could have been a sex game to begin with?"

"Not necessarily. We must check everyone. For all we know he may have been a bisexual. There's no indication suggesting a woman did this."

Steve raised his hand. "We know Jackie and Adam were having a few marital difficulties. She admitted that she cheated on him once. And in return he had cheated on her several times. But Jackie never alluded to him having affairs with other men."

"That's a fair point, Steve," Karen offered in reply. "But we need to cover every angle. He could have been a closet gay for all we know. It wouldn't be the first time that we've come across people who have hidden their sexuality from their partner. We need to avoid stereotyping his relationships."

Steve and a few others nodded in acceptance of Karen's valid viewpoint.

"Anything else that we need to discuss?" Karen asked as she looked around the assembled crowd. A mixture of silent stares and a few shakes of the head met her question.

"Right, we've got a few hours left of the day, so make them count. Those of you on the late shift, call me if you get anything of importance. The rest of you make sure you knock off on time, get some rest, and I'll see you bright and early tomorrow morning."

12

The Uber pulls up by the side of the road. My driver looks over his shoulder and tells me that the fare is four pounds seventy, but we don't make eye contact. No. His eyes dance over my body. I can see the muscles twitch in his face and his mind working overtime as his eyes travel down my legs to my feet. A flicker of life ignites his expression as he imagines what he'd like to do to me, and perhaps even what I look like underneath my clothes.

But I know he can't handle me. He wouldn't last five minutes with me, so he's no different from the others. A filthy, lecherous perv. I can see the wedding band on his finger. He makes no attempt to hide it.

I give him five pounds and tell him to keep the change.

"Hey, are you drinking tonight?" he asks.

I nod. I know where his question leads, so I toy with him. "Yes, I'll be drinking. Lots of it. I'll be so fucking drunk tonight that I won't be able to stand."

“Hey lady, I am on shift all evening. I can pick you up from here and take you home. There are some rough people out there, I want to make sure you’re safe.”

Again, he’s not talking to me, but staring at the gap between my legs as I widen them a little.

“I’ll be fine. I don’t plan on going home alone this evening. I’m sure there’ll be some fit bloke who wants to take me home and… fuck… my… brains… out.”

My words have the desired effect as he repositions himself in his seat. I can see the tent forming in his trousers.

I open the door and step out, not giving two shits about his words, immune to his pleas for me to stay.

The warmth of the summer evening surrounds me and bathes my face. The pubs and bars are too hot, and their punters spill out on to the pavements. In my tight jeans, strappy black high-heeled sandals, and white cropped top, I watch heads snap around to watch my every move. I pause for effect before strolling into the pub. My heels clip against the paving stones, announcing my presence as a gang of guys stand in a circle, nudge each other and watch me walk past.

Inside, the heat hits me in the face like a blast furnace. Wall to wall sweaty bodies press against each other, the heat from one shoulder touching the back of another. There is something magical about blending into the crowd, an ease up in the loneliness that nips at my soul. We act the same, cheer at the same moment, and feel the same emotions together. What I read on their faces is written on mine as I return a smile to the men who stop drinking and watch me.

If I could just melt into this pub, I’d be the vibe, moving

around as easily as fog on a winter's day. Everywhere but nowhere. I'd soak in the laughter and the smiles, back in reality instead of my imaginary dark world. I can hear conversations swirl around me, dozens of conversations told in loud voices, and the stagnant stench of stale beer. A sharp smell of drink wafts towards me, as a hand thrusts a glass in my direction.

"How can I not buy a drink for such a fit woman like you?" says a face from amongst the crowd.

I ignore it, offering a polite smile as I walk past his crowd. The jeers that follow tell me of the ritual humiliation that his friends are throwing in his direction.

The deeper I move into the bar, the louder the music becomes, and I can feel the vibration rising from the floor. I make my way towards the end of the counter and squeeze myself in between two groups. Both are mixed crowds and oblivious to my arrival. From here it gives me a perfect vantage point across most of the pub. I order myself a double TVR. The bartender says it's been a long time since he's heard someone order one of those. And I reply telling him that there is no better combination than double tequila, vodka and Red Bull. A couple of those and it's enough to wipe anyone out.

I take my first sip and enjoy it as it hits the back of my throat. And then I wait.

My eyes scan the scene, moving from group to group, man to man, woman to woman. Having brushed away the advances of several men over the next half an hour, I remained patient, waiting.

Bingo!

Just beyond the two arcade machines in the top left corner, I catch his eyes looking at me. And despite looking away to confirm to myself, when I look back, he's still looking.

I'm ready.

I give him that cheeky, devil smile. Not too little, and not too much. He reciprocates and raises his bottle in a toast. I raise my glass and smile. And before I've put my glass back on the counter, he's weaving through the crowd like a slippery snake through wetland grasses until he's behind me and leaning over my shoulder.

"Are you alone?" he shouts in my ear, so I can hear him over the music.

I turn and put my lips to his ear. "I was until five seconds ago."

It didn't take long for me to find someone. Men are so predictable. We exchange a few glances, and a few more cheeky smiles before he offers to buy me another drink.

He flicks a wrist towards my drink. "What are you having?"

"A double tequila, vodka and Red Bull."

His eyes widen, I can tell he's impressed.

"That's a potent mix," he replies.

I plant the seed. "Well, only a few can handle it. A couple of these and most people are off their faces."

"And are you one of those?"

I shake my head. And tell him it's my drink of choice, and there's not a lot who can keep up with me.

Rising to the challenge, he signals to the barman and orders two more of what I'm drinking, saying that he will join me, and looks forward to drinking me under the table.

Game on.

It gets flirty, and he chances his luck by moving closer under the pretence that the music is too loud, and he can't hear her.

"What do you do?" I ask.

"I work for an event management company in London, and this pub is on my journey home. How about you?"

"I work for a charity organisation," making it sound far more important than what it is. He seems suitably impressed.

And then he trips up by saying that he has a girlfriend, of sorts, but glosses over the fact very quickly by suggesting that we move on somewhere else quieter for more drinks.

I tap his ring finger and accuse him of being a bad, bad boy.

"We have an open relationship, besides what she doesn't know can't hurt her," he replies with a grin.

"Are you sure?"

"Sure, I'm sure. Besides, there's nothing in it, right? Just two consenting adults connecting and letting off steam."

"Steam? Is that what you call it?"

"Well, what would you call it?" he asks.

"I'd say it's two people bordering on doing something very naughty that you *will* regret in a few hours' time."

His words are more brazen now, his bravado breaking through. "Well, we only live once. If we both want it, we should both have it. Don't you agree?" His brilliant white smile stands out against his dark black skin. He's just as good looking in person as his profile, with broad shoulders, warm eyes that undress you, and a fun personality. His line of chat flows in the same way it did online.

I don't offer him a reply. Keeping him hanging on is something I enjoy. I lean back into him saying, "Well, how about I take up your offer of going somewhere quieter, somewhere where we can get to know each other a bit better?"

I can see the excitement on his face as he looks over to see a group of his friends still milling around the arcade machines. A mixture of men and women look in our direction. The women have disgust on their faces. The men have looks of jealousy burning in their eyes.

Perfect.

13

Whilst some of the team were already heading home to have a well-earned rest, Karen's day wasn't over yet. With nervous energy crackling through her, she knew rest would elude her as usual and she'd just sit in her apartment all night chewing the shit out of her thoughts. A flash of annoyance burnt through her, probably aimed at herself. But she felt confused and frustrated, her thoughts like a ball of tangled wool.

If she really wanted to, she could go out and drink herself into a drunken stupor, pick up some guy in town and have some meaningless sex at the end. But waking up the next morning, she knew she wouldn't feel any better. It was as if she needed to stand in a big, open, grassy field, and just let her mind run free in the open space. She needed that room to think. Silence. A place without distraction.

An hour later, she sat beside Jane's bed. Her sister didn't stir as Karen walked in and pulled up a chair alongside her. She took a few moments to look at her sister, taking in her features. She lay peacefully, the rise and fall in her chest ever so slight. Jane always rested in sweet repose, the only way that Karen could recall seeing her for the past few years. Jane's eyelids would occasionally flicker, and Karen wondered what went on behind them. Could Jane hear anything that she said, she wondered if Jane even knew that she was in the room.

Karen fought hard to stop her eyes from welling up. She so wanted to just have a normal conversation with her sister.

"I wish I could tell you about my day. Sometimes it's hard not being able to share the highs and lows with you. I feel so lonely, yet when I come here, I feel our connection and the world doesn't seem such a lonely place. I guess it's the same for you."

Karen rubbed the back of Jane's hand as it lay on top of her covers. The skin was soft, but cold. She wondered what type of life involved being confined to a bed, seven days a week, month after month, year after year. Karen shook her head in despair at her sister's existence. She questioned whether it could be classed as a life because all she knew was this bed, in this room.

Nurse Robyn Allen had given Karen an update as soon as she had arrived. Her sister's day had been comfortable with a moment where she'd been awake. But it was a different kind of awake to what most would expect. Jane's moment of wakefulness included her opening her eyes for a few minutes and staring at the ceiling above, before closing them and drifting off to sleep again.

Despite sitting beside her sister, Karen couldn't stop unhelpful thoughts creeping back into her awareness and spoiling her moment of solitude. Her mind smarted over her encounter with Omar Rashid, and the discovery of

Marvin Harris's disappearance. There were too many things that didn't add up, and every line of enquiry stalled before she even got traction.

Why am I doing this? What do I hope to achieve?

Justice popped into her mind like a flashing neon light, soon to be replaced with something far more potent.

Failure.

Failure sat heavy on her chest, crushing the air from her breath. She had let herself down and those around her, including a witness.

Karen took a break and headed to the communal kitchen to make herself a coffee. On the few occasions she'd ventured into the kitchen, she'd been alone. As she entered the room, another visitor sat in one armchair staring at his cup. He looked up and gave Karen a warm smile, but it felt like a pained smile. Karen returned the gesture before making herself a drink. She wrapped both hands around the mug and leant back against the kitchen counter, her eyes drifting from one focal point in the room to another before they settled on the other visitor. He looked lonely and lost, much the same as her.

"Do you mind if I join you?" Karen asked.

The man cleared his throat and pulled himself up in his chair. "Of course. I often sit here on my own, so it makes a refreshing change to have some company."

Karen agreed with the sentiment.

"I'm Kevin Fenn," he offered with a smile.

"Karen. Karen Heath. Are you visiting a friend, or family member?"

There was a pause as he looked down at his cup, emptiness robbing his face of any expression.

"My wife. Claire."

"I'm sorry to hear that. How is she?"

Kevin shrugged. "The same as she was when it happened. Unresponsive, a vegetative state. A car hit her. Severe brain damage. Life expectancy of less than twelve months." Kevin tipped his head back and blew out his cheeks. "Been here five months already."

Karen noticed his clipped replies. Each one said with effort and resignation.

He glanced up at her with tormented eyes. "How about you?"

"My sister, Jane. She's been here a long time. Much the same as your wife, severe brain damage."

Silence settled between them for a few moments, the company more than making up for the lack of words. United in sadness.

They began talking about life, and how their loved ones had suffered so much already. Karen found it cathartic to talk about the struggles she experienced on a day-to-day basis, many of which stood in the way of her spending more time here. Kevin agreed, even though he was self-employed and ran his own business, he found it hard to visit his wife. It wasn't a time issue, but Kevin alluded to the fact that seeing his wife in an unresponsive state dragged him back to that fateful day. A call from the police that changed his life and how his wife had been hit by a speeding car as she crossed the road near their house.

Without thought, Karen reached out and squeezed the man's arm. She felt the darkness in his soul. Despite the sadness that came with this place and seeing the pain and anguish on so many faces, there was an air of serenity and calmness about each of the rooms, including the kitchen and lounge. Soft colours, comfortable sofas and beds, delicate and refreshing artwork on the walls, and the air perfumed by an abundance of fresh flowers. Everything had been designed sympathetically.

She found the nursing staff were more like friends and extended family than professional healthcare workers. Nurse Allen always had time to stop and talk and give her a reassuring hug. The staff were here for the residents as much as the families. There were no raised voices, no hospital trolleys rattling as they trundled up and down corridors, no plain beige walls, or suspended ceiling signs. It felt more like a large home than a medical facility. And it was the best place for her sister.

Her phone buzzed, interrupting her moment of reflection.

14

We make our way out of the pub zigzagging between the crowds. He waves over at his friends, who raise their glasses and salute and cheer. I keep my head down so they don't get a proper look at me. He leads ahead, holding my hand as I trail behind him.

When we step out on to the pavement, he whistles through his teeth and flashes that white smile at me again. His skin is dark and smooth, there's not a blemish in sight. I allow him to put his arm around me, because it's all part of my plan. I enjoy seeing them feel as if they have a sense of power as they claim me. Little does he know that it's the other way around.

We waited a full hour before leaving and worked our way through more rounds than I care to admit. After several double TVRs, I moved on to gin and tonic, and he moved on to Jack Daniel's and Coke. But I insisted on paying when my turn came, I wanted to make sure I ordered him doubles.

As the warm evening air surrounds us, he sways and rocks as we walk along the pavement. He said his head is spinning. He puts his arm around my waist to pull me in closer to him, using the opportunity to steady himself. I feel fine, but he's well and truly fucked.

His hand keeps sliding down to my arse to squeeze it, and he says he can't wait to get us to a hotel room. He stops every few yards to reach down and kiss the nape of my neck, pulling me in towards him with both hands as he squeezes my arse. I can feel his hard cock pressing against me.

"I've got something better for you. Why wait until we get to a hotel room?" I say.

His brow furrows as he tries to make sense of my suggestion, and I lick my lips for effect. I take him by the hand and lead him through the backstreets to an alley. He questions our destination, and I reply that it's his lucky night. I can hear his breath quickening, words tripping from his mouth as we turn into a darkened corner.

He crashes against the wall as he tries to steady himself. Little does he know that I gave him a gentle push to catch him off guard. I move in closer and let his hands explore me. I unzip his fly and massage his semi-erect member. He groans as he kisses me. He's a shit kisser and can barely keep his head from lolling from side to side. He is so clumsy. Perfect.

I can't tell if it's the heat of the evening, or the excitement that rushes through my veins, that dampens my back with sweat. I can feel the muscles in my jaw flexing as the animal instinct in me rises to the surface. A part of me wants to sink my teeth into his tongue as it reaches into my mouth. I want to hear him scream. I tug harder on his member, pulling it with all my might, his hips bouncing back and forth against the wall. He groans in ecstasy as my hands reach up under his shirt and I draw my nails down his back. He winces for a moment before dropping back into his ecstatic state.

"I've got a treat for you," I say.

"Whaaart, iisss itttt?" he mumbles.

"You're about to find out," I reply, as I drop to my knees and ready myself. I look up to see him staring at me, his eyes rolling in their sockets. I tell him he needs to close his eyes because he'll enjoy this a lot more.

His voice slurs, but he says he wants to see my head bobbing up and down on his cock. I tell him to play by my rules, and either he agrees to it or I walk. Reluctantly he nods before tilting his head back. I hear the thud as the back of his head bangs against the wall. His eyelids become heavier and heavier before they finally close, the alcohol sapping his body of energy, and sending his mind into a euphoric state. His hands drop to his sides, and he waits patiently.

With one hand still massaging his member, my other hand searches around for something that I stashed here a few hours ago. Without taking my eyes off him, my fingers tap around on the ground until I find it. I get to my feet and with all my might I swing my arm around, the brick connecting with the side of his head. The heavy thud sends him flying to one side, and he drops to his knees. Dazed and confused, the second blow renders him unconscious. He falls, his head cracking on the floor.

I sit astride of him and raise the brick in both hands above my head and bring it down on the back of his head. The sickening thud of brick against skull excites me. I wonder how many noises I can make with his head as I keep hitting him. The sharp sound eventually replaced by squidgy wet noises.

Exhausted, sweaty and out of breath, I roll off him and stare at his lifeless body. Fuck, that felt good. It was so much easier than I thought, but then he was putty in my hands the minute I saw him.

I check my phone. Eleven forty-nine p.m.

Game over.

15

Karen swirled around in her chair, enjoying some time to herself. She'd convinced herself that a coffee and Danish from Pret A Manger were the best way to start the day. Her working patterns were so irregular that she found it hard to stick to any sort of routine.

Her coffee was still warm, the Danish quietened her rumbling stomach, and some sleep had helped. If she could, Karen avoided the coffee in any station or police building. She was sure that the powers to be were slowly poisoning their staff with the swill they passed off as coffee. On the rare occasion she had tried one from the machine, there was always a putrid, black sticky mess at the bottom of the polystyrene cup.

Bumping into Skelton this morning hadn't been a great start to the day. He had wanted an update from her, which she began to give him, but she sensed some tension in him. And occasionally was sure he had lost interest in listening to her, his mind preoccupied elsewhere.

Her mobile buzzed on her desk, the vibration causing it to rattle along the surface. The caller ID confirmed it was Wainwright.

"You made it in then?" he asked.

"Of course. If I'm not mistaken, I was under strict instructions last night to be in work promptly?"

"You were, Karen. I was just on my way home last night when I called you, so I didn't have my notes to hand. But I thought I better fill you in as soon as I could."

Karen stared at the papers on her desk. "You could have told me last night before you left work and saved me the hassle of getting in early?"

"Where's the fun in that, Karen? I was hoping by the tone of my voice last night, that I left you intrigued and excited."

"You left me with something, Wainwright, intrigued and excited isn't the phrase that springs to mind. Pain in the arse, sounds more fitting."

"I'm mortally wounded, Karen. And there was me thinking I'm your friend."

"You are, but you won't be for long if you don't get on with it." She laughed.

"Fun over. You can be so boring sometimes, Karen. Anyway. I requested a further toxicology analysis on your body. Nothing came back of significance, other than high potassium levels, which… are perfectly acceptable to most people."

A prickle of awareness travelled up her spine. "I sense some hesitation in your voice."

"Get out of the bloody way, you ignorant fool."

Karen pulled the phone away from her ear and looked at it, before placing it back. "Are you talking to me?"

Wainwright burst out laughing. "Sorry, Karen, I'm driving. I had a bloody ignoramus pull out in front of me without indicating."

Karen rolled her eyes.

"Anyway, as I was saying, I'm not so convinced. And I'll email you my report as soon as I have time to pull up. But I think someone poisoned your victim."

"Poisoned? That's a new one. How?"

"Well I did a bit of digging around and spoke to the chaps at the lab. We discussed chemicals that can get broken down into by-products which are normal to the body but may be enough to kill a human without a trace. After I did the post-mortem, that puncture wound bothered me."

Karen paused long enough to grab a pen. "So, you think our man was poisoned in some way, prior to being killed?"

"I do. And I think potassium chloride may have been used. When it's administered, it metabolises into potassium and chloride ions, both ions are normally found in the body. It's often used to treat people with low levels of potassium."

"So how would it kill him?"

"If too much is administered," Wainwright replied, "it can lead to kidney failure and sudden cardiac arrest. We can't be certain, but my guess is he was injected with potassium chloride in such a large dose that it caused severe heart arrhythmias and mimicked a heart attack."

Karen sat up in her chair, scribbling notes as Wainwright continued his explanation.

"In a matter of minutes, the heart spasms and stops functioning in what we call a sudden cardiac death. And that would correlate with the evidence of high potassium levels. Whenever any muscle tissue is damaged, and of course the heart is a muscle, unusually large amounts of potassium are released into the blood. And there's evidence of damage to the tissues of the heart, which would make sense."

"Shit. You would likely list the cause of death as a fatal heart attack," Karen said. "How much would need to be administered?"

"I can't be a hundred per cent accurate, Karen, but the lethal dose is around two point five grams per kilogram of body weight. A lethal dose for at least fifty per cent of people weighing seventy-five kilograms would be about a hundred and ninety grams."

Karen sprang out of her chair and made her way towards the team as Wainwright finished off his summary with the promise that the report would be to her within minutes.

Karen gathered as many of the team together as possible and broke the news. There was a mixture of surprise tinged with excitement from those gathered as Karen recalled everything Wainwright had told her. Questions and theories bounced around the room. At first some officers jumped to the conclusion that the killer may have been receiving treatment for low potassium levels and had access to the drug. But this was quickly dispelled as another officer did a quick search online and found that potassium chloride powder could be obtained without a prescription from health food stores, fitness supplement stores and even Amazon.

The news quickly dashed hopes that they could start contacting doctors in the local area when Karen realised the easy availability. It gave Karen and the team a further insight into the mind of the killer.

This wasn't a random killing; this was premeditated and planned.

The killer had gone to great lengths to find a way to cover their tracks and had it not been for Wainwright, they may have started looking at the prospect of a random killing.

Jade carried on with the revelations. "We pulled off the phone records from Adam's phone. All the numbers can be traced, but we found evidence of a messaging app called *Don't Talk*, but it's empty."

"Never heard of it," Steve replied.

"I'm surprised you haven't with the number of women you date," Jade fired back.

"What can you tell us about it?" Karen asked.

Jade continued, turning towards her boss. "It's a messaging app that lets users send encrypted text, audio, video or photo messages and becomes a self-destructing messaging app. But you can adjust the timescales within the app for up to six days before it just evaporates."

Karen's eyes narrowed. "This all sounds covert and clandestine, and something that belongs in a James Bond or *Mission Impossible* movie."

"It's astounding to be honest, boss. Quite a few of the dating forums that I've looked around mention this app because users can send texts, messages and media files without worrying about messaging history or tracking systems. This new generation of apps can send messages that delete themselves after a certain period and leave no trace or history on your phone."

Karen crossed her arms and paced around in front of the team. "That just makes our job a lot harder. Does that mean we can't find out who Adam has been talking to?"

Jade shrugged and nodded. "He could have been talking to anyone in the world who had this app, and we wouldn't know. They set all communications with military-grade encryption and there's no server between the sender and the receiver. They've got this secure file shredder built into the app which forensically erases unwanted files. It's a bloody nightmare."

"Once they're read, they disappear forever?"

Jade nodded. "I really don't think there's anything anyone can do to retrieve this information. Even if we contacted the intelligence or military services. I don't think it would help. From what I can gather, the app strips out the metadata from the audio, video and image files, and lets the user set a *Mission Impossible*-style self-destruct timer on anything sent. The app overwrites deleted data with unreadable text, so any deleted data becomes impossible to forensically recover."

Karen shook her head. She had never come across anything of this nature. Technology was supposed to help them to detect and prevent crime and she now found herself in the unenviable position of accepting that technology prevented them from detecting and solving crimes.

"So, there's a possibility that the person who killed Adam may have been using this app to communicate with him.

But we'll never know?" Brad asked, tapping the back of his pen on his pad.

There was a collective silence amongst the team as reality hit them. It perplexed Karen. This was turning into something from an espionage novel. Poisoning by syringe and self-destructing messaging apps. Karen turned towards the incident board and stared at Adam's picture. For the first time in an investigation, she felt lost. The killer's attention to detail astounded her. Her thoughts were interrupted as an officer from the back stepped through the desks and handed her some papers hot off the printer.

Various hushed conversations broke out behind her as officers discussed their own theories and speculated on the profile of the killer. Glancing down at the papers, she scanned over Wainwright's findings, and some points that hadn't been discussed in their phone call.

The semen found on his body belonged to Adam. There were no other hair or clothing fibres found on his body.

Her eyes focused on a few lines. Adam's skin contained traces of hydrogen peroxide and Benzenesulfonic acid. None of this made sense to her as she scanned the notes, her lips moving in silence as she read each sentence.

Karen stopped in her tracks; her eyes unable to get past the few words that screamed at her from the page. Trace elements found on his body were in common household cleaning products, in particular, household detergents and laundry products which produced oxygen bubbles. Her eyes widened at Wainwright's assessment.

The killer had cleaned Adam's body to remove all traces linking them to the crime.

16

Karen stared at the computer in her office and sighed. With little known about Adam's background and friendship circle, Karen had tasked the team with finding out as much as they could about him. His wife had given them plenty of information and a basic understanding of Adam as a person. But with so many unidentified people in photographs on his Facebook page, they had a big task ahead of them trying to eliminate as many as possible.

Part of Karen's job, and that of the team, was to build a much bigger picture of their victim. They needed to know his movements, his interactions with people, and the personal and professional relationships that he maintained. Karen had given the investigating team a list of things they needed to do that included identifying where Adam hung out and to deep dive into his prior relationships. It was a difficult conversation to have with Jackie, but she'd given the names of his past girlfriends.

The task was huge, and the discovery of the messaging app

on his phone hadn't helped it. That opened a new line of investigation. But Karen doubted that they would get anywhere. For all they knew he could have had one conversation or dozens. His laptop from work, and the one he had at home were being analysed by the high-tech unit and data being pulled off the hard drive.

All the MITs followed a framework. Anything of significant value was added to the HOLMES2 database. It always started with a crime scene investigation, followed by the victim or witness interviews before moving to any media appeals. Running in parallel would be house-to-house enquiries, area and intelligence searches that included phone and computer records, CCTV and ANPR footage. Karen believed she was covering most angles and decided to hold back on a media appeal for the time being.

Anyone of these trawls could fire off an important line of enquiry seeking specific evidence which would then help them to trace a named suspect, identify or locate other potential witnesses, or pursue other significant information.

This was the bit she hated most. It felt like a waiting game. She paced around her office going over the information received so far. Whoever killed Adam had chosen him for a reason. That reason eluded her now, but the information from Wainwright carried some significance. She stopped in her tracks and continued reading Wainwright's report before moving again.

The killer had gone to great lengths to clean up the body. Scrapings beneath the fingernails revealed nothing. No dirt, no skin fibres, nothing. There were no clothes fibres on the body and no traces of make-up. Wainwright had concluded the victim died before being burnt with what now turned out to be a paint stripper because had he had been alive, the abrasions around his wrists would have been worse as he struggled to free himself.

Karen grimaced as the full extent of the injuries inflicted on Adam Manners danced in her brain. In a perverse way she felt pleased that he'd died before being subjected to the acid attack. She couldn't imagine what it felt like to be burnt in that way. She recalled the countless times when she'd scalded a hand in boiling water and just how much it hurt as she held it under a cold running tap.

But why?

The chances were Adam was already dead.

Why then continue with the acid attack?

If she wanted to inflict pain on him, then the killer would have done that prior to the injection?

It made little sense to Karen. Her thoughts moved on to the mindset of the killer and what drove someone to do something so heinous.

Was there anger behind it?

Did the killer get off on inflicting as much damage as possible?

Karen needed answers, but as she stood in her office, she wondered where they would come from.

17

Skelton poked his head out of the doorway and checked the corridor in both directions before stepping back into his office and closing the door. He stood facing the glass panel so he could react if someone knocked. Going through his recent call list, he found the number and pressed redial and waited whilst biting his bottom lip. As he waited for the voice on the other end of the line, a black cloud of dread settled over him. His guts twisted, and his sphincter muscle spasmed when his call connected.

"It's me, she's still snooping around. I'm getting alerts twice a day. I thought I should let you know."

Skelton waited whilst Sally remained silent on the other end. So much was his paranoia, he didn't even refer to Karen's name in the conversation in case the calls were being recorded or someone else was listening in.

"That's not good news. You gave me your reassurances you

were handling things at your end. Did you remove what I asked you to?"

Skelton nodded to himself before replying. "Yes. Whatever she searches for, I then remove. Well, not me. I've got someone in IT who is in my pocket. He was nicked a while ago in a knocking shop, sniffing coke off some tom's tits. I made his charges disappear for doing me a few favours."

"Jesus, Skelton, you fucking dick. I told you to sort it, all you've done is added another layer of grief. And you said you would remove all the information."

Skelton could hear the anger bristling in Sally's tone. "And I will. But I can't remove it too quickly. It has to be slow, so it's not flagged up on the system. The case is still open, but it's dormant. Unless any new evidence comes to light, there is no active line of investigation now."

"Who the fuck do you think you are playing with, Skelton? I told you I needed all traces removed. Which bit of that sentence do you not fucking understand?"

"Sal…"

"Shut up. I don't want to hear another fucking, pathetic excuse. I won't repeat myself again, sort it out today."

Skelton had to think fast on his feet. He needed to buy himself some time, temporarily freeing himself of her unreasonable demands. Yes, he could remove the evidence, but he needed time.

"I'll try my best. I'm back-to-back in senior management meetings the rest of the afternoon, so I will be here late."

"Skelton, I said no excuses. I'll see you tonight, and it better be sorted by then."

The line went dead before Skelton could say another word. He stared at his phone as if expecting it to reconnect. The constriction feeling grew, as if someone had their hands wrapped around his neck, choking the life out of him. He stared up at the wall clock, and listened to the ticks, like the timer on a bomb. He couldn't stop it, reverse it or slow it down. Each tick dragged him forward, helpless and nervous to this evening. He could no more avoid it than the beating of his own heart as it pounded with futility against its cage of bones and cartilage. The dread was like an invisible demon sitting heavy on his shoulders and only he could hear the sharpening of its knives. The first signs of sweat erupted on his forehead, as he became pale, then the tremor in his hands began. His head became a little giddy and his stomach nauseous.

Skelton paced his office, walking from wall to wall, as his mind tried to make sense of the situation. He had removed as many records as he could without causing too much alarm. Karen continued to snoop and hadn't heeded his warnings. He needed to warn Karen off. The last thing he wanted was Karen at the bottom of the Regent's Canal, but without knowing the identity of those she was up against, she played with fire and there was little chance of her winning. He wasn't her keeper, and if she went after the Connells, it would end only one way for her.

Dead.

Needing to calm his nerves, Skelton slipped out of his office and made his way to the toilets. He glanced over his shoulder a few times just to see who was about, and when the corridor was empty, he darted in. He pushed the door to each cubicle to make sure none were in use before he made his way to the far end cubicle and shut the door. His breathing was heavy and laboured, his forehead damp, and his jaw ached from clenching his teeth so tight.

He reached into his pocket and pulled out a small plastic packet of white powder. He dropped the lid on the toilet seat and emptied the contents of the packet on to the flat lid before shaping it into a thin line. With a spare ten-pound note from his wallet, he folded it into a thin tube and snorted the line, waiting for the dust to do its magic. Skelton closed his eyes and leant back against the wall of the cubicle. In just a few minutes, a wave of relaxation washed over his body and a smile broke on his face. He could have visited the brothel again, but he'd been there last week.

Skelton always had a line before going to fuck that eighteen-year-old Albanian called Greta. Despite her youth, she had the body and the sex appeal of someone twice her age. In a few years her ravaged figure would reveal the hundreds of men she'd slept with, and the drugs pumped into her by handlers to keep her compliant. But it hadn't gone well the last time he had been there. After paying her one hundred pounds for some coke and sex, he had wanted another go with her as a freebie. She had asked for another hundred pounds, and he had refused. The bruises he had left her with would ensure that she never argued with him again.

18

Tired eyes and weary bodies surrounded her as Karen convened the team for an end of day briefing. The team were following up on the key action points per Karen's direction. As a result, the team were thin on the ground, with many out on enquiries.

"Ladies and gents, I'm sure you're just as knackered as I am, so let's keep this brief and then get out of here. I'm going over the road to the Havelock's for a quick drink on my way home so any of you are more than welcome to join me."

"Is it your birthday?" one officer asked in jest.

"You found the combination for the lock on your purse?" another one shouted.

A ripple of laughter spread across the room as Karen put her hands on her hips and joined them.

"Hilarious. We are known to shout the team a drink. I just think you lot have been working hard on this case, and it's been challenging. So, I think we deserve a bit of chill time. If you want to throw that gesture back in my face, you can all piss off."

They met her words with jeers and heckles.

"Right back to business. Are there any updates before we get out of this sweatbox?" Karen blew out her cheeks as she looked towards the windows, brilliant sunshine streamed through them casting a blanket of dappled light across the office. The building could never get its air conditioning right. In the winter it would belt out cold air and they would sit wrapped in coats. And during the summer, it threw out hot heat which made conditions unbearable.

Brad started first. "Ma'am, we've been looking into Adam's background. He is one of two brothers. He has a younger brother who works in Dubai and has returned to the UK after being contacted by his parents following Adam's death."

"Where do his parents live?"

"Norwich. They're coming to visit Jackie tomorrow."

"Any more on Adam himself?" Karen asked.

Brad nodded. "He graduated from Nottingham University with a 2:1 honours in business and marketing, and in his spare time does a lot of cycling. He joined Arrows Cycling Club, and we are contacting them."

"Update the incident board and database when you get the chance. Jade, how are we getting on with his previous relationships?"

"We spoke to Jackie again, and he was in a long-term relationship prior to their marriage. Since being married he has had several affairs. Well, not affairs, more like one-night stands with loads of flirting. He assured Jackie that neither lasted longer than a week."

Karen couldn't help but roll her eyes. "It sounds like he's tried to play down each affair. To me that looks more like damage limitation than anything else."

"Possibly, ma'am. She's given us their names, and we've got officers tracking them down. From what we can gather, neither of them lives in London. One lives in Leeds now and the other in Cambridge. We will arrange for local officers to interview them both."

Karen gave Jade the thumbs up. "Good work. Let me know what they say. There is the possibility that one of those relationships, if you can call them that, ended on a bitter note, and she took revenge. But as I said at the beginning, if it was revenge, this is a whole new level."

Karen hoped for news on the laptops that had been seized. But they were still with the high-tech unit pulling off the data from hard drives. With very little else of interest, Karen called it a day. What she needed more than anything was a seriously chilled bottle of Pinot Grigio and judging by the dozen or so officers that joined her, they needed a stiff drink, too.

SKELTON STARED up at the darkened ceiling, counting his lucky stars. Just prior to logging off and making his way to Sally's, he had contacted the IT guy and given him a list of files to delete. The lad had reluctantly agreed to the request.

By the time Skelton had arrived, Sally bristled with anger.

Normally she was dry, blunt and had a twinkle of mischievousness in her eyes. This time her eyes looked dark and menacing like thunder. Her lips were drawn into a thin pencil line, and when she spoke, she spat each word out with venom. But he had pacified her.

He'd assured her he had taken the necessary steps to remove evidence from the case files. She had wanted him to remove all the evidence, but he'd managed to make her see sense when he'd explained that it would raise more questions if investigating officers opened the case again.

Skelton rolled over to Sally's half of the bed and nuzzled in behind her. He loved to feel the warmth of her back on his chest, and the roundness of her arse on his thighs. Skelton enjoyed lying by her side and feeling her heart race from the sex they'd enjoyed just moments ago. He wrapped his arm around her chest, his hand resting on her sweaty breast.

"I can come over again in a few days if you want me to?"

"We'll see. And though you're good in bed, you ain't half give me a fucking headache," Sally replied.

"I know. I'm sorry. But I'm doing my best. The last thing I want is to lose my job. Think of it from your angle, you'll lose a man on the inside. And that's not going to help anyone, is it?"

"You think you're that valuable? You love yourself a bit, don't you?"

"Well, who's kept your firm out of trouble? Your lot could have been banged up years ago if it wasn't for me." Some of Skelton's bravado came back.

Sally brushed his arm off and sat up on her side of the bed reaching for her cigarettes. The glow of the lighter lit up the room for a few seconds before she took a deep drag and blew out the smoke. "Who says you're the only person we have on the inside?"

"What? You must be fucking kidding. There isn't anyone else. You're just pulling my chain. I don't have to heel every time you threaten me."

"You keep thinking that, Skelton, and you might believe that one day. I could drop you off the face of the earth within the hour and no one would ever… ever see you again."

A chill of fear prickled Skelton's skin. Her words held a coldness that tore through him. He knew he had got away with it but was fast running out of excuses. And though he wanted Karen out the way, a part of him wanted to save her, for her own sake. Whether it was guilt or the fact that Karen was another serving officer, he wasn't sure. But if there was one thing he didn't want; it was Karen's blood on his hands.

He was torn from his thoughts as Sally got up and made her way out of the room. Her parting words left him bewildered and confused.

"I need you to come with me tomorrow. No questions asked."

19

Karen stood at the start of New Inn Broadway, glancing around. Whenever the job phone rang, Karen knew it signalled a development or something of significance. Often, the news wasn't good. Occasionally, she was lucky enough to have a call confirm they had apprehended a suspect, but on this occasion, it was the news she feared the most. The discovery of a body during the night.

She took a moment to familiarise herself with her surroundings. It wasn't an area that she had been to. She glanced at the artwork on the side of the building. Against a black wall canvas, there was an artistic impression of a bird in flight and a hand holding an envelope. The intricate artwork outlined each fold and crease in the fingers, but her eyes were drawn to a stunning mural of a black woman holding a blue orb with white strips of light breaking through long slits in the orb. It took her a moment to realise that the long slits and white colouring spelt the word future. She was holding the future in her hand. Karen thought it was brilliant.

Karen turned towards a scene guard and signed in before retrieving her protective coverings. "What's that building over there?" she asked, flicking her head backwards.

The uniformed officer looked over her shoulder towards the artwork on the wall. "I believe that's the London College of Fashion and some art college, ma'am."

Karen nodded. "That figures. Impressive artwork."

The officer shrugged and nodded. He appeared neither impressed nor interested as he took the pen back from Karen and lifted the blue cordon tape to allow her through.

The road was narrow as two lanes merged into one. Karen imagined that at night the road took on a far more sinister feel. She could see a hive of police activity just up ahead of her as Steve made his way towards her, dressed in a matching protective suit.

"What have we got, Steve?" Karen asked, as she studied the old brown brick buildings that surrounded them, their bright red doors and window frames a marked contrast to the drab and dreary brickwork.

"Ma'am, Wainwright is examining the body now, and SOCO are busy doing a sweep. Jade's arriving shortly. I've had a quick look, and there's not much left of his face."

Steve handed Karen a clear evidence bag containing a gent's wallet. "We believe the victim is Dulani Kalagho, aged twenty-nine, reported missing yesterday mid-morning when he didn't arrive for work."

"Anything on his last movements?"

"He was out with friends the night before last, and they reported him leaving the pub with a woman."

"And that's the last anyone saw of him?"

Steve nodded.

"Who found him?"

"There's a bakery around the front, and one of the workers stepped out of the rear doors to dump a load of rubbish. She saw a pair of legs sticking out from behind the bin. She freaked out before nearly passing out, and that's when her manager called the police."

Karen looked over towards the open doors of the ambulance and saw a woman's head poking out from the top of a red blanket that cocooned her. A female police officer sat beside her taking notes.

"Are we getting a statement?"

Steve followed Karen's eyes. "We're trying to, but the witness is in a state. One minute she's lucid, next minute, she's falling to pieces."

"Any chance this was a robbery?"

Steve shook his head. "Unlikely. There's loose change in his pockets, and two hundred and fifty quid in his wallet. His mobile is in the back pocket of his trousers and he has a roly."

"A what?"

"A roly, ma'am. It's a street name for Rolex. He's got a Rolex on his wrist. Easily ten grand upwards."

Karen widened her eyes in surprise.

Steve nodded. "Seriously. Those things are worth a bomb. Even a basic used submariner will set you back about six grand."

"Blimey, how can people afford that? I mean, ten grand. You could buy a second-hand car for that."

Karen and Steve moved towards the body to get a closer look. SOCO continued their examination of the scene, their work overseen by Mason Brophy, the crime scene manager. He was giving them instructions and making sure that every angle was photographed and documented. Karen could see the victim lying face down with a severe injury to the back of his head, with his trousers around his ankles. In fact, describing it as a head didn't do it justice. It appeared to be nothing more than fragments of brain, bone and blood matter formed in a congealed mess that created a red halo.

She wondered what degree of force had been applied to create such catastrophic injuries. She recalled attending a road traffic collision as a uniformed officer where the driver of the car lost control and hit the back of an articulated lorry at high speed. The victim had lost most of their head.

She scrunched her face as she watched Wainwright examine the body. The extent of the damage sent waves of nausea through Karen, but Wainwright appeared unperturbed. After about fifteen minutes, he stepped outside of the inner cordon and approached Karen.

"Blunt force trauma, at least two, possibly three, blows to the head," Wainwright explained as he sighed. "Well to be honest, it could have been more than that, ten perhaps, there's so little left of his head that it's hard to determine how many times he was struck."

"Any sign of resistance?" Karen asked, shaking her head in disbelief.

"Not from what I can see. His fingertips are clean, and there're no scratches or abrasions on his hands. I'll know more once I get him back on the table."

Karen looked around the scene. Discarded boxes, empty Costa coffee cups, the occasional sandwich packet and remnants of food littered the ground. "And they say love is dead. It's one thing having al fresco sex, and all the excitement and thrills it can bring, but a quick shag in an alleyway, a dirty alleyway, really doesn't rate that high on my bucket list of things to do."

"Agreed."

"Time of death?"

"I'm not sure, to be honest. But considering he was in a bar over twenty-four hours ago, and with no sightings since, I'd say somewhere between twenty-four and thirty-six hours."

Karen turned towards Steve. "Any other witnesses or sightings?"

"Nothing yet, ma'am. We are checking the other buildings to see who's in them and whether or not anyone saw anything suspicious."

By now Mason Brophy had joined them and given them the debrief on the actions of his team. They would soon complete the initial stages of their investigation, but he anticipated that some members of his team would remain here for the next few hours whilst extending their search cordon.

"When we turned the body over earlier, the victim had

suffered what appears to be severe burns to the groin region, it looks like some form of toxic liquid may have caused that injury."

"Really?"

Brophy nodded. "Yep. It's not the type of injury you would receive from a splash, this is more extensive."

Karen and Steve exchanged a glance. Their thoughts collided, and the likelihood of it being linked to the first case. There were similarities between both cases, though the MO was different. But both within a week.

Karen's mind drifted as she watched SOCO move in systematic waves across the crime scene. One investigator placed half of a red brick in a clear evidence bag. Brilliant flashes of light bounced off the surrounding walls every few seconds as they continued to photograph the scene.

If the team weren't stretched already, she now had another murder on her hands.

20

With the news relayed back to the team, and live cam footage from Steve, most of the team were up to speed by the time Karen returned to the office. They jostled for positions as they gathered around Karen. Another incident board sat beside the first, with information surrounding a second victim.

Karen rolled up the sleeves on her blouse and took a sip of water to cool herself before pinning up images of Dulani Kalagho. "Okay, team. If you thought you were busy before; things are about to heat up quickly. No pun intended. We've got our work cut out for us now. Steve and I have just returned from the scene. And as most of you have seen from the footage, it's not a pretty sight." She looked around at the gathered crowd. "If none of you have seen the footage, I suggest you do that as a priority as soon as I finish this briefing. I need you all up to speed as quickly as possible."

Karen nodded in Steve's direction. He rose and joined her side.

"The victim is a twenty-nine-year-old male, Dulani Kalagho. Having spoken to the pathologist, and the crime scene manager, our initial thoughts are a blunt force trauma injury as the cause of death. He had his wallet on him, so we know that he lives in Bethnal Green. He had a girlfriend but didn't live with her. And, she wasn't the person he left with."

"What else do we know about him, Steve?"

"Ma'am, he had a business card in his wallet, and from what we can gather he worked for an events management company in London. Social services records confirm that he came from Malawi in Africa at three with his mum. They received refugee status when the authorities deemed it unsafe for them to return to their home country for fear of retribution." Steve elaborated further on the information they had received. "Malawi's main religion is the Sunni Muslim, Kalagho's family were Shia Muslims and faced persecution and death. That's why his mother fled, for their safety."

The fact he and his mother escaped persecution and imminent death for a better life in the UK, only for Dulani to lose his life prematurely, wasn't lost on the team. A respectful silence fell amongst them for a few moments.

"Thank you, Steve."

"Ma'am."

"As well as the significant injuries to the victim's head, he also suffered extensive and severe burns to his groin area. So that's why this case interests us."

An officer amongst the crowd interjected. "But ma'am, it's a different MO. The burns are the only similarity."

Karen agreed. There were no signs of robbery, but as with their previous case, there was possible evidence of sexual activity, which Karen was at lengths to explain to her team.

A female officer that Karen knew as Tracey Martin offered the information that she had gathered so far. "Obviously, we need to check this in person, but from what I can gather, there is no CCTV leading up to the approach where he was found nor is there any within the alley. But we should be able to get CCTV footage from outside of the pub where he was last seen, and there are a couple of other cameras situated close by."

Karen instructed Tracey to dispatch officers to grab any footage from nearby cameras from two nights ago.

"He was seen leaving the Bell pub with a woman. And then failed to turn up for work yesterday morning."

"The chances are he was killed not long after leaving the pub?" Brad asked.

Karen nodded. "His girlfriend won't be making a formal ID for obvious reasons. So, we can begin the post-mortem quickly. She will need careful handling, I'm sure the news has devastated her. But we'll need a statement from her at some point."

"Ma'am, I had a quick look, and Dulani had a Facebook profile," an officer commented.

"Well, that's a start. Print off his pictures and take them with you to see if any bar staff remember seeing him. Jade, can I leave it with you to get some officers to take witness statements from the group of friends he was with in the pub?"

Jade nodded her approval as she flicked through some

crime scene photos that were being passed amongst the group.

"We need to do the usual again. Check out all of his social media profiles and see if we can get access to his phone and bank records. If this was a robbery, then it would have been straightforward, the fact nothing was taken suggests that it was more personal. As Steve pointed out, he was still wearing his roly." Karen stressed the word roly by doing air quotes.

Karen paused and studied her team. There was a mixture of concern and excitement etched on their faces. She could see several processing their own theories as they stared into thin air.

"This concerns me, and it will become a big issue. That both victims were doused in acid suggests the two cases are linked. I've never in my career heard of something like this. It's just too much of a coincidence to ignore. Find that link and we may have a chance of catching the person who has committed these acts. And yes, before anyone asks, my gut instinct tells me it's the same person, because both are on our patch, both within a week, and both had their groins melted off with acid."

21

"They took a long time to find him," I say to myself as I watch the lunchtime news. I wonder just how clever the police are and whether they will make the connection? I hoped that by killing in different locations and different ways, it would throw them off the scent for a while and buy me time to enjoy this even more.

It makes me laugh as I watch the commotion play out on TV. The blue cordons, the police cars blocking off the street, and the puppets in white suits that try to look important and mysterious.

My mind flicks back to the last few moments of his life, and the sound that his head made as it cracked and split under the force of my blows. God, it felt so good. I can still feel the power and excitement that surged through me as I hit him repeatedly. He put up no resistance. In fact, it was a little too easy. I like it when they struggle a bit or plead for their lives. But I misjudged how much he could drink, and lucky for him he didn't know what was coming when the first blow hit him.

Men will never learn. You show them a bit of attention and they become putty in your hands. Why are they so easily influenced? That question has challenged generations. Maybe it's a genetic weakness, or years of conditioning, or goes right back to the days of their ancestors where cavemen hunted and procreated. That was their only purpose in life, to hunt, bring food home for the family, and have sex. What a simple life they lived.

Who knows? And do I care? No!

They were both easy to talk to. It didn't take long to turn them on. And when I started sending pictures of my naked body, I knew I had them. Especially Dulani. He couldn't get enough of them, begging me for more. But I was discreet with him and kept my face hidden in pictures which is why he didn't recognise me. It would only end one way for him.

I planned every single stage with him. My initial profile, the first contact, warming him up, and finding out as much as I could about him. I knew his movements. I knew what he liked and didn't like, and more importantly, I knew where he would be. My eyes look back to the windowsill and the small bottles of colourless liquid that sit in line, waiting their turn. I wonder if I'll use any of them again. Seeing Adam freeze, his eyes widening as he shut down, looking confused. All of it had caused a swell of joy to surge within me.

We are just bags of meat in their eyes. The weak bow down and the strong devour them. They always say that women are the weaker sex, but I disagree.

Men are the weaker sex; they can't say no. And when they can't walk away, I reel them in and enjoy exploiting their vulnerabilities and taking their lives. My thoughts tumble back in time to a distant memory from the past. Albert Johnson. A man who lived one street away from me as I grew up. He was a pest and a dirty pervert. I remember hearing from the other kids that he was a kiddie fiddler.

He tempted me with sweets and cakes when I was out playing with my friends. And I resisted the urge. And then on one occasion I succumbed. He attracted me in a way that no boy or man had, and thinking about it now, I hated it. When he pushed me against the table and touched me from behind, I grabbed the long screwdriver I'd seen on the table and drove it straight into his belly. I watched his eyes, fuelled with fear and surprise.

Within seconds, pain distorted his features further and he collapsed to his knees. I then stabbed him with it over thirty times. His belly, his back and his neck punctured with raw and bleeding wounds. I loved the sickly-sweet smell, and how warm the liquid felt between my small fingers. It was like nothing I'd felt before.

To this day they have never found the killer, nor the weapon. How could they when the screwdriver sits at the bottom of the pond in my local park?

I open my phone and flick through to my favourite app. I spend the next few hours just trawling through the different profiles. Old men, young men, fake smiles, and some more intimate photographs which you can only see if you friend someone. So much choice, and so little time. There's a certain criterion that I look for in a man, and I don't get to find out until I've spoken to them a few times. I realised quickly that their profiles are full of bullshit. It's only when

I ask the more direct questions or swap photographs that I discover the real them. There's only one thing on their mind. It's those that I am after. I better carry on looking to see who I might want to meet next.

22

The hours were ticking away as Karen sat at her desk reviewing the information gathered from this morning's crime scene. At times like this she felt the most impatient, whilst waiting for new information and feedback from their initial enquiries. A nervous energy kept her heart beating just a little faster than normal and made her fidgety.

The uncertainty around each case frustrated Karen. Sometimes every aspect of a case would fall into place, and they'd get a result in a matter of days. Then there were cases that sat on the system and remained active months later. Often those cases lacked evidential matter or witnesses which meant the chances of reaching a successful conclusion were limited. And from experience Karen knew that as time progressed, the less the chance of success, too.

That wasn't always the case, especially cold cases, because with changes in forensic technology and forensic sampling, it meant they were able to get more information and evidence than they would have been able to get ten years ago.

Karen felt a tinge of excitement as she received a call and made her way through to the video room. A sense of urgency fuelled her steps as she sped down the corridor. The room wasn't the biggest of spaces, and with the combination of the monitors radiating heat, four junior detectives hunched over their own screens, and heat from outside, the room felt stifling and stuffy as Karen burst in, breathing heavily.

Jade had tasked the detectives to trawl through CCTV footage from the pub and surrounding shops close to the location of the victim. One detective had struck lucky and had identified the victim in the pub talking to a woman.

"What have you got, Chris?" Karen asked as she grabbed a chair and squeezed into the cubicle alongside the detective. She had worked with Chris frequently and found her a competent and thorough detective. Chris wouldn't miss a lot when tasked with trawling footage. Her meticulous attention to detail had earned her the assignment.

Chris smiled as she wrapped her mousy blonde hair behind her ears and winked at Karen. "Images are a little dark and grainy, but I've zoomed in as much as I can without pixilating the images any further." Chris moved the recording backwards and paused the tape.

Karen watched as the tape stopped on a still image of the victim talking with a young woman. Chris had portioned off her screen so that half showed the video footage, and the other half showed four pixilated images of the woman. Karen checked the timestamp and then tutted. Unfortunately for most of the recording, Dulani Kalagho faced towards the camera. The woman he was talking to faced away.

"Clever, very clever. If I had to guess, I would say that she was teasing us," Karen said.

"She knows the cameras are there. We get a sideways glance from her when she looks towards the bar. But she doesn't turn around."

Karen studied the still image of the woman and grimaced. They were tantalisingly close to getting their first insight into the woman that may have killed Dulani. From what Karen could see, the woman had brown long bobbed hair, a slim figure and wore a white cropped top. But that was all they could see. Amongst the crowd of people, they couldn't see any further past the middle of her back as the couple nestled in between the crowd at the bar.

She leant in further, resting her elbows on her knees attempting to get a closer look at the screen. "Bollocks. Get out of the fucking way," she muttered as other customers obscured their view as they came back and forth from the bar. One minute they had a clear view of the couple, and the next their heads disappeared in a sea of people.

"Any other sightings of either of them?"

Chris shook her head. "Nothing yet, ma'am."

Karen hoped the footage would reveal more, but they'd have to settle for the occasional side glance. It wasn't a great start. But it was a start.

The chances were that she was likely to be the last person to see Dulani Kalagho alive.

23

"How certain can you be that this is the last person to see the victim alive? Especially because you're still yet to identify any further sightings of him afterwards."

The tone of Skelton's questioning riled Karen. There wasn't an ounce of encouragement in his voice, his tone harsh, dry and aggressive. But then again, he was like that with her most of the time, so she should be used to it by now.

Karen watched her boss as he rested his elbows on the table and kept rolling his fingers round and round in a ball as if massaging them. His eyes narrowed into thin slits that matched his mouth. There wasn't much about him that she admired or liked. Even though he wore a suit to work, he always appeared scruffy because he left his tie hanging loose around his neck. Pulling his hair back in an unshapen lump, he just made his large forehead even bigger than normal. He just looked weathered and tired as if the job and his life had drained any energy and vigour out of him.

"It's certainly a start, sir. I've still got some of the team going through footage from other premises along the road. I think it's only a matter of time before we identify him and the female again. And if we do, then at least we'll have some idea of where they went afterwards."

"That's all well and good, Karen, but what happens if they left the pub, and then went their separate ways. For all we know they said goodbye to each other outside and that's the end of it. Have we got footage from outside of the pub?"

Karen's heart sank. "No, sir."

"Well, that proves my point then, doesn't it?"

"But…"

Skelton cut her off with a dismissive and arrogant flick of his wrist. "Until you get more definitive evidence that he left with her, and you can place her at the scene where the body was found, or close by, then you're clutching at straws."

Karen, unwilling to give up, defended her corner. "That's what we're working on, sir. In the meantime, we aim to take the still images of both Dulani and the female to the bar now. We want to show them to the staff and the punters in the hope that we can jog some memories."

"Do that, because the chances are, you'll get more results by shoving those pictures in the faces of people, than making assumptions."

UNWILLING TO BE PUT off by Skelton's lack of support,

Karen and several members of the team headed to the Bell pub.

For early evening, the pub was standing room only. It appeared that the spell of hot weather brought out the crowds, and many stood around on the street outside enjoying the last of the sun whilst sipping on their pints and having a cigarette. Karen was not surprised why so many of the punters were outside as she stepped in and felt suffocated by the lack of fresh air. Any pub she walked into had this distinctive aroma, she couldn't quite put a finger on it, but she put it down to a fusion of the smell of alcohol, stained wooden floors, and the stale smell of tobacco.

Karen instructed the team to split up and circulate images of both the victim and the girl. Karen headed towards the bar and attracted the attention of the nearest member of bar staff. A woman with a rosy smile, dark brown hair tied back into long ponytails, and a green tight T-shirt, stepped over in Karen's direction.

"What can I get you?" the woman asked.

Karen held out her warrant card. "We're conducting enquiries following the suspicious death of a man not far from here. He was seen in your CCTV footage talking to a woman with brown bobbed hair. Do you recognise either of them?" she asked, sliding across two still images.

Just the words suspicious death wiped the smile from the woman's face as she furrowed her brow and studied the pictures. Her eyes flicked between the images as she shuffled them in her hands.

She shook her head. "I can't say that I recognise either them, to be honest. The last couple of weeks have been crazy in here. We've been mobbed in the evenings. Each face just blends into another. For all I know I could have served them, but half of the time I'm literally just listening with one ear for what they want, serving them, and taking the money, because I'm getting shouted at by another half a dozen thirsty customers further along the bar."

"Do you think any of the other staff would have recognised these two?"

The woman shrugged and turned. "Joe, have you got a sec?"

Another bartender a few feet away stopped taking the freshly cleaned glasses from the dishwasher and stepped over in their direction.

"Have you seen these two in here in the last few days?"

He shook his head in reply, then shrugged and walked away.

Karen rolled her eyes at the man's lack of interest. She thanked the woman for her time before joining the rest of the team to question the other customers who were milling around.

FOUR HOURS LATER, Karen returned home exhausted. She was so tired she could have fallen asleep on the Tube, and the fifteen-minute walk home felt like an hour.

She was too tired for a shower, but the smell of cigarettes and alcohol clung to her clothes like an invisible cloak. She groaned as she stripped off and dragged herself to the bathroom. Karen lost track of time as she stood in the shower, her head bowed beneath the jets, the pulses of water prickling her skin. Waves of relaxation rippled through her body and if she could have crawled up into a little ball in the shower tray and fallen asleep, she would have done.

Her mind tracked back to the still images of Dulani and the woman. They were clear enough for anyone to identify either person, but on this occasion, they had drawn a blank. They could have worked with the native originally recorded material.

But with no added compression or recapturing to ensure maximum clarity, Karen had taken the footage to the forensic team who used advanced forensic strength deconvolution technology to literally undo as much of the blur as possible. She had been fascinated by the enhancements they could achieve as they repaired both out of focus blur and motion blur in the images. The technician she sat with had spoken about how they processed frames by combining more than seventy available filters. They did this in unlimited ways to restore specific defects or to clarify certain features in an image. She watched the technician as he moved around on a computer screen, picking on different features whilst he took specific linear and 3D measurements of the images.

The results of this state-of-the-art technology had been good enough for Karen and her team to use as they circulated amongst customers in the pub. And yet, nothing. She had dispatched another officer with the images of the woman to Jackie Manners to see if she recognised her. It was a risky move, which might be considered inflammatory. Considering that Jackie had just lost her husband, Karen felt she had no choice. She wanted to chase down every angle to identify this woman, and she wouldn't rest until she had.

Karen towel-dried her hair, and slipped on a thin T-shirt, before heading to the kitchen to retrieve a cold bottle of Pinot Grigio from the fridge. She poured herself a glass and enjoyed the chill as it bathed her lips. Since she'd fed Manky when she had got home, at least he wasn't wrapping himself around her ankles. She padded through to the lounge and sat on a sofa, tucking her feet beneath herself. Taking another sip, she stared at the wall in front of her, desperate for her mind to switch off.

Even though she needed some downtime, a part of her just wanted to rush back in and do something, anything. But she had covered every angle, and now it was just a waiting game. But it didn't stop that feeling in her gut that said, "there's a killer on the loose," and, "what if they strike again?"

24

The sound of wood splintering and heavy thuds shattered Karen's sleep. At first, she thought it was part of a horrendous dream, one of the many nightmares that seemed to haunt her. But it felt real this time. Karen felt the vibrations through the floor that crept up through the frame of her bed. But the sound of the front door crashing against the wall pulled her into full consciousness. With heart pounding, her eyes searched the darkness as her mind spun out of control.

Desperate to get her bearings in the dark, she had little time to react as her bedroom door burst open and two dark shadows appeared in the dull illumination, their silhouettes blending into the blackness that surrounded them. Before she had time to react or even sit up in bed, their heavy feet thundered towards her. Karen went to scream but a strong muscular hand grabbed her throat in a vice-like grip, pain erupting around her neck as his fingers pressed hard.

Any chance of moving faded as the full weight of his body smothered her, pinning Karen to the bed. Panic tore through her. A scream lodged in her throat as she clenched her hands into fists and attempted to lash out. Her mind wanted to flail her legs and kick out, but her body felt paralysed. Her eyes searched for any sign of recognition, but they were nothing more than shadowy monsters, dressed head to foot in dark clothing, their faces blackened behind balaclavas.

Total darkness enveloped Karen as the men placed something over her head, robbing her of her sight, and muting the surrounding sounds.

She felt hands grab at her arms, pulling her in different directions as they wrenched her from her bed. Her feet fell to the floor as they dragged her head first out of the bedroom. Karen kicked her legs and squirmed, desperate to get some traction, but they were pulling her too fast through her hallway towards her lounge.

Dropping to the floor, she had little time to gather her senses as they placed a soft object over her face. The feeling of losing her breath frightened her. She threw her head from side to side, her screams never going further than her lips as she fought the overwhelming surge of panic and fear that threatened to engulf her.

Is this what it feels like to suffocate and die?

I don't want to die.

I can't breathe.

Please someone... help?

Her breathing grew more frantic and laboured as she gasped for air. The heat built, and the sense of feeling trapped escalated.

The first blow shook her to the core. She sucked at the air like it had suddenly thickened and become almost too difficult to draw in. The force doubled her up as her insides screamed in hot, searing pain, like someone had hit her with a red-hot poker.

The second and third blows had Karen curling up in a ball, her arms and legs shielding her from the worst of it. Each kick or blow, she wasn't sure what they were, pummelled her like a piece of meat.

As quickly as the attack had started, it stopped. A man's voice bellowed in her ear, "If you want to live, stop sticking your nose in where it's not welcomed!"

Karen pulled herself in tighter waiting for the next assault, then she heard footsteps disappearing in the distance and down the hallway. The attack had lasted no more than a minute or two but felt like it had gone on for ages.

Karen pushed aside the cushion and ripped off the hood, gasping for air. After her first ragged inhale, she put her hands to her sweaty, clammy and hot cheeks. Her hair clung to her face and she couldn't tell which part of her body hurt the most. Pain from the attack spread through her body in pulsating waves. Her heart clambered to escape from her chest as she struggled to control her breathing.

She lay on her back for a few moments, her mind in turmoil, her body limp, spent of all energy.

A few moments passed before she heard more footsteps creeping up the hallway, followed by screams of concern. "Karen, Karen, are you okay?"

25

Skelton waited at the instructed location. He checked his watch; it was a little after one thirty a.m. The heat from the day hadn't dissipated, still close and humid. He had rolled up his sleeves, and pulled off his tie, before slinging his jacket over his shoulder. At this time of the morning nothing more than a few cabs scuttled around and the odd N205 night bus breaking the silence as it cruised past.

He took another drag of his cigarette and blew out a slow plume of smoke that hung over him like a grey blanket. He tried to calm himself as he waited, apprehension and concern twisting his insides. At this time of the night he would always go to hers. A change of location surprised him.

He checked his watch again, one forty-eight a.m. Any second now.

On cue, he heard the rumble of two Range Rovers approach, their bright neon lights punching the darkness and causing him to squint. As they pulled up alongside, the blackened rear passenger window on the second Range Rover slid down to reveal Sally sitting on her own in the back.

"Get in," she said before looking away.

Skelton knew not to ask questions and bit his bottom lip as he walked around the back of the car and joined Sally on the other side.

"Where are we going?" he asked.

"We have some business to sort out."

"What sort of business?"

"Skelton shut up. You'll find out when we get there."

Her acid tongue did nothing to appease him. An icy chill raced through him despite the heat. Whether it was fear, or the cool air conditioning, he wasn't sure. Regardless, it left tension lingering in the air. The driver and another heavy who sat in the passenger seat alongside neither spoke nor turned around.

They made their way out of Shoreditch towards East London and the A13 beyond. It was a short journey, lasting only twenty-five minutes. They drove at a steady pace, not wanting to attract any attention on the deserted roads. Skelton didn't dare look in Sally's direction, instead he chose to stare out of his window, checking all the landmarks and locations unsure if his life was in danger. He wanted to get his bearings just in case he needed to make a run for it.

Skelton recognised Barking as they continued along the A13 before turning off on to one of the many large industrial estates. The car bumped and jolted hitting potholes before they arrived towards the back of a large industrial unit shrouded in darkness. Everyone exited both cars and gathered in a large group. Malice and tension tightened the air as Sally and Skelton moved towards a shipping container about twenty feet away, surrounded by six of Sally's men. All thickset, dressed in dark clothes, with confidence and aggression in their swagger.

A shiver of panic snaked up his spine. The situation didn't feel right. He didn't know whether to shit himself or cry as he clenched his teeth. He was way out of his depth and outnumbered. Sally had put him in precarious positions before, but this time it felt different. There was a coldness in her attitude as her men hung around her like obedient Rottweilers waiting for her command. He watched Sally as his eyes darted from her to the other men.

She gave the two men nearest to the container a nod. They unlocked the large steel doors and pulled them apart. A blackness greeted the assembled group inside.

Skelton's heart hammered liked an over-revving engine. He had underestimated the situation as fear drained him of strength. *Is this it? Am I expendable? Surplus to requirements?* He tried to remain cool and level-headed as the two heavies stepped forward followed by Sally. She motioned for him to follow. At first something firmly rooted his feet to the ground, his mind screaming to run.

"Well? What you are waiting for?" Sally asked him.

Unable to find the words and fearing that anything that did come would sound squeaky and terrified, he stepped forward and followed a few steps behind her. The sound of their footsteps echoed inside the cavernous chamber. Torchlight punctured the darkness as one of Sally's men pointed the beam towards the corner.

Skelton's eyes followed the beam to see a man cowering in the corner, his hands chained to the side, his mouth taped. An overpowering smell of shit and piss made Skelton gag.

Sally turned towards one of her men standing by the doors. "Dan, close the doors." The clanking of the doors signalled finality as they stood in the torch's illumination. The heat and the vile smell sent bile rushing to the back of Skelton's throat. His face felt cold and clammy, and his bowels twitched. He fought to control his breathing, as a panic attack loomed.

"We're here to clean up unfinished business. If there's one thing I don't like, it's loose ends," Sally spat.

All eyes fell to the man who cowered in the corner, whimpering like a wounded dog. He pulled his knees in closer to his chest, his emaciated form looking weak and dirty. The man's terrified eyes searched them out in the darkness, squinting as a bright beam penetrated his retinas, mumbling incoherent and muffled words.

Despite the man's dishevelled appearance, Skelton recognised the large birthmark that covered part of the man's face. He had come across him many times, Two-tone Charlie.

Sally gestured to one heavy, who pulled out a handgun from his waistband and aimed it towards their prisoner.

The realisation dawned on Skelton. He wanted to take two steps backwards and run through for the doors, but what good would that do?

The sound of two gunshots rang out, the echoes bouncing

from one metal wall to another. Skelton jumped, his whole body in shock, his ears ringing like he was inside a huge church bell. His head thumped as if someone had hit it with a baseball bat. His eyes refused to blink as he watched Two-tone Charlie crumple into a lifeless form.

Sally turned to Skelton. "As I said, I don't like loose ends. It's dangerous for business."

Skelton understood the reference, Karen and himself. He tried to swallow but his parched mouth wouldn't allow it.

Sally burst out laughing and gave him a gentle tap on his shoulder. "Don't worry. I know what you're thinking. We've got her covered."

Skelton's mind was awash with confusion, fear and panic as he read into her cryptic reply.

He watched as she walked back towards the doors and thumped hard on them. The doors opened, and she stepped outside followed by her two heavies. Skelton hurried out after her. Several deaths had been attributed to the Connells, but he had never witnessed one in person. Being here compromised his position, and as a result, his connections with the Connells had just deepened.

Skelton took one last look over his shoulder into the bleakness, his eyes fixed on the dark silhouette of Two-tone Charlie's body hemmed into one corner.

"Stay close to your phone, Skelton. Something big will be going down soon and we'll need your help. I'll be in touch in the next few days," Sally said as she stepped into the rear of her Range Rover.

Skelton made his way towards the second car to join Sally, when Dan stepped in the way, and barred his path. "Where the fuck do you think you're going?" he said in a caustic tone.

"I'm getting in the car with Sally. I'm not hanging around here. I need a lift back."

"No, you fucking ain't, mate. You can make your own way back, unless you want to join him," Dan said, shoving Skelton in his chest.

Skelton staggered back a few steps as he watched the heavy return to the second vehicle, and the two cars glided away, their red tail lights disappearing into the distance.

Skelton's vulnerability frightened him. He stood just yards from a dead body and had witnessed a murder. For all he knew, someone may have been watching the whole thing and had alerted the police. They could just be minutes away, and an overwhelming urge to run flooded his body. His thoughts were torn between the little sense of justice he carried, and the fact he was in bed with the Connells in all senses of the word.

He needed to get away from here. His best bet was to get back to Ilford and order a minicab from there. Walking as quickly as he could, he made his way from the industrial park, sticking to the side roads. He was still hours away from home, but the quicker he got back, the quicker he could block out what he had just witnessed.

26

The news of Karen's attack spread like wildfire, with a steady stream of officers popping their heads in to check on her and to pass on their best wishes. Despite their genuine concerns, Karen felt embarrassed by the extra attention. The attack had dented her pride, exposing her vulnerabilities and showing it could happen to anyone. Random violence spared no one, regardless of whether they were a member of the public, or a serving police officer.

Except my attack wasn't random.

Skelton poking his head around the door caused a jolt of surprise to rocket through her.

"Karen, I've just got in and heard the news. Are you okay?"

Karen waved off his question. "I'm fine, just a few bruises."

Skelton clucked his tongue like he actually gave a shit. "Did they say anything? Was anything taken?"

"No. My laptop was on the table in the lounge, along with my phone and purse, but they didn't take them. Maybe they intended to rob me, but I think my neighbours disturbed them."

"That's good to know. But did they say anything? Anything that might help the local force to track them down?"

Karen shook her head. "No, they said nothing." She looked down at her paperwork as she muttered those last few words, unwilling to meet his eyes.

"Well, listen, I suggest we get a panic button fitted in your apartment. It might sound like an overreaction, but I need to know that you're safe. We all need to know that you're safe."

Karen scrunched up her nose and pulled a face. "Sir, that's a bit of an overreaction. I'm fine, the motivation was probably robbery, but they shit themselves when my neighbours came to investigate." The half-truth stalled in her throat, but it had to be close enough to convince Skelton.

"Karen, you can cut the macho bollocks. You were attacked, and your safety both inside and outside of work concerns me. Think about the panic button, and I'll catch up with you later today once you've had time to think about it."

THE CONVERSATION with Skelton gnawed away in her mind as she joined the rest of the team for a briefing. She knew they were looking at her with a degree of sympathy and shock, and despite their questions, she glossed over the event and moved on before anyone had a chance to say anything else.

"Team, let's do a round robin. Who wants to start?"

Various members of the team looked at each other, unsure who should start.

"Come on, you lot. We haven't got all day. Steve?"

Steve pulled his notepad off the table and flicked through his notes. "Forensics have come back with a small fine hair fibre that they found on the bedding belonging to victim one, Adam Manners. They've eliminated both Adam and his wife Jackie. So, this belongs to someone else. There is no corresponding DNA profile on the national DNA database."

The news excited Karen. She felt like they were chipping away at a block of ice until they got to its core. And the news was getting better.

"They also found short black fibres on one corner of the bedding. They cross-referenced it against his and Jackie's clothes, again there was no match. So, there's a strong possibility that they belong to the suspect."

"That's good news, Steve. A positive result. We now have a person of interest, a DNA profile, and fabric fibres from the crime scene. Have we found much more about Adam's social circle?"

An officer sitting next to Brad cleared her throat and chipped in. "We haven't been able to identify all the people in the photographs on his Facebook page. We have identified a pattern of bars and restaurants that Adam went to, and we're following up with visits to see if they recognise his picture."

The officer also confirmed that they had made enquiries into his past relationships but hadn't been able to identify anything of significance. There was no suggestion of malice or bad blood from his past relationships.

"I've been thinking about the profile of the suspect. My feelings are that she's not in a relationship, but I'm undecided. Would anyone disagree?"

"If she is, then I feel sorry for her partner," Jade replied. "He must sleep with one eye open."

They met her suggestion with a ripple of laughter, and a few crass replies.

"We need to keep an open mind. This is an individual who can display extreme rage but appears perfectly normal on the outside. When we reviewed the CCTV footage from the Bell pub, the individual seemed capable of holding down a sensible conversation and feeling comfortable in a social environment."

Karen turned to look at the pictures on the incident board taken from inside the Bell pub. They discussed how Dulani Kalagho was five feet eleven inches, and the woman was considerably shorter. The team concluded that she was around five feet two to five feet four inches, so was physically at a disadvantage and had to be good at persuasion.

"And carrying on from what you are saying, ma'am, I would say that the attacks suggest wanting control and exerting authority. Adam was tied to the bed and left helpless, and Dulani was left in a public alleyway with his trousers around his ankles. I'd say she's got the art of persuasion nailed."

"I agree, Jade. Both cases suggest domination, and that may have been reflected in her personal life with men who controlled her? People who have hurt her both mentally and physically? It's worth considering."

Karen asked the team to continue digging and following up all potential leads and enquiries. And in return, she would contact the press department to put out a press appeal and get a bulletin put on the Crimestoppers website now that they had more information, and a person of interest.

"MA'AM, HAVE YOU GOT A MINUTE?"

Karen looked up from her computer to see Steve by her door. "Of course. What's up? Everything okay?"

Steve took a few steps into her office and stuffed his hands in his pocket. "I think I should ask you that question."

"How so?"

"Just worried about you. You got a bit of a kicking last night, and I know what you're like. On the outside you will play this down, but on the inside, you're pissed off."

Karen smiled. "I don't need babysitting. There are thousands of victims up and down the country who've been assaulted. We must get on with it. I'm a big strong girl; I can handle it. But I appreciate your concern, Uncle Steve," Karen teased, as she winced in pain from her bruised ribs.

"Well, you know where I am if you need me or want to let off a bit of steam."

No matter how hard she tried to push it to the back of her mind, the caring attention from her fellow officers kept her replaying the incident in her mind.

Several of her neighbours had come to her rescue after hearing the commotion. And Essex Police had responded within minutes.

Epping police station on the high street had closed three years earlier due to budget cuts, so the closest units came from Loughton and Harlow to reach her. Luckily, police officers always rushed to the assistance of fellow officers as a matter of urgency, but on this occasion the suspects had cleared the scene long before their arrival. SOCO had given the flat a once-over, but she was doubtful whether they would find anything of significance, other than the footprint on the front door.

Karen hadn't allowed herself the time to process the events of the night. At first, she could have taken it as an aggravated burglary, they were common enough. But it was the words that her assailants had used, and the veiled threat, that lingered in her mind. She hadn't told that bit to the local officers who had attended.

She felt the swell of anger rise in her chest and drove it back down; this was not the time or the place.

27

Needing a break from the office Karen took up Wainwright's offer of a spot of lunch at a local sandwich bar. Despite not feeling hungry, she welcomed the opportunity to be away from the office.

They grabbed a small table inside, preferring the opportunity to sit in the cool than outside in the blistering heat. Karen ordered a chicken and pesto panini and a diet Coke; Wainwright opted for a roast beef and pickle sandwich and a bottle of sparkling water.

Straight after the briefing, Karen had attended the post-mortem for Dulani Kalagho. Because of the significant head trauma, a formal ID by his girlfriend hadn't been possible. Instead, identifying marks on his body including tattoos and moles were used along with DNA referencing from the victim's toothbrush.

Wainwright had confirmed that Dulani's death was the result of blunt force trauma, and impressions left corresponded with the brick recovered from the scene.

"That was a messy one," Wainwright said nonchalantly. "You're getting the wrong end of the stick with the cases landing on your desk."

"I must have been terrible in a former life. There's blunt force trauma injury, and then there are these catastrophic injuries that we've just seen."

"Blunt force trauma injury is blunt force trauma injury," Wainwright answered, lifting a shoulder and letting it drop. "You can get blunt force trauma injury in a variety of scenarios. Car accidents, pedestrian struck by vehicles, people falling from heights or even blast injuries. They're all the same. It doesn't matter whether the person had been struck by a fist, a crowbar, a baseball bat or even a machete. The only variable is the degree of damage."

Karen wiped her mouth with a napkin. "I agree. But what we've just seen goes beyond the realms of violence."

"How much progress are you making?"

She filled him in on what they had identified so far but admitted that she was at a loss for the time being regarding the motive.

"Well, you have some similarity amongst the cases, but the method by which they died is different, I'll give you that. But it's the acid attacks that I find fascinating."

Karen stared at him in awe. "I wouldn't say I agree with the word, *fascinating*, Wainwright. That's just sadistic overkill. The poor fucker was dead already. Why continue the assault? It makes little sense."

Wainwright leant back in his chair and crossed his arms across his chest. There weren't many people inside the café which gave them the opportunity to talk freely. He noticed two workmen sitting in the corner tucking into something that looked cholesterol-busting. A middle-aged couple sat two tables to their right picking at their sandwiches. There were a few other customers taking lunches outside and enjoying the sun.

"I agree, Karen. It makes little sense. But it's as if the killer is destroying their manhood and what a man stands for."

Karen narrowed her eyes and stared at Wainwright, deep in thought, processing each of his words again. She cycled her finger to encourage him to continue his train of thought.

"The killer is thinking through how they can execute each murder. To me it doesn't look spontaneous or random. It's well thought out and executed. It takes a certain degree of, pardon the pun, balls to do something like that."

Karen nodded. It was something they both agreed on.

"I've seen the effects of acid attacks, but they have been aimed at the upper torso and face. I've seen victims where their groins have been damaged either by having their penises cut off or having boiling water poured on them. Those cases are clearly documented. In fact, the last one I read involved a girlfriend taking revenge on her cheating partner by pouring a kettle of boiling water over his groin whilst he slept."

Karen winced as she visualised the scene in her mind.

"Anyway, enough of business. How are you holding up? I heard about that nasty business last night."

"You are probably the hundredth person today who's asked if I'm okay."

Wainwright held out both of his hands, palms facing

towards her. "I'm only asking. Besides, it must be nice knowing so many people care."

"I know. I know. It's lovely that people are concerned about me. And I appreciate it. But if truth be told, I'm fucked off that I couldn't defend myself. I think I can handle myself in most situations, but last night, I felt like a wilting daisy."

"I don't doubt it. You're one of the toughest women I've met."

"I'm not sure if that's a compliment?" Karen said furrowing her brow.

They both laughed, enjoying the moment.

"Karen, it was a compliment. You have to remember that they took you by surprise, in your own home, where you thought you were safe. It was the middle of the night, and you had no opportunity to react. Every single person in your situation would have struggled to respond. I'm just glad that you're safe."

Karen welcomed his thoughtful words. Though it didn't take the sting from the situation. A dangerous message lurked behind the attack relating to her own investigations into the hijacking. Someone was trying to scare her off.

The lunch with Wainwright had been a welcome distraction. She always felt at ease when she was with him, and he was one of the very few people she would open up to.

But something stuck in her mind from the conversation. It had been enough to pique her interest, and now back at the office, a thought formed. She pulled up Google and started a search. Over the next few hours she found articles relating to a string of cases where women had sought revenge on their cheating partners.

One case involved a woman setting fire to her cheating boyfriend's genitals whilst he slept. Another involved a woman carrying out an acid attack on her boyfriend's genitals after he'd put their sex tape online and it had gone viral. The woman had been utterly distraught by the humiliation and betrayal. She sought revenge by launching an irreversible attack which left him having to use a tube to urinate.

The more she looked, the more she uncovered where women had sought revenge. The reading was uncomfortable but lent weight to her current cases. One carried similar parallels. It involved a woman who had drugged her ex-partner, who then woke up several hours later with his wrists and feet bound to the bed. He could not defend himself as she stabbed him multiple times in the neck and groin before she cut off his penis.

Case after case opened in front of her of men being run over and killed by their partner, being stabbed to death, sexually mutilated, or drugged and killed. Karen pushed back her chair and headed towards the incident room to find Jade.

"Have we been able to gather any evidence on the possibility of revenge porn in our cases?"

"I've had no feedback from the team to suggest any evidence of that. Why?" Jade replied.

Karen spent the next few minutes detailing her conversation with Wainwright and her subsequent research.

Jade nodded. "In theory, revenge porn ties in with the first victim, Adam Manners. He's cheated on his wife before and had affairs. Jackie's alibi is watertight, and there's no evidence of large cash withdrawals from their bank. But she could have arranged for someone else to do it."

"I agree, Jade. She could have arranged it. Highly unlikely, I know, but what happens if he was having a bit on the side again and she found out. After the promises they had made, she would have been devastated."

Jade agreed with the hypotheses but felt the savagery suggested something more than a simple case of cheating.

Karen asked Jade to investigate Jackie's background in more detail later, but for the time being they needed to visit Dulani Kalagho's girlfriend.

28

Dulani Kalagho's address took them to a small row of town houses in Hoxton. Karen rung the communal buzzer before being let in through a double set of black railings that formed the entrance to both the building and the residential parking at the back. A small woman with dark brown hair pulled tight in a ponytail greeted them at the door. Karen and Jade presented their warrant cards, and the woman greeted them with a weak smile before inviting them in.

"I'm Dorothy, Antoinette's mum. This is my husband Sunil," she added, as an Asian male stood behind her, his features heavy with sadness.

Dorothy took them through to the lounge where a young woman stood by the window, her arms wrapped protectively around her waist, a tissue scrunched in one of her hands.

"Antoinette?" Karen asked.

The woman looked in her direction, dark circles around her

eyes, a lattice of red lines etched on her eyeballs. She nodded once to confirm.

"I'm Detective Inspector Karen Heath, this is my colleague DS Jade Whiting. We're very sorry for your loss, but we need to ask you a few questions."

Antoinette dropped her head and fell into a nearby sofa.

The room had a warm comfortable feel. Soft sofas, green walls, and little feminine touches like framed photos lined the windowsill, whilst small lamps sat in the alcoves, and framed quotes hung on the wall. Karen's eyes were drawn to one whiteprint that said, "Think Less, Love More." *If only life was that simple.*

"Have you found who attacked him?" Antoinette asked. Her voice was soft, breaking as she forced each word out.

"Not yet. The investigation is ongoing, and we're covering every angle."

Antoinette shook her head in disbelief. "I can't… believe… he's gone. It feels like a dream. A nightmare."

Karen understood the younger woman's horror, along with deep shock and trauma. Judging from their surroundings, the couple had set up a comfortable life.

Antoinette's parents came and joined her on the sofa, each one taking the seat either side of her, her mum placing a reassuring hand on her knee.

"What can you tell us about Dulani?"

The woman shrugged, unsure where to start. "He was a lively, fun guy. A bit of a party animal, but he was just beginning to quieten down a little."

"And how long have you been together?"

"About eighteen months. He was renting a place before that and spending so much time over here, I suggested he move in. Our working schedules meant it was difficult for us to meet, but we would always call each other every day. But that wasn't enough for me, I wanted to see Dulani more."

Karen gave her a reassuring smile. "Did he have any disagreements or fallouts with anyone?"

Antoinette stiffened on hearing the question. A pained expression darkened her features. She shook her head. "No. He wasn't like that. He hated confrontation. To think he might have got into an argument and been killed… That's not him."

The police hadn't revealed the circumstances in which they had discovered Dulani, nor that he was semi-undressed. Karen remained undecided whether she should reveal that information for fear of causing more distress. But she needed answers.

"What about previous relationships? Do you know much about them?"

Antoinette's mother appeared more annoyed about the question than anyone else in the room. "I'm sorry, Inspector. What does that have to do with Dulani's death?"

"We are looking at all aspects of Dulani's life so we can build a better picture of him, and now we need to keep all of our lines of enquiry open. His past life is just as important as his present."

"Well, I see it as insensitive, in my opinion," Dorothy replied.

Karen understood her objections, but time was working against them, and she was treading a fine line between sensitivity and directness. “Antoinette?”

Antoinette cleared her throat and wiped her nose with the back of her hand. “He had two serious girlfriends before we met and a couple of flings. I needed to know all those things, because I believe in openness. The flings were nothing serious and I only know the name of one of them, but I do know the names of the other two that were serious. In fact, we met one of them again about a year ago at a wedding. She seemed pleasant enough.”

“So as far as you’re aware, none of them ended on a sour note, no more than usual?”

“How do you mean?” she asked.

“None of his exes threatened him with revenge or violence or even malice?”

Antoinette frowned and shook her head in frustration. “No. What the fuck has that got to do with this? Are you telling me one of his exes might have killed him?”

“No, I’m not saying that. But we need to look into his past to build a full picture of his life.”

Over the next few minutes, Antoinette provided them with the names of Dulani’s exes. Karen passed them through to Jade who excused herself from the room to feed that back to the team in the office.

Karen opened a brown envelope and passed still images of Dulani in the pub to Antoinette. Rather than just showing pictures of him with the woman, she had included other pictures of him standing with his friends. Antoinette had placed a few faces that she recognised amongst his friends but could not identify the woman he had been talking to at the bar. It was a risky move on Karen's part, but despite Antoinette's upset at seeing a picture of him talking to another woman, she had been unable to confirm the woman's identity.

"WHAT DID you make of her, Karen?" Jade asked as they made their way back towards the Tube station.

"Either she was completely besotted with him, and didn't see any warning signs, or he was a very good actor. It looks like he copped off with a woman in the pub and paid with his life."

"She didn't have a bad word to say about him. I didn't get anything from the interview that was of substance."

"I know. It still needed to be done. Any updates whilst you called the office?"

"Lots of work in progress. Dulani had a Facebook profile, so the team are contacting his friends. They're also analysing his phone and bank records as we speak. We've also had officers visit the event management company, and they reiterated Antoinette's thoughts. A nice guy, friendly and helpful. And he loved a good party."

Karen's frustration grew. It felt like a case of déjà vu. There was nothing out of the ordinary with either victim. But the last revelation from Jade meant that another piece of the jigsaw had fallen in place as a thread of commonality surfaced. Dulani had been using the same messaging app found on Adam Manners' phone.

29

I couldn't have picked a worse time to be on the Tube. In this heat you sweat just sitting, yet alone moving. I read somewhere that some Tube lines broke temperature records during the summer months, hitting the mid-thirties, which exceeded the EU limit of thirty degrees, the maximum temperature which livestock could be transported. And yet here we were, melting in the stifling, sweaty heat.

But everything has a purpose, and I'm watching him. I'm keeping my distance and can see him at the other end of the carriage. I know his pattern off by heart. I've never known him to sit in the middle of the carriage. He always chooses the end seat next to the glass partition.

He plays the game well. Every morning during the week he leaves the house no later than seven twenty a.m. and kisses his wife and daughter on the doorstep. He follows the same route religiously to the Tube station and stands in the same place on the platform. Every Saturday is family day where the three of them go to the local park for a walk, his daughter gets pushed on the swings, and he occasionally slips his hand around his wife's waist as they both lovingly look at their daughter squealing like a pig as she goes back and forth.

His wife seems oblivious. She happily waits for her husband to come home so they can be a family again. Every Thursday morning, she goes to the local Tesco superstore and does her weekly shop. I've noticed that she hovers a lot in the fruit and veg aisles, pondering over the validity of whether she should pay those extra pennies for organic products. But she is a creature of habit, her shopping trolley always filled with the same products week in and week out.

Little does wifey know about her husband's other pastime when he sneaks off for lunches with a female colleague. How they meet in random spots, looking around to see if anyone notices them. How they pick random pubs and small backstreet coffee shops for their clandestine meetings. Only then do they kiss and cuddle.

I've watched them whilst they disappear into the Ace Hotel after work, emerging ninety minutes later, their faces telling the tale of the naughty guilt.

That's why I had to have him. He couldn't resist it when I brushed against him in the bar. It was a crowded lunchtime with standing room only. His other bit went to the toilet which gave me the perfect opportunity to sneak past. I gave him that look that I always give them as I squeezed my body past his in the lunchtime crowd. Our eyes met, and I knew I had him then. A twinkle in my eye, the corner of my lips just turned up a little allowing my look to linger for a few seconds longer than needed.

Those chance encounters happened on two further occasions, and when given the opportunity, I slipped my details into his hand as I walked past. I had him hook, line and sinker. He took the bait, and how could he resist? He was a man. Men think with their cocks, not their brains.

I watched him from across the bar as his woman returned. She had her back to me, but I saw his lips moving in conversation. Surprise, surprise. He wasn't looking at her, he was looking over her shoulder at me. I'm sure he was talking to me, too. But I wouldn't have long to wait. I might be invisible to others, but not to him. He might be interested in her, but his life was about to change because I would be the last woman he would look at.

I spent the next few weeks nurturing him online, our messages being exchanged in secret, never to be found. But that didn't matter. Each message achieved its aim, pulling him in to me. And unknown to him, each message brought him closer and closer to the fateful moment where he would breathe his last breath.

I laughed at some of his cheesy messages. I thought chat-up lines like that went out with the dinosaurs. I mean how would you react if someone said, *"I would say God bless, you, but looking at your pictures, it looks like he already did"*?

But I played the game. I teased and tantalised him. I think I tipped him over the edge when I sent him a nude picture of myself and told him that I wasn't looking for anything heavy, just a bit of NSA fun, and it didn't matter whether he was with someone or not. And he replied he wasn't either because he was married.

At that point he crossed the line, and he was fair game.

He said he liked my openness, and the more we talked, the more our messages became more extreme and explicit. But I kept him waiting despite his insistence on wanting to see me and *ruin* me. I think he wanted me because I played hard to get, but when I indicated that we should meet to explore it further and suggested a hotel, he didn't need a second invitation.

30

I scan the room; it's perfect for what I have in mind. And it should be for one hundred and eighty-eight pounds a night. A double bed, a thick luxurious mattress, funky bathroom, but just the slightest aroma of staleness in the air from lack of ventilation.

With five minutes until he arrives, I prepare myself and dress to impress. I'll only get one chance to make this work. I place a knife under a pillow and my bottle beneath the bedside table, and my rope and duct tape on top. Everything is in place.

I stroke the bedsheets; they're cool on my skin. I want to lie down and wrap myself in them but there's a knock on the door.

He's here.

I take my time and amble towards the door, imagining how much tension he must have boiling up inside him as he waits nervously in the hallway. I peer through the spyhole and he looks up and down the corridor. I open the door, and his mouth drops as he stares at me. Judging from his face; it looks as if I'm the answer to his dreams. I wear stockings, suspenders, crotchless knickers and a push-up bra. I finish the look with chunky clear plastic high heels, the slutty heels that pole dancers wear.

"Oh man, I wasn't expecting this," he says with a big grin on his face.

His eyes travel up and down the length of my body. "I hope you're not disappointed?" I reply.

"Disappointed? No way. You're perfect. Sex on legs."

He shuts the door behind him and skips the small talk as we paw each other. He's hungry and ready judging by his firmness pressing against me.

"I need you out of these clothes," I plea as I tear at his clothes.

He tries to push me backwards on to the bed, desperation in his voice as he grunts, "God I need to fuck you."

I push back against his chest. "You'll have to wait because I'm in control and I want to give you a special treat."

I spin him around and push him on to the bed, before reaching for my rope. His eyes widen, a mixture of surprise and uncertainty.

"You're going to enjoy every minute of this, and I promise you that you're about to experience something that no other woman has done to you before."

My words only excite him even further.

"I can't wait, the dirtier, the better," he moans.

I tie his wrists and ankles to the bed, and by now he's a pent-up ball of sexual energy and putty in my hands. I tear a bit of duct tape off and place it over his mouth. I can tell there's concern mixed with excitement in his eyes. I tease and play with him, gently pulling my nails across his chest, before placing a pillow over his face. I encourage him to explore the boundaries of sexual ecstasy as I continue to push my hips against his.

Just when he can't take any more, I reach beneath another pillow and grab the handle of my knife. Lifting it with two hands above my head before bringing it down and thrusting it deep into his chest. Muffled screams tear through the pillow. I stab him again, and again. Each time I push the blade into his body until it can go no further. I lose count. There's blood over the sheets, and his body twitches and shudders before coming to a stop.

I wipe the sweat from my face, my bloodied fingers streaking my skin. I get off the bed and admire my handiwork. My heart thumps, and I can feel my pulse throbbing in my neck. Adrenaline shoots through my body, causing it to twitch and buzz.

I retrieve the bottle from beneath the bedside cabinet and pour the contents over his groin. I stand and watch for a few minutes, mesmerised as his skin sizzles like meat on a barbecue.

I step back into the bathroom and take a shower to cleanse myself of him. I don't want a fleck of his filth on my skin. I'm in no hurry to leave and enjoy soaking under the waterfall of warm water. Wrapping myself in a towel, I go back into the bedroom and look at the broken remains of the man who just a few moments ago was filled with the excitement of having the best sex of his life. Once dressed and assuming my identity, I head towards the door taking one last glance over my shoulder before leaving.

I feel nothing.

31

Karen had spoken to the high-tech team regarding the *Don't Talk* messaging app. In her eyes it was a significant development that both victims were using the app, and only confirmed what she suspected, that it linked both cases.

Despite Karen's insistence, the technician she'd spoken to assured her that there was little they could do to retrieve any erased data. The developers had designed the app to erase messages based on predefined criteria and there was nothing they could do.

It could have been sheer coincidence that both victims had this app, it was one of a dozen apps freely available to millions of users.

Feeling like she was going around in circles, she had left work, stopping at Tesco for a bottle of wine on her way home. The front door had been replaced and there were no signs of damage from the night before. However, it felt odd being here. Even though the door was firmly secured when she opened it, she took a few moments to tiptoe around the flat as if expecting further intruders lying in wait for her.

They had invaded her privacy, and she now understood how the victims of burglary felt. She had chosen to live far away from work, and yet somehow, someone had tracked her down and ruined her haven.

Emotional pain seeped from her pores as she walked into the lounge and stared at the spot where the attack had taken place. Cold shivers ran through her as she tried to grit her teeth in defiance. The bedroom evoked the same chilling feeling. She started to question whether she could stay here this evening and sleep in her own bed. The thought crossed her mind about grabbing a room at the Bell hotel down the road but dismissed the thought the very next second. Staying away would only make a return harder. If she couldn't stay here tonight, would that mean she could never bring herself to stay here again?

Though she had tried to process the events of the night before, an unsettling feeling lingered inside her. It was something that she didn't enjoy experiencing. It left her feeling vulnerable, scared and isolated. Perhaps Skelton's suggestion of a panic button wasn't so bad, but that would mean they'd won.

She felt emotionally and physically drained as she collapsed on to the sofa overcome with waves of frustration, sadness and fear. With a heaving shudder, Karen burst into tears. It was like the floodgates opened, and she had no way of controlling it. It was more than crying; it was the kind of desperate sobbing that came from a person drained of all strength. Struggling to keep her tears silent, her face creased, and her fists closed so tight she could feel the heat trapped inside them. She pounded her thighs as tears zigzagged down her face and dripped off the end of her nose.

Karen couldn't tell whether her outburst was the result of feeling violated last night, or the build-up over the past twelve months and the sense of injustice and failure that she felt.

Perhaps it's both.

But the harder she thought, the more upset she became. When she cried, there was a rawness to it, like the pain was still an open wound.

"Fuck!" she yelled, a swell of anger rising inside. "I refuse to be beaten."

She couldn't remember the last time she had broken down like this. But whichever aspect of her life she turned the spotlight on, the more fragmented and broken it looked.

"I must look like shit," she muttered as she wiped the snot from her nose with the back of her hand. "I doubt I'll win any beauty contests looking like this. Pull yourself together you wet muppet."

Karen stayed rooted on the sofa, unable to move or think straight. Tears continued to stream from her eyes, though she didn't know why. Maybe it was the hijack, or the pain that she felt for her sister, or the job? The job was enough to get her down on a daily basis. But had she buried all these feelings so deep that the break-in was the final straw? Thoughts tumbled through her mind.

Manky sat on the floor in front of her watching with curiosity, patiently waiting to be noticed.

"Yes, I know, and I'm sorry. You want your dinner. Come on then."

Manky followed her, meowing his approval, as she padded into the kitchen. She emptied some food into his bowl, before reaching for a wine glass. But she paused in mid-movement. "Fuck it. I need something stronger." Karen opened the cupboard to her right and pulled out a bottle of Glenmorangie. She poured herself half a glass and downed it in one, the bitterness lighting a fire in her throat. Her shoulders shook in the aftermath, and her face twisted in repulsion.

Karen poured another and convinced herself that she would need a few more of these to build up the courage to sleep in peace tonight. She hoped that she could get through the night without adding to the nightmares that already haunted her.

32

The morning briefing hadn't been running for long before the call came through. There had been little progress overnight in relation to the first victim, Adam Manners. There were no revelations in his background that warranted further investigation. Much of the investigative work had been fruitless. His social media profiles, his personal life, past relationships and even his computer hardware had revealed nothing.

The only point of interest had come from the door-to-door enquiries. Neighbours either side of the Manners had come forward to report that they had heard a series of blazing rows a few months back. She had thrown his clothes out in tatters, having cut them up. They reported her screaming that she fucking hated him, and he'd ruined everything.

It came as a surprise to the team and put the spotlight back on Jackie Manners. Karen parked the idea of bringing in Jackie for an interview but asked the team to double-check with her doctor to confirm whether she had been experiencing any mental health or emotional issues.

They had just started to discuss Dulani Kalagho, and the outcome of continued forensic investigations which had identified synthetic brown hair fibres on his clothing. But the call had come in that a body had been found in suspicious circumstances and that Karen's team were needed immediately on the scene. The team dropped everything they were doing and scrambled towards the location.

THE A10 WAS busy as three job cars weaved in and out of traffic, the sirens and flashing blue grill lights pushing cars to the side of the road as they screamed through in close convoy. The road was one of the main feeder routes that took drivers from North London straight into the heart of the city, so was busy with taxis, delivery vehicles, couriers on mopeds and general traffic. A lay-by outside the Ace Hotel normally reserved for buses in between shifts was awash with police vehicles. With nowhere to park, the three-vehicle convoy pulled up on to the pavement as PCSOs kept pedestrians at bay.

As Karen left the vehicle she had been travelling in with Jade, she took a moment to gather her bearings. The hotel itself was an impressive six-storey building with a modernistic grey brick exterior that stood at odds with the rest of the street. Opposite were a few clothing stores, a Persian restaurant, a dry cleaners and a bar and grill that took ground floor space in three-storey buildings that maintained their Victorian façade.

The first officers dealt with preserving the scene whilst tackling the panic amongst residents of the hotel. Karen arrived just before lunchtime, as a gathering of guests were just about to check-in. From her initial enquiries, Karen gathered that a female had booked into room seventy-four but had failed to check out by the obligatory eleven o'clock. The maid had let herself in only to discover the bloodbath.

With the hotel in lockdown and swarming with police, it took Karen a while to make some sense of the timeline. The hotel itself was urban and chic. The front reception desk had T-shirts and baseball caps for sale, and the front of the desk had loads of twelve-inch vinyl records on display creating a record shop kind of feel. There were lots of trendy breakout areas with relaxed seating and spaces to work on laptops. It transpired that the Ace Hotel was part of a chain with other hotels in major US cities which explained its character.

The team followed Karen along the corridor until they arrived at the room. Several other rooms close by were open and vacated. From what Karen could see, most of the rooms carried similar features. A multicoloured blue check patterned bedcover sitting on a brown base close to the floor. It reminded her more of a futon bed than anything else. Funky metal conduit piping ran across the walls and ended with light fittings. They had gone beyond the standard tea and coffee making facilities, with trays full of chocolate, crisps, pot noodles and biscuits.

A police officer stood on guard outside room seventy-four. Jade and Karen signed into the scene log and put on protective suits, foot coverings and gloves. Steve and Brad took the opportunity to scope the rest of the hotel including entry and exit points.

The officer stood aside as Karen and Jade went in. On first impressions the room looked no different from the others that she had passed, but when they turned into the main bedroom area the twisted scene unfolded before their eyes.

A man lay tied to the bed, with most of the bedsheets now stained a dark red. Karen couldn't go further as crime scene investigators continued their detailed forensic analysis of the scene. She glanced at Wainwright, who sat on his knees by the edge of the bed examining the ligatures around the victim's ankles.

Mason Brophy, the crime scene manager, was overseeing his two investigators and recording information that they were relaying to him.

"Don't come in much further," Mason said. "We've still got a lot to cover, including the bathroom. But I'll come and find you as soon as I can."

Karen didn't hang around and walked back into the hallway to give them space to work, followed by Jade.

"The poor bloke didn't have a chance," Jade said.

Karen nodded and took a deep breath as she pulled her face mask off. "To be frank, that reminded me of the first vic, except more violent."

Steve and Brad were downstairs in the general manager's office when Karen and Jade found them.

"What have we got, Steve?"

"Ma'am, this is the duty manager and the maid. It was the maid who found him."

The woman was visibly distressed, her eyes stained red, and her hands trembled in her lap. She bit her bottom lip as she stared at the officers around her.

"The deceased is Harry Kruger. SOCO pulled his wallet for us. He's on the system here and has used the hotel frequently. He's got a South African ID card in his wallet, and his mobile phone was sitting on the bedside table. SOCO have got both bagged up as evidence."

"Brad, can you nip outside and find out what you can on this Harry Kruger?"

"Yes, ma'am."

"Steve, can you arrange for officers to attend the address and inform the next of kin? We'll need a formal ID, anyway. And make sure we assign a FLO."

Karen pulled up a chair and sat opposite the two members of staff. "I'm Detective Inspector Heath, I'll be overseeing the investigation."

The duty manager placed a hand on his chest. "I'm Lorenzo Romano, and this is Maja Banic," the man said in his thick and heavy Italian accent.

"I know that this has come as a massive shock to you both, but whilst we are here, we need your full cooperation and help."

Romano nodded. "Of course. My staff and myself are available to you, but can I ask how long you will be here? We have had to turn away many guests on arrival. And the ones that are here are very worried. They want to leave and want a refund. This situation is not good for business."

"I appreciate that, Mr Romano. But we are dealing with quite a horrific suspicious death, and until we have completed all our investigations, we need to keep this hotel in lockdown to avoid confusion, and contamination." Karen kept her voice neutral though she seethed inside. What she wanted to say was, "don't you realise someone's been fucking murdered upstairs and all you're worried about is losing business, you greedy piece of shit?"

Romano shrugged his shoulders as if not bothered by their investigation.

"We'll need a full list of everyone on duty last night. And I would like to see your CCTV footage from the camera you have in reception. Can you arrange for that?"

Romano took Karen and Jade to the office behind the front desk. They were met by a thin figure of a man perched on the seat in front of a large monitor with what appeared to be six live feeds. Romano instructed him to pull up footage from the night before.

From what Karen could see, the live feeds were mounted at the front of the hotel, the back of the hotel, the reception desk and one each for the fire exits on either side of the building.

Romano confirmed what time the room had been booked out, and the man in front of the monitors pulled up footage to correspond with thirty minutes prior to that.

Karen asked the man to pause the tape at the point when a woman entered the hotel and made her way to reception. She signed in and picked up an electronic fob for the room. Karen and Jade exchanged a puzzled look. The woman in the footage appeared different from the Bell pub stills. She wore large black sunglasses, and a baseball cap, which Karen thought was an attempt to disguise her face. But this woman had blonde hair cascading over the back of her shoulders and down her neck. The image was clearer than those they had captured from the bar, and they could make out many more facial features, but it didn't add up.

WITH A COPY of the footage secured, Karen and Jade took a moment to walk around the hotel before making their way outside.

"Do you think that's the same woman?"

"I'm not sure, Jade. Certain facial features had similarities, and the height and build of the woman looked about the same. But she was clever. Not only did she hide her identity, but she paid with cash."

"But we've got a name now?"

"Andrea Hobson. My guess is that if she's gone to the extent of paying with cash, and disguising her appearance, I doubt that's her real name."

Karen looked up and down the street. She couldn't see any visible signs of CCTV footage on the front of the buildings opposite. Nevertheless, she would instruct uniformed officers to do door-to-door enquiries in case they had seen anything, or more importantly, had cameras inside their buildings which looked out on to the street and beyond.

Wainwright, who had completed his assessment, joined them. "I think you've got your hands full here, Karen. Your victim was attacked similarly to your other victims. And once we have samples sent away for analysis, they might confirm that this victim had the same chemical substance poured over his groin."

Karen had nothing to say as she listened to Wainwright, her mind making sense of the pattern of attacks.

"Oh, I've had more detailed results come back on the substance used. It carries the same chemical constituents as a paint stripper. It's a liquid either similar to or is Nitromors. We had a match for methylene chloride in the samples taken from the other victims."

"And it can do that much damage?" Karen asked.

Wainwright nodded. "Get it into your eyes and you can blind yourself. Breathe in the vapours, and it will burn you and make you woozy. Splash it on your skin, and in sufficient quantity, and it will burn you quite badly, even through your clothes."

Karen knew that Nitromors was available in every DIY shop like B&Q. The chances of tracking down where the attacker had purchased theirs would be too difficult. It felt like another dead end for her.

With three killings in one week, each one carrying a different MO, but one common similarity, Karen had a serial killer on her hands. But a shadow of doubt hung on the horizon as to whether the attacks were carried out by the same person. They had conflicting CCTV footage. The question crossed her mind, were they dealing with two killers?

33

With some detectives still on scene, and others beginning the arduous task of doing door-to-door enquiries, Karen addressed a smaller group back at the office.

The savagery of the attack wasn't lost on those gathered around the incident board. As each victim had been discovered, the level of violence had increased. It wasn't unknown for serial killers to adjust their methods as they moved from victim to victim. Nor was it uncommon for each victim to be on the receiving end of more extreme elements of violence as the killing spree continued. That's why in Karen's experience tracking down a serial killer was challenging and difficult.

Karen, along with the others, stared at the evidence pinned to the incident board. Still images of Harry Kruger tied to the bed and brutally slain, were pinned alongside the other two victims.

"We haven't got a lot to go on with our latest victim. All

we know is that his name is Harry Kruger, aged thirty-seven, married with one child. From the enquiries conducted so far, he has been in the UK for five years, and carries a South African passport. He has the right to permanent residency here because of UK grandparents."

"Any idea what he did as a job, ma'am?" asked a junior officer.

Karen shook her head and tapped the whiteboard with her black marker as she pursed her lips and examined the crime scene photographs. "We should have that soon. Jade and I will be visiting the family, so if we haven't found out by then, then we should know once we've visited."

"On the face of it, there doesn't seem to be much of a connection between all three men?" Jade pointed out.

"It appears that way. *If*, it's the same perp, then it looks like they're picking men at random. But I'm not so sure. They may have been killed in different ways, but the attack to the genitalia suggests a connection of some sort."

"There's some sick people out there," muttered another officer.

Karen continued, "Whilst I was at the scene, I had an opportunity to talk to Mason, and look at the victim's phone. I swiped through the different screens, and found the same messaging app, *Don't Talk*, so that gives us another connection."

"And, the other connection, whether it's relevant, is that they were married or in a relationship. Although, I don't know if that has any bearing," Jade added, rubbing her sticky forehead, and blowing out her red cheeks.

Karen handed out still images of both women captured on

CCTV, their images side by side on each handout. She stayed silent for a few moments whilst those gathered took their time to examine the images. One or two officers pulled the images closer for a more detailed inspection, whilst others held them at arm's length for comparison.

"As you can see, there is some similarity between the two women. They have a similar height and build; the shape and angle of their facial features appear similar but they have different hair colour."

"Can we get these images enhanced through facial recognition software?" someone asked.

"Already being done. I'm not hanging around anymore. We need to move on anything quickly. It may be the same person, or a pair of females."

"Sisters?" Steve offered.

Karen dropped her head to one shoulder whilst she stared at the photos. "Could be. Or it could be the same woman, but she's dyed her hair?"

Karen emphasised the need to keep an open mind until they had further information.

"We have uniformed officers and members of our team making general door-to-door enquiries as we speak. We've sent images of Harry Kruger and the two women to the phones of all officers. Perhaps if shopkeepers see the photos, it might jog a few memories. I'm hoping it flushes her out," Karen said.

"Or *them* out," Steve added. "I mean, someone must have seen Kruger. He may have popped into one of the shops prior to arriving at the hotel. We've got officers interviewing every single hotel guest and employee. So, it's going to take a while to get all of that information back."

"I agree, Steve," Karen replied. "The fact he came alone may make it harder for anyone to remember him. I mean, how many people come and go through your average hotel every day? Especially so close to London."

Karen tapped a finger of one hand on each finger of the other as she relayed all the different guests. "Holidaymakers, business people, people passing through, people meeting for illicit encounters, and people who don't want to be found."

"What do we need to do next?" Steve asked.

"Set up an incident room number and circulate the details of all three victims to every single shop, pub, restaurant and hotel in the area. That way we keep it fresh in their minds, and they can report anything suspicious, no matter how small. And whilst we're at it, can someone, I don't care who, search the prisoner release database for the last twelve months. We need to know of any females released recently for assaults or murders that might carry a similar MO."

"This is turning into a fucking PR disaster," Skelton barked as he stormed on to the incident floor. "I'm getting fucking grief from the super, the press is hammering our press department for information, and it's been a week with no breakthroughs or progress. Why the fuck not?" he fumed.

It wasn't unusual for Karen to witness Skelton freaking out like this. He liked everything to run smoothly, and whenever senior officers poked him with a stick, he'd growl at everyone like an angry bear. But his outburst only created an awkward silence that fell across the team. Many officers didn't know where to look and chose the safer option of looking down at their notepads.

"I wouldn't say there's been no progress, sir. The first two victims have been added to the Crimestoppers website. Leaflets have been handed out at all locations where their bodies were found, and door-to-door enquiries have been conducted. And…"

"That's all basic legwork, Karen. There's nothing there of substance. I could do a better job with my shoelaces tied together and one arm behind my back," he spat.

Karen felt like reminding him that he was the SIO, so in theory headed up all three cases but decided against challenging him in front of the team.

"And, as I was about to say, we've identified the likely substance used to inflict severe burns on the victims. We've found hair and clothing fibres from the first crime scene, admittedly we haven't had a match, but nevertheless I see all those things as progress. And now with the third victim, I do think a press appeal would be helpful."

Skelton fumed, "The last thing we need is mass public panic that we have a serial killer on our hands. We should have gone to the press from the start."

"Sir, doing a press appeal after the first victim probably would have caused more panic."

"We need results, Karen, results. Not backchat," Skelton shouted as he turned on his heel and stormed through the double doors.

Karen went off in pursuit, and followed him into his office, before shutting the door behind her.

"I don't wish to speak out of line, sir. But don't you dare try to humiliate me in front of my team. You're the SIO, but you always leave it to me to run the show. And then when I run it, you don't like it. That's hardly fair, sir." Karen held back a tide of anger, her words were clipped, but regretted the second they left her lips.

"Don't you see, Karen; I'm trying to give you a break. It's an opportunity for you to prove yourself and get back some of that credibility you lost. But you're like a loose cannon, one eye on the job, and one elsewhere. Everything takes twice as long with you, and you dither about making decisions."

"I refute that. And what do you mean, one eye on the job and one elsewhere?"

"Snooping, Karen. Snooping. You're here to do a job. But all I keep getting are alerts on the system that you are investigating the old case. You need to drop your personal crusade to find those responsible. It's not healthy and we're not paying you to do that. Do you think it's just me who gets those alerts? The bosses get them. And I'm trying to protect your arse from getting a kicking."

Karen bristled, on the verge of losing it. Her personal credibility was being challenged as an officer. "Sir, with all due respect, I nearly lost my life, not forgetting the other officers who lost their lives. And from what I can see, nothing is being done to find those responsible. I'm doing this for them as much as me."

"Are you really? Because from where I stand, it looks like a selfish quest, because you're screwed up."

Their argument continued for a few more minutes, their

voices rising with each counterargument. It was enough to turn heads of those who walked past Skelton's office.

Skelton didn't want to hear any more and sent her away. Karen stormed out of his office and headed back towards the incident room where her team sat in stunned silence. She continued with the briefing, her heart hammering in her chest, her breathing short and rapid as adrenaline flooded her system.

Meanwhile, Skelton sat back in his chair and closed his eyes. The final images of Two-tone Charlie played out behind his closed eyelids like a movie. Karen was treading a thin line, and he was trying to avoid her ending up the same way. Despite his hatred for Karen, he didn't want her death sitting on his conscience for the rest of his life. But he had the niggling feeling that there was little else he could do to help Karen if she continued her current path.

34

A warm, dodgy tuna sweetcorn mayo sandwich from the local Tesco Express, and a mug of tea were her company this evening as she sat in her office staring at her computer. She'd forgotten to put the sandwich in the fridge earlier today and regretted it now as the sandwich felt limp in her hand.

Whilst some of her team were off for the evening, no doubt enjoying themselves, Karen was stuck in the office finding things to keep herself busy. She felt fidgety and tense.

"Room for one more?" Jade asked as she appeared in Karen's doorway.

Karen glanced around her office. "Well, I'm hardly packed to the rafters with a sea of people, so come on in and join the party."

Jade settled into the chair opposite Karen and yawned. "Aargh… I am so tired, Karen, that I haven't even got the energy to go home. I think they should offer a few beds in every office and station where officers could get their head down for a quick nap."

Karen smiled. "Like the hospitals?" She was referring to the doctors and consultants who sometimes slept during their night shifts in small rooms for medical staff.

"Yeah. We do some crazy fucking shit hours. How can we function on so little sleep when we come in here and do twelve- or fourteen-hour shifts? And sometimes even more. It can't be good for us…" she added, taking her dinner out of a Pret A Manger bag.

Karen felt embarrassed by her measly little sandwich as she watched Jade pick through a delicious chicken salad. It appeared more appetising than her sandwich.

Neither of them addressed the elephant in the room but exchanged awkward glances which suggested that it played on both of their minds. It took a few more moments before Jade plucked up the courage to say something.

"Are you okay?"

Karen furrowed her brow.

"I mean after the way the DCI had a go."

Karen rolled her eyes. "It's not the first time he's flipped out and had a go at me, and I doubt it'll be the last time. I'm not his favourite person, and all that concerns me is doing a good job."

"I know. And you do. It's not for me to say, but he could have taken it off-line and had a chat with you in private."

"He could have done, but every so often the DCI needs to flex his muscles and let everyone know that he's still around. That's what it was about." Karen glossed over it and chose not to say what she really felt. Skelton may have embarrassed himself, but she wasn't about to. She needed to rise above the name-calling, vindictive stares, and jibes about whether she was up to the job.

"The main thing, Jade, is that we do whatever we can to the best of our capability. We've got a triple murder investigation, and many teams across the country wouldn't have the ability to deal with the same situation. Most officers wouldn't deal with a triple murder enquiry in their lifetime. These types of cases take planning, more research, we have to get out there and talk to more people, and all of that takes time. I'd like to say that the perpetrator would just knock on our door and say, "yes, I did that!" But this is the real world, and we can often find ourselves chasing a bunch of dead-end leads that get us nowhere. It takes just one conversation, one sighting, and one tangible and credible lead for us to bust a case wide open. And that's what we need to hold out for."

Jade grinned. "And that's why I enjoy working with you. Do you think we are getting any closer?"

Karen nodded. "Definitely. It doesn't look like that now, but we have DNA evidence, we have images of the perpetrator, or perpetrators, and we are building a picture of the type of targets."

"When you put it like that, it sounds like we're on the cusp of something good, but Christ it gets fucking annoying after a while."

"I know. But you're good at your job and solving these cases would be a lot harder without you."

Jade wiped her mouth and put her food down to pop open a can of Coke. She took a couple of hefty long gulps and placed a hand over her mouth to stop the escaping bubbles coming out as an ear-shattering burp. "Thanks, Karen. I appreciate your endorsement."

By now Karen had got sick of her sandwich and had placed the last quarter back in its packet and tossed it into her bin.

"Karen, can I ask why you joined the force?"

Karen dropped her head back and rested it on the back of the chair and closed her eyes. The relief was instant, and all she wanted to do was fall asleep.

"I'm not sure, really. Probably lots of different reasons. But I remember one," she said laughing to herself. "Back in primary school, we had a visit from two police officers who talked about their job, and as a little kid I sat there and thought they looked amazing in their uniforms. There was an air of invincibility around them, and they terrified most of us as we listened. No word of a lie, we were genuinely scared. And at the time I thought I wanted to be wearing that uniform."

"And look where you are now?" Jade whistled.

Karen didn't reply but let out a grunt of frustration. "Yeah, a washed-out forty-year-old, who lives on her own and has a cat as her best mate. And to be honest, I don't know what else to do. This is the only job I've done. But I don't imagine doing it forever, I'm an old bird now and can't hack the pace any more."

"You're forty, not seventy-five!"

"Yeah, yeah. I've heard it all before. Besides, you still have the option of following in the tradition of your family and going into the City as a lawyer, banker or financial analyst. They come with respectability. Do your parents not see the role of a police officer carrying responsibility and respectability?"

Jade shrugged. "They do, but not the same level. They call jobs in the City, proper jobs. My father is a bit of a snob. He feels that anyone can become a police officer."

Karen agreed to a certain extent. Some of the new junior trainee constables she had come across could hardly string a sentence together. And with graduates being fast-tracked into trainee detective roles, it had led to animosity amongst long-serving officers. Karen wondered if a graduate not long out of university would have enough life skills, knowledge and experience about policing to be an effective detective. The counterargument was old-school thinking, that people had to earn respect by spending time in the trenches first.

"Why don't you get out of here and do something tonight, Jade?"

"I was going to see a film, but I had too much to do."

"I was just looking forward to going home and getting an early night. God, I sound like an old woman." Karen sighed.

Both women laughed in joint sympathy.

Jade left to finish the last bits of work hoping to take the opportunity of a late-night showing at her local cinema.

Karen checked to make sure no one was in her immediate proximity before she logged on to her computer. With Skelton's words still ringing in her ears, she couldn't help but snoop. A thought crossed her mind earlier that a mobile phone had been discarded at the scene of the hijack. At the time they'd assumed it belonged to one of the attackers.

Within days of the attack, the phone had been analysed, found to be a burner phone, and all the numbers on it were unregistered. But no matter where she looked in the case file, there was no reference to the phone being recorded in the evidence log. Yet again, information had been tampered with.

The whole case, and subsequent investigation smelt corrupt. It was the only conclusion that made sense. It was as if a deliberate attempt was made to ensure that this case was never solved.

Sabotage.

Whilst she had an opportunity, Karen picked out another witness statement. A woman in her late fifties, Barbara Murphy, had jumped out of the way as a car careered towards her. The woman had got a brief glimpse of the occupants. Karen noted her address and number before calling her. Under the pretence that she was continuing to investigate the case, Karen arranged to visit Barbara the following evening.

35

It's almost too easy now. Thoughts of murder consume me every waking moment. Taunting me. Urging me forward. Sometimes, the things I see in the shadows are more than just shadows, but then I get so tired of watching. I want to be doing something. And as I walk the streets, I don't feel in control. That's why I stick to the side streets, where there are fewer people. Because as I look at others, if they stare at me a heartbeat too long, I'll be tempted to pluck out their eyes with a knitting needle.

The first time I was careful. I learnt what I needed to know to kill and take care of the details. I was doing all those people a favour, because they had nothing to offer, and they were bad people. And in that world beyond sanity in life, demons constantly look for new recruits, both in the living world and the spiritual. I consider myself the facilitator, taking people from one world to another.

Bloodshed is the only choice left for me now. Bad news for them, good news for me. Because people come to me for pain. For suffering. And I'm the one that gives it to them.

But in a weird kind of way I like the sound of screaming. It's the sign that people can't take much more and they want it to be over and done with.

And the part I enjoy most? How quickly I can destroy their skin. Something so perfect, that can be reduced to nothing more than a bubbling, sizzling mess of fat and tissue in a matter of minutes. I could sit and watch for hours, but time is never on my side.

Yes, it almost seems too easy. I can imagine the chaos and the frantic running around as the police try to fit all the pieces of the jigsaw together. I can almost hear them behind me, the long arm of the law reaching out to snatch away my joy, but I think I'm doing enough to keep them at bay. Three deaths in one week. That's enough to test even the most competent copper.

And now I find I am here again, teasing them. It's in the same place where I met Dulani. The Bell pub. I know it's taking a risk, but I enjoy the thrill and the chase. I'm dressed to impress with skin-tight jeans, and a figure-hugging and revealing bodice that's peeking out from beneath a thin black jacket. I've squeezed my feet into the tightest stilettos I have in my wardrobe and as I walk along the street, I know I have caught the look of many driving past. And that attention continues as I enter the pub.

Looking around the bar, I check to see if anyone recognises me. And yes, I get plenty of looks, but I'm unsure whether they are because of the way I'm dressed, or because they recognise me. But I guess I'm about to find out. I've seen some grainy images of me pinned in the windows of shops as I walk by. Police notices appealing for help. So yes, they're looking for me; the question is whether they'll find me.

I'm certain there's probably a few more of these flyers behind the bar, or in the office beyond. A sheet of paper with my picture on it, but will they be able to recognise me looking like this?

I order my usual drink and hand over a fiver before sitting in the perfect spot, in full view of the CCTV camera, its lens pointing straight at me. I'm not one to shy away, and I acknowledge its presence by staring straight into the lens. I give it a few more minutes, and still no one takes any interest in me. I've blended into the background. A few fellas give me some cheeky smiles from across the bar, but none pluck up the courage to come and talk to me. That's disappointing. I continue to look around but the person I'm interested in isn't here. I thought I'd try to catch him unaware.

I slowly nudge my glass towards the edge of the table and send it tumbling to the floor. The sound of breaking glass turns heads. Customers and bar staff alike glance in my direction in curiosity. I've been in many places where the sound of breaking glass signals the start of a fight. I remember being in a bar one evening called Brodie's in Canary Wharf when I heard a pint glass smash, and moments later beer glasses flew in both directions. Screams, blood, swearing and shouting as two rival groups of men charged into each other. So, I guess people have a right to be nervous when they hear glass breaking.

I have a coy smile on my face, but I wonder if anyone recognises me yet?

I watch a server come out from behind the bar with a dustpan and brush. I apologise, and she comments how it's not a problem, it happens often. As she stands, she gives me a look that lingers a little too long. And after she's gone,

I wait for a further five minutes before I grab my bag and slide through the crowd. I make sure that my body rubs up against as many people as possible. I need them to recognise me. I need them to pay attention. There are looks of curiosity from the women I pass, jealousy and envy etched on their faces. I enjoy the cheeky smiles from the men who find it hard to avert their gaze from my breasts.

Stepping out on to the pavement, I breathe in the warm evening air and smile contentedly.

The sound of sirens in the distance heralds my exit. I would love to be a fly on the wall when they pile into the pub, but you need to catch me if you can.

36

With many officers off for the evening, including Steve and Brad, Karen dragged Jade from her workstation and they made their way towards the Bell pub as soon as the call came in. Jade weaved in and out of traffic, the blue lights of an approaching police car enough to cause other motorists to slam on their brakes and pull over to the side. Drivers haphazardly mounted the kerb or pulled into bus lanes to create space as Jade pushed through the gaps left in the wake of the marked squad car in front of them.

Karen gripped the door handle, her seatbelt straining to hold her as she gave a running commentary to the control room requesting extra uniformed backup.

"Jade, I know I said hurry, but my tuna mayonnaise sandwich is about to make a reappearance over your dashboard. I feel like I'm on a roller coaster at Alton Towers."

"Karen, you said, 'get there as quick as you can,' so that's what I'm doing. This is why I drive, and you don't. I can handle it. You can't. Besides, you turned down the opportunity for advanced driver training."

Karen turned towards Jade, gasping. "How did you know I turned it down?"

Jade held back her laugh. "It was the talk of the office. Everyone knows you don't enjoy driving, so we weren't surprised when you bottled it!"

"I didn't bottle it. For your information. I just didn't see the need. Besides, I rarely travel alone in a job car, so I passed over the opportunity to allow others to do it instead."

"Yeah, yeah. I believe you. Go on, admit it. You get motion sickness."

"Um, yeah. Because of your driving."

They raced through multiple red lights as the traffic thinned. The squad car in front pushed close to fifty-five miles an hour as it tore through the traffic. Jade did her best to keep up as shopfronts and side streets became a blur.

The sound of sirens and two police cars approaching like charging chariots caused onlookers to stop in their tracks. Customers from the pub who were having a cigarette outside gawked, a mixture of curiosity, surprise and excitement etched on their faces.

Karen and Jade threw open their car doors and raced through the front doors of the pub, followed by two uniformed officers. Further sirens wailed in the distance signalling the backup. She instructed the officers to split up and search for their suspect. The two uniformed officers disappeared into the crowd as Karen and Jade made their way towards the bar. A bulky character, a small beer belly poking through his T-shirt, and a dishcloth that hung off his shoulder met them. He introduced himself as the bar manager, before pointing to a female member of staff who had alerted him. She stood beside her manager, with one arm wrapped around her chest. She looked nervous and worried as crease lines formed on her forehead.

"I'm Detective Inspector Heath. I understand you had a sighting of a person of interest to us?" Karen asked looking at the woman.

The waitress nodded. "It's that woman in the photo that some of your officers left here. I think it's the same woman who came into the pub last time. She even had the same hair style, a brown bob."

"Do you know if you captured her on CCTV footage?" Karen asked looking back towards the bar manager.

"I should think so. If you follow me to the office, we can have a look at what we have recorded."

The manager and waitress led Karen and Jade around to the side of the bar and through a door that led up some steps towards an office above the pub. As the manager rewound the tape, the waitress gave a running commentary of what she had seen.

"I just heard what sounded like glass being dropped and broken. It happens all the time, so I'm not fussed about it. It's just one of those things that happen. So, when it did, I just grabbed the dustpan and brush and went to clear it up."

"And did you get a good look at her?" Jade asked.

"Not at first. I needed to clear the glass away to begin with. You go into automatic mode. It was only when I stood up that I thought she had a familiar face. And for the life of me I couldn't place it. I thought she was another customer, and that's where I recognised her face. But it wasn't until I got behind the bar and was throwing the glass away that it came to me. I realised she had a similar resemblance to the picture."

"And you're absolutely certain it was her?"

"As I said, I wasn't sure to begin with. When I had a look at the picture, I thought 'fuck me'. My hands started to shake; I could feel my chest heaving. You see it all the time on TV, but you don't expect it to happen in the pub you work in. For a minute I just froze. I honestly didn't know what to do. And that's when I spoke to Nigel," she said nodding towards the bar manager.

"You did brilliantly. You reacted quickly, and that allowed us to respond immediately."

The waitress smiled, feeling pleased with herself.

"I need the glass that you threw away." It was a slim chance, but Karen hoped that some of the pieces may hold a legible fingerprint or a sample of saliva to allow for a DNA profile. "Jade can you go with this lady and retrieve the glass. In fact, secure the whole bin as evidence. We can leave it to SOCO to sift through it."

"It's in a lot of pieces, but the stem was intact," the waitress added, as she led Jade back out of the office.

"Here it is," the bar manager interrupted.

Karen watched the footage on the screen. She saw the suspect wander into the pub, before making her way over to the bar. Karen noticed both male and female customers taking cursory sideway glances as the suspect weaved her way through the crowd.

Karen and the bar manager watched as the suspect took a seat in full view of another CCTV camera, and the manager switched to that feed.

Cocky and confident, Karen thought as the suspect looked towards the camera and continued staring at it. There appeared to be no hesitation or attempt to shield herself from view. It was a blatant attempt to get noticed, either that or her way of sticking two fingers up at the police.

Together, they watched as the suspect slowly pushed the glass towards the edge of the table, before sending it crashing to the ground.

It was bloody deliberate.

Karen asked the bar manager to rewind and play the tape twice more but at half the speed.

Yep, exactly as I suspected. The falling glass wasn't an accident. It was deliberate. She knew she was being watched, she wanted us to see this.

37

It was gone eleven p.m. by the time Karen returned home, tired and brain-dead. Ever since the break-in, she had become wary about returning home and the feeling didn't sit comfortably with her. She'd usually get off the train at Epping and start to relax, but since the break-in, she'd felt uptight, checking over her shoulder in case she was being followed.

She had fallen into the habit of checking and double-checking the street outside her apartment for any signs of suspicious activity. Cars parked up with their engines running. People hanging around in the shadows, or anyone near the entrance to her apartment block.

Karen hated the sense of vulnerability that she felt. Sometimes it rushed through her for a fleeting moment. Other times it would sit heavy with her and cause her mind to spin in turmoil.

Having locked the front door, she peered from her window into the street below looking for any changes in her surroundings before feeling reassured that the coast was clear.

She kicked off her shoes, fed the cat and made herself a gin and tonic. The CCTV footage had fascinated her. It played over in her mind. With a copy on a flash drive, she plugged it into her laptop and downloaded the footage. Taking a sip of her drink, she sat back in her chair and watched the footage play out several times. Karen paused it on each occasion and held up an image of the woman against the side of her computer screen and compared the two. The cheekbones were aligned in the same way, the shape of her eyes, the angle and line of her jaw looked the same and even her nose carried similarities.

The harder she looked the more she realised that they were looking for one woman. She had taken to disguising herself by changing the appearance of her hair. In Karen's opinion, the woman was dying it, or wearing a wig. She was switching between being a brunette and a blonde, and then from short to long hair. Karen shook her head.

Karen was sure this was her suspect.

Despite this, she felt frustrated. The team were going round in circles. Just as Karen thought they were on the cusp of a breakthrough with a sighting of their suspect, she slipped through their hands.

Karen blew out her cheeks and closed her eyes for a few seconds. Sleep was calling her name, but she couldn't quieten her mind. They hadn't found much connecting the three men other than the fact that they were all using the same messaging app. They all had different lifestyles, careers and interests. One more commonality plagued

Karen's mind. All of the victims were meeting other women behind their partners' backs.

The press team had put out an appeal for information. It was now another waiting game. They had received their fair share of crank calls, and each call needed to be assessed on its value. They had released different images of the woman, hoping it would jog memories. The incident room hotline had fielded dozens of calls, most were irrelevant. Several calls had come in from concerned members of the public who believed the woman lived down their street, which had led to more than eighteen streets being mentioned.

Two wine bars had also contacted the hotline believing that they had seen someone matching the description within the past week. Again, the calls needed to be followed up, and officers would be dispatched to those locations. It was a labour-intensive job, but every call needed a thorough risk assessment to determine its relevance. As far as Karen was concerned, it was a fucking logistical nightmare, and a huge drain on resources.

It felt like they were hunting a ghost. Karen cursed herself at how close they had come to tracking down this elusive woman. She hoped that the broken wine glass might yield some useful information once the forensic teams started work on the broken pieces, but she knew that was a long shot. It was a case of second-guessing the woman's next move. For whatever reason only known to her, she targeted men and the only natural conclusion Karen could come to was that the killer bore a grudge against men who cheated.

Why?

The million-dollar question and one without an immediate answer.

Karen's mind drifted back to those left behind, two wives, a girlfriend and a child. They no doubt had many unanswered questions why their partners had been targeted. And at some point, soon, the penny would drop for them as well.

MY HEAD SPINS with euphoria over the games I'm playing with the police. Despite my being in full view, they still couldn't catch me. I gave myself to them on a plate and they were fucking useless.

I sit on the end of the bed and stare into space, wondering just how far I can push the boundaries. My work isn't complete yet.

Not by a long shot.

I pick up the hammer on the floor and take a wild swing; it connects with his toes and a muffled scream tears from his throat. He looks so pitiful and scared. He can't move, nor can he say anything and that's just the way I like it. I'm sure he's being missed, in fact I know he is, but he's mine now. Sweat gathers on his brow, and a fine sheen breaks on the surface of his chest. His face is bloodied and swollen from where I performed my extraction.

"I know you're suffering. And it's cruel of me. It's like opening a birdcage to let the bird fly out, whilst all the while it's tethered by its leg, and freedom is only an illusion. You see, you had the chance to get away, but you couldn't help yourself. You wanted more, and the more I played with you, the more you fell for it. Addicted. Like a drug."

The man flinches and tries to break free from his restraints, each tug on the cables cuts deeper into the open wounds his ligatures already created. They're red, weeping, bloodied and sore, but that's the least of his worries.

"I've heard that in situations of captivity, the perpetrator becomes the most powerful person in the life of the victim, and the psychology of the victim is shaped by the actions and beliefs of the perpetrator." I walk around the side of the bed and lean over until my face hovers just inches above his. My hair falls over his face creating a darkened shroud. He only has eyes for me. "What do you think? Do you think that's true?" I whisper.

He tosses his head from side to side. Squeals, grunts and groans rattle in his throat.

"Hmm, that's what I thought. You want to know about the place called hell? There is no hell; hell is here." I run my finger up his arm before pressing my thumb into an open wound around his wrist as hard as I can. He screams as pain shoots down his arm. I grit my teeth and feel the ecstasy rush through my body like a natural high. Who the fuck needs drugs when you can create so much misery? "When one faces pain daily, one either learns to live with it or lets it consume them. Which one is it going to be for you?"

I place my ear closer to his face. "What's the matter? Cat got your tongue? Oh, I forgot. I've cut the end off already."

I really thought this one would be fun, but he's no different from the others. It started well, but he gave in too easily. I think he lost it completely when I told him that he was going to die and that my face was the last face he would ever see.

He's getting weaker and becoming less of a challenge. But he still has his purposes and I'll enjoy playing with him for a little longer.

Before I close the door, I take another look over my shoulder and wonder how many more days he'll survive.

I wonder when he'll have his last breath?

38

An officer from her team knocked on her open door and stepped in before she had a chance to answer. Glancing down, she realised she hadn't even had time to fire up her computer, let alone engage her brain in work mode. DC Craig Martin had a sense of urgency in his body language, which appeared to twitch with an abundance of energy. He was always smartly dressed, appearing to have nothing but grey suits in his wardrobe, because that was all Karen had seen him in over the past year.

Craig had been a trainee detective constable for a short while but passed with flying colours. He was intelligent and enthusiastic, perhaps a little overenthusiastic in Karen's opinion. Craig had his feet firmly planted in the yes brigade and would do whatever was asked of him. Sometimes Karen wished he had more of an edge to him and challenged the status quo.

But she liked Craig. He was still young and bright, and she liked that freshness about him. After graduating from

Durham University in history and politics he had joined the police and done four years in uniform before applying to be a detective. She wished she still had that level of enthusiasm. Society hadn't poisoned him, or the things witnessed by seasoned detectives, not yet anyway.

Karen dropped back into her chair and rested her arms on the table in readiness for a heavy dose of eagerness.

"Morning, ma'am, how are you?" Karen teased as she raised her brow at Craig.

Craig flushed, a hint of embarrassment in his face as the corners of his mouth twitched. "Sorry, ma'am, I…"

"Don't worry, Craig. I'm just pulling your leg. What's up?"

"I wanted to give you an update on the calls we received during the night before I clock off. We had eleven in total. We discounted three as drunken pranks. Two are being followed up, and six were from different pubs or bars. Each one of them claimed to recognise the image circulated by the team and the press office in the last twenty-four hours."

Karen pinched her chin with her thumb and first finger as she listened. "That sounds good. Let's pause you there and let's gather our motley crew together and you can share anything else that has come out of these calls."

The team was about half strength with some officers not clocking on till two p.m. and a few others already gone for the day having covered the night shift. Those who remained swivelled in their chairs to face Karen by the incident board. She asked Craig to repeat what he had just told her.

One officer piped up. "It sounds like the killer is trawling the bars and pubs looking for suitable victims?"

"Absolutely," Karen replied. "It would explain why she's visited the same bar twice, and why it's been difficult finding much of a connection between three victims."

Craig continued. "One call was of particular interest. It came from a bar where one of the male members of staff tried to chat up the woman of interest."

"Well, let's hope it wasn't successful," came a voice from somewhere within the team.

Karen couldn't help but agree with the sentiment and pushed Craig for further information.

"He got a name, but whether or not it's real is a different matter. Her name was Bethyan, Beth for short. The bartender mentioned that the strange name stuck out in his mind."

"We need to get officers over there to get a full statement from him when he's back in. And if he's not, then we need to know his home address so we can pay him a visit this morning."

"Ma'am, it's already been organised during the night. I acted on the information and went to see him first thing this morning. Poor bloke got woken by us. He talked about how he went on to serve other customers but kept exchanging glances with Beth who sat at the bar drinking alone." Craig glanced down at his notes before continuing. "The bartender said she looked wired, like she was buzzing on something, and kept giving him the come on, so he made a hit on her and asked her what she was doing after he finished his shift."

"Which was what time?"

"Just before midnight. Anyway, she handed him a napkin

with a breakdown of her name. A bit weird he thought at the time. Most people scribble a number, but she wrote something weird. He stuffed it in his pocket and didn't think more of it. It was lying on his table at home along with a load of other bits and pieces when I arrived." Craig produced a clear evidence bag with the napkin and handed it to Karen.

Karen looked at the front and back of the napkin and then read out what had been written.

"B is for bewitch; my charm is undeniable.

"E is for ecstasy.

"T is for teasing.

"H is for horny.

"Y is for yours.

"A is for arousing.

"N is for nightmare, need I say more?"

The team exchanged puzzled looks unsure what to make of it. Karen stared at the writing again.

Karen chewed on her bottom lip. "It sounds odd. I wonder if there's a cryptic message in it. Like code for something else?"

"I don't know, ma'am. The next time the bartender looked up, she was gone," Craig answered.

"Craig, take this down to forensics immediately and see if they can lift anything from it. Our focus must be researching this name. I agree with you Craig, it's weird, so I'm not surprised the bartender thought the same. It's unusual enough, and that helps us because I can't imagine many people with the name spelt like that."

"It could be fake, ma'am?"

Karen agreed, but it was all they had to go on. Besides, the woman delighted in taunting the police. Perhaps she was brazen enough to use her real name, or an iteration of it. She looked at the images of the woman on the incident board and wrote the name down beneath them with a question mark.

"If this Bethany," Karen corrected herself, "Bethyan is the person we're looking for, then we need to find her and find her fast. We are looking at a female, either dark brown or blonde hair, most likely a wig, probably aged in her early twenties to early thirties and more than likely local to the area because she keeps visiting the same locations."

"It looks like we're getting closer, ma'am?" Brad said as he fidgeted on his seat like he normally did.

"Definitely. In the last twenty-four hours we've discovered more about her than we have done in the whole week. We've no phone records, so there are no call logs that we can download. The victim's phones were clean other than this messaging app, so this individual is smart and very clever. She is not leaving much of a digital footprint for us to find and that's deliberate on her part."

"And she's been very certain in her actions. She's making herself visible in public places and playing a game of cat and mouse with us," Brad added.

"Yes, and that really pisses me off, Brad. We need to find her, if for nothing more than to eliminate her from our enquiries. We need to follow up on every lead and every phone call. I need you to go back out there and knock on doors, because we need to jog people's memories."

There was a collective round of approving nods as the officers returned to what they were doing before, a sense of urgency in their actions.

39

Karen sat at her desk and stared at her growing to-do list. She had more than a dozen case review files to go through from her officers, each one with a twenty-eight-day expired marker. To add to that, three of her officers and herself were down for officer safety training which would take them out of the office for a whole day, something that none of them could afford to do whilst in the middle of a triple murder investigation.

She logged into the HOLMES2 database and looked through all the evidence logged on to the system including witness statements, crime scene information and forensic evidence. To begin with, most investigations were convoluted and a confusing mess. With evidence, information and leads being pulled in through so many channels, the database was nothing more than a storage vessel. However, as investigations progressed, the volume of information started to come together, and that's what Karen hoped for.

Checking her watch, Karen knew she needed to be somewhere else, but the images of the three victims kept pulling her in. Her team had trawled the major social media sites, they had checked off phone records, referenced computer data, but so little of it made sense. Karen's team had made two calls to the US developers of the app with no success. She had made contact as well but had been fobbed off with the excuse that their software was developed and designed in the US and therefore were not obligated to adhere to UK law.

Their stonewalling had only infuriated Karen. She'd asked Skelton to escalate it up the chain, even as far as the commissioner, but he remained doubtful. Karen recalled recent cases in the US where the FBI had wanted Apple to unlock the phones of those who had committed domestic and international acts of violence. If Karen recalled correctly, the FBI hadn't been able to get Apple to comply, so the chances of the UK police getting an American firm to bypass their own layers of encrypted software seemed unlikely. Whether it was true or not, the developers stressed that the way in which the software had been designed meant that all data was removed by the inbuilt shredder, leaving no digital footprint.

Karen scanned through the documents and clicked her tongue against the roof of her mouth.

There must be something else. She's selecting them for a reason.

Perhaps she's a woman scorned? But then that would sum up half the female population, me included, she mused.

Karen reviewed the CCTV footage captured in the Bell pub. She watched the woman appear in shot, home in on Dulani Kalagho, before disappearing with him later. She personified the pickup artist. Smooth with her words, deadly with her appearance, and lethal with her mind. Second-guessing the woman's next step kept Karen up at night. For all she knew, the woman could be out there stalking someone, chatting to an unsuspecting victim in a coffee shop, or scouting the next location for a kill.

"Ma'am, have you got a moment? Craig thinks he's on to something," Jade said as she appeared in Karen's doorway with Craig.

"Twice in one morning, Craig? Anyone would think you're after some brownie points."

Craig gave her a tenuous smile.

She nodded for both to come in and grab a seat opposite her. "Okay, super sleuth, show me what you've got."

Craig cleared his throat. "I've been looking at her movements and the places where all three victims have been found. And all of them appear within a two square mile radius. She knows the area well, or lives within earshot of all these places."

Karen looked across her desk at Craig. "Yep, I think we were coming to that conclusion anyway."

"Yes, I know, ma'am, but with more sightings of a female following the press appeal, and through door-to-door enquiries near the hotel and pub, there seems to be a pattern to her visits. That's if the sightings are her. She's revisited the place where she met Dulani Kalagho. She was seen in three other pubs within the Shoreditch High Street, Old Street and Great Eastern Street areas."

Craig unfolded a map and placed it on Karen's desk. He pulled a red marker from his pocket and ran red lines between three points on the map. The shape he drew was a triangle. "This is her stomping ground."

Karen studied the map, her eyes moving from one point to the other and the various locations that Craig had circled already.

Craig then narrowed down the area on the map, and drew a square that covered Bateman's Row, Curtain Road, Shoreditch High Street and Old Street. "I then began to cross-reference everything we had on the database, and the results from trawling through three hundred and twenty hours of CCTV footage."

"And we found more evidence of her in this area?" Karen asked, pointing to the red square.

"Yes, ma'am. We've got CCTV footage that catches her coming out of Bateman's Row and walking north up Curtain Road on two separate occasions. She was also spotted on CCTV at the Strongroom bar in Curtain Road, less than twenty-four hours before our vic three, Harry Kruger, was murdered. It's only a four-minute walk between those two locations."

Karen sat up in her chair and studied the map. She tried to put herself in the mind of the woman and pictured herself walking down the very same streets.

"I told you he was on to something, ma'am," Jade chipped in as she raised a brow.

Karen nodded. "This is good. This is really good."

"And to top it off, she was seen last night in the Lighthouse bar on Rivington Street where Dulani Kalagho often went. We've been able to find a small piece of footage from a few days back where Dulani was in the bar, and the same woman appeared about twenty minutes after he arrived. They didn't make any contact, she stayed back and out of view, hidden behind other customers. But we can see her looking in Dulani's direction for a good ten minutes before she left."

A million and one ideas floated into Karen's mind, jockeying for position as she pieced together conversations and snippets of information taken in over the past week. "This is encouraging. She's out there a lot. I think if we look hard enough in this small area," Karen started, pointing towards a red box, "then we might have a good chance of spotting her. We need to set up an op tonight and flood the area with surveillance."

40

Karen waited patiently outside one of the meeting rooms. She kept glancing through the glass panel in the door waiting to see if they had concluded the meeting. The bare-bones of a plan formed in her mind as she paced up and down the hallway, staring at her feet. She couldn't help but think about this evil woman's actions and mindset. Karen shook her head unable to make any sense of it.

The door to the meeting room flung open, startling her. Karen waited for each of the officers to file out before catching Skelton's eye.

"Sir, have you got a moment? It's urgent."

Skelton looked neither phased nor concerned. His face adopted the usual bland expression, before he flicked his head in the direction of the meeting room.

Karen updated him and what the team had been working on, and what Craig had pulled together.

"And how certain are you, Karen?" he asked after hearing her request to mount a surveillance operation.

"As certain as I can be, sir. The team have been working hard, and it's making sense. She is targeting a specific area and often. I think we have a good chance of spotting her. We've already come this close to apprehending her last night," Karen said as she held her thumb and index finger about one inch apart.

"But we didn't get her. And there's no guarantee that you can get her tonight either, is there?" he challenged.

What. A. Prick.

Despite his contrary attitude, Karen knew that she needed to butter him up more. "There's no guarantee in anything, sir. But the press appeal that you allowed paid dividends. People are spotting her. Without the press appeal we wouldn't have even got that. And that's down to you."

Skelton licked his lips, as his eyes darted from left-to-right processing what Karen had told him. "It's a big ask. A press appeal doesn't really involve much in the way of resources, but a surveillance op on this scale would require dozens of officers drafted in from other teams."

"I agree, sir. But there will be other departments and units on tasking this week and we could request their help. I'm telling you, sir, this is the person we are looking for. She is slippery and dangerous. Her MO is the same, she picks up a guy in a bar, lures him to a secluded place away from prying eyes where she kills them. We've got a list of venues she visits frequently, and she repeats her route. I realise that it's a tough ask, but we need to find this person before she kills again."

"Karen, I'll authorise it. But just for this evening. If any of your team get eyes on, they must not try to apprehend her on their own, call for backup. We must make sure she doesn't do another disappearing act on us. Understand?"

Karen agreed and rushed off. She would ask Jade to organise a suitable location nearby like a sports hall, where the briefing could be conducted. In the meantime, Karen had a few hours, which just gave her enough time to rush off.

FOURTEEN GRUELLING FLIGHTS of stairs later, Karen stood on the landing, gripping the stair rail. Her chest crushed her breath, and a fine sheen of sweat glistened on her forehead. "Why the fuck don't elevators ever work in these bloody tower blocks," she fumed.

Waiting there a few minutes would allow her to catch her breath before knocking on the door. Without the luxury of air conditioning, the stairwell and corridors were hot, musty and smelly. With little natural light, and even less fresh air, the environment was oppressive like the rest of the building and the local area.

By not turning up in a squad car and making her way by foot, she hoped she hadn't attracted the attention of the local street gangs that roamed menacingly around the base of the tower blocks.

Karen blew out her cheeks, her knuckles hovering just inches from the door. She knew that this was a crazy move and one that could backfire, but the overwhelming urge to continue seeking the truth pushed her on.

She rapped on the door and waited. After a minute or two she tried again and heard footsteps approaching from within.

The door opened and a slim tall woman appeared from behind the door.

"Barbara Murphy?"

"Yes, that's me," she said in a timid voice.

Karen held out her warrant card. "I'm Detective Inspector Karen Heath. We spoke on the phone. I haven't got long, but have you got a few moments?"

"Of course, please come in."

Barbara led her through to the lounge and offered Karen a seat, before joining her. "Can I get you something to drink, some tea, perhaps a coffee, or even in this hot weather a cold drink?"

Karen shook her head, and thanked her for her hospitality. Karen thought she seemed nice enough. She had small eyes, and a thin face. But for someone in their late fifties she had a classic look about her, with silver-white hair in a pixie cut hairstyle. Karen couldn't tell how much of it was natural or coloured. She wore a deep red blouse, with several of the buttons undone to just above her bra, and wore skin-tight denim jeans, finishing off the look with a pair of white Converse trainers.

"As I said, I haven't got long. But I'm investigating a case from about a year ago. And you were a witness to it. It was when two police cars were ambushed."

Barbara folded her hands into her lap, and Karen noticed her knuckles turning white.

Karen laid it on thick about how she was still investigating the crime, and yet no one had been brought to justice. She was pressing to find those responsible so the families of the two deceased officers could finally get some closure.

Barbara listened intently and offered a lot of sympathy but remained tight-lipped.

"From your statement, you gave a very clear description of the events that unfolded, and how you were nearly hit by a car driven by those responsible. Can you remember much about what the men looked like?"

Barbara drew her lips into a thin line and shook her head. "I'm not sure. It seems such a long time ago. I'm sure whatever I saw at the time I provided in my statement."

"Oh, you did. I just wondered if you'd had any further recollections. Often to begin with people are in shock. But once things settle down, you'd be surprised at how much more detail people are able to recall," Karen reassured her.

"I'm sorry. I really don't remember much at all. It's an episode I'd like to forget."

Karen sensed the woman's voice cracking, and her answers being evasive.

"Did you hear them say anything amongst each other whilst the ambush was going on? Maybe a person's name, an accent?"

There was a lengthy pause whilst Barbara wrung her hands in her lap. She shook her head when nothing came to mind.

"Barbara, I know this is hard for you. But it's just as hard for me. As I said on the phone, I was one of the officers present. It shocked me as much as it shocked the bystanders who witnessed it. You must have seen something else. Perhaps the way they walked, their physical build, any characteristics that stood out?"

Barbara shook her head again. "Inspector. Please don't pressurise me. I gave everything in the statement. There isn't anything further I could add at this late date. In fact, looking back on it now, I'm not even sure that half of the things I said in there were relevant. I think I was in shock, and just said anything."

Karen furrowed her brow. "Are you saying that you're not sure about the statement you provided?"

The woman's body stiffened, and she drew her shoulders back. "No, inspector. I'm certain in everything I said. All I'm saying is that perhaps what I saw wasn't exactly what had happened. My recollection is somewhat vague," she replied firmly.

Karen leant forward and rested her elbows on her thighs. "Can I ask why you were happy for me to come here? As I said on the phone, I had a few questions to ask about the case. If you felt that you had nothing to add, why did you agree to see me?"

Barbara didn't have an answer and shrugged. "I don't know what I expected. But I'm not in a position to help you. I'm really sorry if you feel you've wasted your time."

Karen stood and sighed in frustration. "Far from it, Barbara, you've been very helpful, in fact, you've made things even clearer for me."

BARBARA STOOD on the other side of her doorway with her

ear to the door. She listened as Karen's footsteps descended the stairs, the sound becoming quieter until silence returned. She bit her bottom lip and picked up her phone and dialled the number.

"Hello… hello… um… It's Barbara Murphy here. You know you asked me to call if anyone contacted me… well…"

SKELTON PRESSED the red disconnect button on his mobile and pushed his chair back. He stretched out and rested his heels on his office desk and stared up towards the ceiling. He whistled through his teeth before sitting back upright and bringing up Google on the screen. Things were hotting up.

41

Karen had enough time to head back to the office for a change of clothes. Her conversation with Skelton troubled her. At first, she thought Skelton was tampering with the files and that would make sense. But his remark about not being the only one who got the alerts, caused her to wonder who else in the chain of command had a vested interest in this case. For the first time, she considered the notion there was some form of cover-up across the police hierarchy.

Karen had changed into a pair of trainers, jeans and a thin long-sleeve T-shirt. She, along with the other officers, needed to blend in tonight. Shoreditch and the surrounding area were full of young urbanites that hung out in trendy bars and restaurants. To them it was much more about enjoying the vibe than dressing to impress, and officers on surveillance had been briefed accordingly.

All available officers made their way towards the small community hall in Shoreditch they had commandeered for the briefing. Plenty of traffic congested the roads as rush-hour approached, so their journey to St. Hilda's went slower than Karen would have liked. Karen used the time to think through her plan of action for this evening. Much hinged on the outcome of their efforts and though they had a large area to cover, she hoped with enough officers, they could cover the main points of interest.

Jade and Steve followed Karen into the community hall. Brad had booked the evening off, citing that he wanted to visit his ex-girlfriend and hoping she would allow him to see their two boys. Though Karen needed him on the op, she accepted that he needed personal time and understood his predicament. They had spoken several times about the difficulties he faced in his personal life, and how not seeing his children affected his emotional stability.

Though Karen only heard one side of the story, she couldn't understand why someone would use children for leverage. According to Brad, it all extended from the fact that his ex-girlfriend wanted money above and beyond what he already paid in maintenance. Ten grand was a figure she had plucked out of the air but when pushed by Brad, she hadn't been able to explain why she needed the money.

The DCI had been good on his word for a change. He had pulled the right strings, and more than forty officers filled the hall. About a third of them were from her MIT, and they had drafted the others in from different departments and teams. Karen recognised a few faces in the crowd, although she couldn't remember from where.

"This is the person we are looking for." Karen handed out pictures of the woman with both brown and blonde hair images. "She's elusive, cunning, very good with her words, and above all else, volatile and dangerous. As you can see, she dresses to impress and from the video footage that we have secured, can turn heads wherever she goes."

"Does she have a preferred hair colour between these images?" an officer asked.

"Not as far as we are aware. As you can see in some images, she had long blonde hair, and in others she had a short brown bob. We believe they are wigs, so your guess is as good as mine which one she turns up in tonight if she's out there."

"How do you want us to play this if we see her?" someone asked.

"If you see her, do not approach her or apprehend her until you've spoken to me. She is a slippery character and the last thing we need is getting her spooked and doing a disappearing act on us again. I would much rather get as many available resources together in one spot so we can cut off all exits. If we work together, we have a greater chance of success. I'm not looking for any mavericks here, we work as a team. Do I make myself clear?"

Karen scanned the crowd and most of them nodded in agreement.

Jade walked amongst the group and handed out another sheet of paper.

"DS Whiting has just given you a list of establishments that our suspect has been to on more than one occasion. I would suggest that these locations should be our priority. I need you to blend in with the crowd, keep your eyes open, and act normal. And I repeat, do not get too close to her. If she sees you looking at her for more than a few seconds, she will clock you and slip out the door."

Karen spent the next few minutes describing the suspect's MO, and how she wanted the teams to cover the locations. Ticking each venue off the list, she assigned officers to each of the locations, and the remainder of the officers were asked to scour the streets, paying attention to side roads, alleyways, and access points.

A rumble erupted around the room as the briefing ended. Sporadic conversations broke out amongst the officers, chairs scraped across the floor, and a buzz of energy flowed through the group as they made their way towards the exit.

I SIT on the edge of my bed and stare at the mannequin heads that face me, each one with a different hairstyle. It's like something out of the living dead, white non-descript faces staring back at me, their pale complexions in sharp contrast to their hair. A blonde bob, long blonde hair, a brown bob, brown ringlets, a fuzzy perm of copper. So much choice, so little time.

They're clever, but I'm smarter than them. I'm sure right now they're looking for me, expecting me. The e-fits pinned in the shop windows carry a good resemblance to me, so I need to stay one step ahead of them. They'll be looking for someone who matches those descriptions, so I need to do something different. I make my way towards my bedroom door and look at the outfit hanging on the back of it. This will throw the cat amongst the pigeons.

I have just enough time to go for a shower and enjoy

running my soapy hands across my skin and enjoying the sensation. I'm loving every minute of this journey, and shivers of excitement flow through me. I spent a few hours at work today, and that was so dull in comparison. Smelly, dirty cast-offs. I can't remember how many hand sanitising gels I've gone through, but it must be hundreds now. I think it surprised them when I handed in my notice.

It's high past time to go. I've been around here far too long, and it's time to move on again. I rarely enjoy staying in one place longer than a year. It's too easy to get sloppy and make mistakes. Last year I was in Manchester. The year before that I was just outside of Skipton in Yorkshire. But I didn't stay there that long. Skipton was remote which was good, but very small, my tally there was only one before I left. London has been brilliant. It's so easy to blend into the background and become another face in the sea of faces. The police are stretched which means their detection rates are lower, and that's bought me more time.

My taxi driver hates me. I make him drive around the houses, travelling one way down the street before turning back on ourselves. We must have travelled up Shoreditch High Street on three separate occasions, turning left and then turning right. He keeps asking me where I want to go, and I tell him around here somewhere, but I'm too early. I just need him to drive. At first, he balks, and keeps mumbling to himself in a foreign language which I don't understand.

Fucking rude bastard!

But when we pull up, I give him an extra fiver as a tip which surprises him.

I stop for a moment and check my reflection in a shop window. This is a big departure for me. I look nothing like the e-fit and that gives me the edge.

Tonight's going to be a good night.

42

I walk in full view of everyone, but I'm a nobody. A lone female going from point A to B. The busy streets allow me to blend in. I'm not going too fast or slow, just taking my time, glancing in windows as I pass by the shops.

The Reliance, the Hoxton Pony, and so many other bars I walk past are filling up. I'm in no hurry as I weave in and out of the roads and check my phone. I think my appearance is having the desired effect. The looks still come my way from every man I pass.

It's time, I say to myself and make my way towards my meeting point. Level D became a firm favourite of mine the first time I visited it. The music's loud, the drinks are cheap and the place is small. It's a strange place where drinks are served from two bars, the ground floor and the basement. I noticed on my first visit that as the evening wore on, more customers would head downstairs which featured more of the garage vibe, with louder music that rumbled through the floor and up through your feet. The flashing lights were probably powerful enough to trigger epilepsy in someone, and a space so small that you were hemmed in on all sides.

I order a drink from the bar and glance around. Men try to chat up women, the women enjoying the attention, and the drinks flow freely. At first, I take a few moments to move around the bar, stopping every few minutes to scan the crowd. I can't see him and a few minutes pass before I see his face at the bar where he orders a drink.

Game on.

I push my purse into my back pocket and squeeze through the people in front of me before standing beside him. Whilst he's being served, another waitress takes my order. When she returns, I rummage through my handbag and claim to have had my purse either lost or stolen. He hears me having a discussion with the waitress about my inability to pay, and the waitress's concern. And he plays right into my hand by interrupting and offering to pay for my drink.

He looks the same as his pictures. He flashes that same charming smile, and I thank him for helping me out.

"Are you meeting friends?" he asks.

"Yes, fifteen minutes ago. But they're not answering their phones. So, I have no idea where they are," I lie.

"Well, whilst you're waiting, perhaps I can keep you company? I'm Lee."

"I'm Beth," I reply with a smile.

We get talking, and he can't resist laying on the chat. He doesn't recognise me, Why would he? My make-up is different, my hair isn't blonde, and I'm wearing flat strappy sandals, and not the heels he's seen in my pictures. He said he had a thing for redheads, so I couldn't let him down, could I?

"Do you know, you ain't half reminding me of someone."

"Is that good?" I ask.

A wide smile breaks, and I can almost see the wheels turning in his mind.

"Oh, trust me, it's a good thing. But I've got a soft spot for redheads, and I love your hair. It really suits you. You're stunning."

He's engrossed in me, but the only thing I'm thinking is how long I have to listen to his drivel. He's been on a charm offensive ever since we first messaged each other. I remember him saying I looked a bit of a plain Jane to start with, so I spiced it up by sending him pictures of me dressed like a pole dancing slut. That did the trick, and since those first few photographs, I've been reeling him.

A little shiver travels up my spine. Something doesn't feel right. I'm sure the couple at the other end of the bar have looked at me more than once. The man has his back to me, but the woman keeps glancing over his shoulder in my direction. And now it's my turn to place her face. I'm not one to be paranoid, and I'm good at spatial awareness, but that woman must have glanced in my direction more than a dozen times in the past ten minutes.

And then it comes to me. I saw her just thirty minutes ago a street away. She was walking in the opposite direction. Alone. I looked at her, but she looked straight ahead, not even a cursory glance from her.

And now she's here.

Coincidence? Possibly.

It isn't unknown for customers to go for a bar crawl around here, but the fact she keeps looking in my direction worries me.

I take Lee by the hand and move him deeper into the bar away from prying eyes, and behind a pillar. I tell him that it's a bit quieter here and a little more personal where we can get to know each other better. I think he's taken aback by my forwardness. He carries on talking about what he likes to do, much of it I ignore as I scan my surroundings. I vaguely recall him talking about football, playing nightfall or fortnight or some shit like that. But it's the least of my worries. Five minutes later the same couple have shifted position and once again I can see them.

Their hovering is too much of a coincidence. I move location once again with Lee, and within minutes the couple are there standing in the same spot I just left. They seem engrossed in each other. He leans into her, whispering in her ear and she smiles. I remain calm, teasing Lee with some random shit whilst my mind spins through a dozen possibilities. I move in and give him a hug which gives me the opportunity to look over his shoulder. They're still there.

I make my excuses and tell Lee to meet me elsewhere as I need to go to the cashpoint, but before I leave, I need to go to the loo. I circle around the bar, darting amongst the crowds, before leaving via a fire exit. Thankfully, bar staff left it open so they could take empty bottles outside.

With another pang of trepidation, I escape. Something isn't right.

43

Karen wanted to listen in on the Airway radio, but it would have been too obvious. Instead, she relied on her mobile phone. She stood in a bar with Steve; it made sense for them to go as a couple. Jade was with another female officer in a bar further down the road. One by one, Karen made calls to her officers to get a sit-rep.

Though she tried to have sensible conversations with Steve, he appeared distracted by female customers around them.

"Wind your tongue in, Steve, you're not here to pull. Mind you," Karen looked around, "that wouldn't be hard."

"Ma'am, I'm not doing anything."

"Yeah, but you'd like to. Look at them. They're falling over themselves to get a better look at you. I mean, couldn't you find the worst clothes in your wardrobe to wear this evening?" Karen continued, looking Steve up and down.

Though he was dressed no differently to most of the men here, his boyish good looks, and Steve McQueen features, made him attractive whatever he wore.

"Any updates from the others?" he asked.

"Nothing yet. It might be worth our while moving on again to another bar. I can't see anyone here that matches her description."

Karen tapped her redial button and scrolled through her list before hitting Jade's number. "Jade, anything going on with you?"

"No, ma'am. No one here matching her description."

"Jade try somewhere else. We need to keep moving."

No sooner had Karen disconnected her call with Jade, her phone rang again. "Heath."

"Ma'am, we are in level D. We thought we saw someone who looked like her, but she was a redhead. She was with another guy, but we lost sight of her. We've searched the whole premises and outside."

Karen swore into her phone. "Fuck. Do you think it was her? Perhaps with a different colour wig on?"

"We can't be a hundred per cent certain, ma'am. The make-up and hair were different, and she was dressed low-key, to be honest. Skinny jeans, flat sandals, and a long-sleeved blouse that looked a little big for her."

Karen continued to get an update from the officer whilst telling Steve to contact the other teams for sightings of a redhead.

The feedback was negative. No one had seen anyone resembling the description or the pictures. Karen's stomach sank. But with a few hours, remaining, she instructed all teams to move to different locations before coming back to her with further updates.

I MOVE to another location just to be safe. This is a new one for me, but I need to make sure that no one is following me. My initial plan didn't work out as I had hoped, but I still have time to salvage it. I text Lee and tell him where I am.

Fifteen minutes pass whilst I wait in the shadows of an alley until I see Lee arrive and go into the pub. I'm keen not to rush in, so I wait a few more minutes just to make sure he's not followed, or that couple is nowhere in sight. I check that the coast is clear before making my way to the pub. This one is a little less crowded, and quieter. It's off the main drag, so less likely to be discovered by the passing crowds.

Lee waits at the bar with two drinks in hand. I can tell he's pleased to see me as he gives me a soft kiss on the cheek. We carry on from where we left off, asking questions about each other, and me reeling him in.

"So, do you have someone special in your life?" I probe.

"Nah, to be honest, I'm a bit shy, so it's not easy approaching anyone I like."

"Yeah right, you were confident enough to approach me."

"That's down to this," he says waving his drink. "Dutch courage."

"There's lots of ways to meet someone. Online dating sites, online apps. Come on, you must have been on PoF?"

"I've heard Plenty of Fish is full of fake profiles. Besides, those type of things aren't for me," he sighs.

Fucking liar.

"So, why does a good-looking fella like you find it so hard to meet women?"

Lee shrugged and rolled his eyes towards the ceiling. "Ever since leaving school, I've worked in London in male-dominated industries, like insurance and banking, and found it hard to meet women."

Whether or not that's true I don't know, but he's probably bullshitting like most men.

I think the time is right to reveal myself. I hold up a picture of my profile on my mobile phone, the same one that he's been responding to. And his jaw drops as he looks at me.

"You were supposed to be meeting her tonight? Well that's me."

He's speechless, unable to find the right words. His eyes dart back and forth between the picture on the screen and me.

"No way. That isn't you, is it?" he asks as doubt tinges his words.

"It is. But as you can see, I was blonde in those photographs, but you said you liked redheads. Well, this is my natural look."

He seems lost for words, before a smile returns on his face.

"Hold on a minute. Do you have matching cuffs and collars?" he teases.

I roll my eyes. "You'll have to find out, won't you?"

"So… all those fantasies you talked about in our messages. Were you just pulling my leg, or did you mean them?"

"Put it this way, I didn't lie in any of those messages. You and I were on that app for only one reason. No strings fun. Like everyone on that app. So you can cut the no confidence crap. You want it as much as I do. Whilst you were tossing off over my pictures, what do you think I was doing when you sent me pictures of your knob?"

He likes the naughty talk as he takes half a step closer to me. His face hovers within touching distance of mine.

"I fucking fancied you the first time I saw you on there. You looked fit as fuck. When you asked to meet up with me, I jumped at the chance."

"All this bollocks about you being shy with women… it's just that, bollocks?" I said through gritted teeth as I brushed the back of my hand across the front of his jeans.

He rocked his head back in laughter. "It's a fair cop. You got me on that one."

I've got you.

"Do you remember the fantasy I told you about?"

Lee looks up towards the ceiling for a few seconds. "Which one? If I'm not mistaken, you had a fair few."

There's a glint in my eye. "About being fucked against the wall outside…"

THE LACK of feedback from the teams ate away at Karen. As her patience wore thin, her aggravation grew. The team became restless and as annoyed as Karen over the lack of action.

"Try the next place, ma'am?" Steve asked.

Karen shook her head. "We've been to three places already. And I think between all of us, we've been to over twenty bars and pubs. And there's no sign of her."

"Maybe she's not out tonight? Or worse, moved on to a different patch?" Steve suggested.

Karen didn't want to entertain the idea, but a part of her agreed with Steve.

Stepping out on to the pavement, Karen took in a deep breath and tried to steady her nerves. This was a big deal tonight. Forty officers waited on instructions from her. Skelton expected a result, and her reputation once again hung out on the line.

Not wanting to give up, Karen jumped into the job car with Steve and asked him to drive around. She was fed up of being static and wanted to scour the larger area.

For over twenty minutes they drove up and down streets. Random street names flashed by, Redchurch Street, Calvert Avenue, Holywell Lane, Willow Street. Street names that carried no significance but meant the world to her. Karen just stared out of the passenger window, her eyes darting from one face to another as they passed by. Somewhere amongst this tangled mess of roads their prime suspect pursued her next victim. Her hunting ground, and like hunters in the wild, they never strayed further than their familiar territory.

She was here somewhere.

Where are you?

44

The excitement of the chase lasts just a few minutes for me. I'm not there to make friends, find a boyfriend, fall in love with my future husband or meet my soulmate. I only have one thing on my mind, and it isn't what Lee has on his.

His face erupts into a grin more fitting of an eleven-year-old boy who just got the latest Xbox console for Christmas. He can't wait to finish his drink and leave. And that's fine with me, this evening has left me edgy. The vibe isn't there for me, and the same face in the crowd worries me.

One thing is certain, regardless of what happens this evening, it will only end one way.

Causing pain is my addiction that no rehab can ever cure. I should never have been let loose because like any addict, I need my fix. Lee is the poor fucker who's fallen for my charm and is spending his last night on earth.

I let him lead the way but nudge him in the directions I want to go. I've been around here a few times during the day, holding my phone, pretending to be lost, as I follow the map on my phone. But as a willing participant now, Lee can't move quick enough.

We head down a side street and away from the crowds and traffic. The odd minicab whizzes past as it takes shortcuts to avoid the traffic. His pace quickens as the prospect of a fuck looms nearer. I pull him to a stop and push him up against the wall, before kissing him hard and deep. I bury my nails into his arse cheeks, the short sharp stab of pain seems to excite him further as I feel the bulge in his jeans press against me. His eyes feast on me, picturing what comes next. I pull away. It's just enough to tease and tantalise him before he marches off, a sense of urgency and desperation in his movements as he pulls me along.

The further we navigate the backstreets, the quieter it becomes. The sound of traffic dulls into the background, replaced by the sound of our breath and the tapping of our shoes. This street is perfect for us. It's narrow and hard to get anything down here bigger than a Mini. It's dark and confined, the walls closing in on us the deeper we venture into the alley.

"Keep going. The road ends up as a dead end, so we won't be disturbed."

The gloom melts into complete blackness as we stop in a doorway.

"Do you know where we are?" he asks as he glances up and down the street.

"I don't work far from here, so I knew it was somewhere we wouldn't be disturbed," I lie.

He pushes me against the wall and cups my face in his

hands before kissing me deeply, leaving him breathless. His hands move down and start massaging my breasts, and I push my hands down the back of his jeans to pull his hips into mine. He responds.

"Slow down. I don't want you dropping your load too soon." But I'm uncertain that he's heard me. His breathing is hard, and he's desperate to please. I press myself into the wall and open my legs. He moves and stands in between them, pressing his firmness against me. I undo the button on his jeans, and then his flies, before sliding his jeans and boxer shorts down to his thighs. I massage his cock. He's firm and straining to let go.

"I hope you're going to please me?" I whisper in his ear.

He grunts in response. "I'll do anything you want me to. I wanna fuck you so bad."

"Well, you're going to have to work for it," I respond as I undo my own jeans and slip them down. As I push his shoulders, he drops to his knees, his lips and teeth tugging at my knickers. I can feel the heat from his breath pressing through the fabric. *He's in another world, and just where I need him.*

My fingers reach for the small craft knife concealed in my bra and I push on the orange button to extend the blade. Even in darkness, it still catches a shard of light as I stare at it, mesmerised. It's a thing of beauty, so delicate and yet so powerful. Able to inflict so much pain and misery. It's captivating, and for a moment I forget about Lee, desperate to please.

"Try harder," I taunt.

He shuffles around on his knees to get a better angle,

pushing my thighs apart with his elbows. I let him get closer, only to push him back, before allowing him back in. His face is hot with exertion; his hands are sweaty with greed.

With one hand, I grab the back of his hair and pull his head back, whilst running the knife across his throat. I feel the warmth of blood spurt across my hand as he stumbles back, fear and panic tearing through him as he tries to steady himself and get to his feet. I stand there and watch him fighting for life. His hands wrap around his throat. The thought crosses my mind to run the blade through a second time, but I want him to suffer. It's better this way; the darkness entertains my imagination as I see his silhouetted form crumple to the ground. I can see him flapping on the ground like a fish tossed from water. Squeals of pain are replaced by gurgling, and retching sounds as blood fills his airways.

I remain fixed in place waiting for the shaking to stop.

And then there is silence.

I reach into my handbag and take out a pair of latex gloves. I take my time and snap them on, since I'm in no hurry. The last time I stood here, I waited for over an hour and didn't see a soul. So I know I have time on my side. I pull out the bottle of liquid and empty its contents over his groin. After about five minutes, I hear the sizzling of skin, like meat on a barbecue.

Game over.

THE LAST REMNANTS of adrenaline course through my veins

as I pull a bottle of beer from the fridge and squeeze off the lid. The bottle trembles in my shaking hand as I bring it to my lips and enjoy its coolness quenching my thirst. I stare into space, no thoughts, no feelings, just blackness that clouds my mind. The strange thing is I feel nothing each time I do this. There's no guilt, no remorse, fear, or apprehension. Just nothing but an emptiness deeper than any canyon in the world. One part of me wants to go down the road and pick up a Domino's pizza and settle down in front of the TV. The other part wants to watch snuff movies on the Dark Web and run amok down a busy street slashing and stabbing people at random. I'd love to see their faces, the sheer look of panic and terror as people flee in every direction.

I open the door and watch his squirming body. The smell of his shit and piss isn't as bad now. I've not fed him for four days. I've given him some honey every day, because I read somewhere that honey helps open wounds. It heals them or some bollocks like that. I also read that honey makes blood taste sweeter. Though I'm not sure about that theory, because I licked the open wounds on his wrist yesterday and his blood tasted foul.

He senses me coming closer and flinches. I reassure him it's just me. He really is a pathetic specimen. He started out fun, but now fears his own shadow. I sit beside him and release the blade from my craft knife. I run the tip lightly across his chest, the score marks creating little rivulets of blood that bubble to the surface. A deep groan of a scream rattles in his throat as he arches his head back and buries it into the pillow.

I run the blade in random directions across his chest and down his stomach, each score line sending shards of pain through his body like he is walking on broken glass. God it's a beautiful sight. Skin that appears to be impermeable to water tears so easily at the hands of a knife. How can that be?

I glance down his body. It's greasy, sweaty and creased from where he's lost weight. I slap his flaccid cock. It's unresponsive.

"You thought you could use that with me, but looking at it now, it's pathetic, don't you think? I mean, why the fuck were they created?"

I stand to leave; he sweats from where he tensed to fight the waves of nauseating pain that torture his body.

"Hang on in there, not long to go."

45

Karen couldn't face going home after the op last night and settled into her office chair. Over the next few hours, she went through moments of drifting off to sleep, to sitting wide awake, to staring at a blank computer screen drained from having spent hours thinking about their suspect. In her eyes, it was a complete disaster. She had dispatched officers to many locations and had cruised the streets hoping to track down their suspect. The evening had yielded nothing.

Nothing!

It wasn't uncommon for surveillance operations to end without result, but in Karen's eyes she'd fought for resources and only ended up with an epic failure. She needed to get a result to prove to those around her that she was back, and on top of her game. This case was personal.

What she didn't need was an ear bashing from Skelton when he arrived for work.

"Well, that was a complete waste of time. I was prepared to

give you the benefit of the doubt and go along with your hunch. I ran around to get the extra officers, because you thought the suspect might commit another crime."

"Sir, it wasn't a complete waste of time. You know as well as I do, that sometimes these things work out. On this occasion, it didn't."

"You think so?" Skelton barked.

"I know she's out there. She's out there every night. It just so happens that last night we couldn't find her. We had a lot of ground to cover, and we scoured as many pubs, bars and clubs as we could."

Their argument continued. Skelton stressed the efforts he had gone to. And Karen in her defence kept pushing that whilst she had officers at those locations, it had disrupted their killer.

"Karen, this isn't going to help if we need to mount another surveillance operation. Can you imagine how much the overtime bill is going to be? It will go back up the chain, and I'll face the questions," Skelton pushed, jabbing his own chest with his index finger.

That's it, you worry about yourself, and what your bosses will say. Meanwhile, I'm trying to catch a killer.

Skelton paced around the room and spun on his heel ready to launch another verbal volley, when Jade knocked on the open door. All three of them exchanged uncomfortable glances amongst each other in the silence that followed.

"Sorry to disturb you, ma'am, sir."

"What is it, Jade?" Skelton butted in before Karen opened her mouth.

"Our suspect was out last night, and we missed her."

Karen furrowed her brow. "Come again?"

"Our suspect, she was out last night. There's another body."

JADE AND KAREN shot out of the office, leaving Skelton in the dust. As Jade made her way to the location, Karen felt bittersweet. On the one hand she felt vindicated in mounting an operation last night but saddened over another dead body. If this victim was the work of their suspect, they had been moments away from preventing another death.

Blackhall Street was sealed off with blue and white police cordon tape as Karen and Jade made their way on foot from where they had parked the car. Two officers stood on guard fielding questions from curious onlookers. Karen swore under her breath. The street was on the other side of Great Eastern Street and no more than a few minutes away from where they had mounted the surveillance operation.

Having signed in on the scene log, and kitted up in Tyvek suits, they made their way down the narrow road.

"It must be a place where artists or painters hang out," Jade remarked as they walked past small units and lock-ups decorated in an abundance of graffiti. One graffiti tag blended into another as they walked past. Jade cocked her head from left to right to read some of them. She had to admit that some of the graffiti was actually very good. She didn't see this as vandalism, but an expression of art.

Karen walked past a sign which said CCTV in operation. Checking her surroundings, she figured that warning served more as a deterrent than anything else when she couldn't see any cameras. The further they walked down the road, the narrower it became to where the white scientific services vans were half parked on the narrow pavement.

"She picks her spot. You could drive past the street without noticing it." Karen began to wonder how much preparation had gone into killing the victim. She doubted that the location had been chosen randomly.

Mason Brophy, the crime scene manager, walked towards them with several clear plastic evidence bags in one hand.

"Please tell me it's not one of ours?" Karen asked.

Mason shrugged. "On the face of it I think it is." He held up the evidence bags. "There's no sign of a robbery. We've got the victim's mobile phone and his wallet. The driving licence picture matches the victim. Lee Barnes, aged twenty-nine."

"I didn't want to hear that. Tell me this is a fucking nightmare, and I'm going to wake up, and everything smells of roses, and I'm sitting at Wimbledon eating a punnet of strawberries and sipping champagne."

Karen followed Mason towards the victim. Two SOCOs examined the body. Wainwright had been delayed but would be there within the hour. When Karen neared the victim, the corpse left her in no doubt as to its link. The victim's trousers and underwear were down to just above his knees, and his genitalia and the surrounding flesh were a gnarly, red and blistered mess. His head rested in a dark red pool of dried blood, and she could see a large laceration across his throat.

"Fuck," Karen said, feeling annoyed with herself.

"A different MO again, but carries similar hallmarks," Jade added.

Both officers stood in silence whilst they examined the victim. Karen mentally pieced together his dying moments as Jade walked off to find out more information about the victim.

Karen looked back over her shoulder to where the blue cordon tape held back a growing crowd of onlookers. Thankfully it was too far for them to see anything, and Mason's team were setting up a white forensic tent to cover the worst.

"Who found him, Mason? Because I couldn't see many of these units open as we walked down."

"Coffee shop worker found him on her way to work. She uses this alleyway as a cut through from Paul Street to Leonard Street."

"I bet she regrets that now." The scenes were becoming all too familiar to Karen. The suspect was killing at random. And despite forty officers being only ten minutes away, the killer had committed another heinous act right under their noses. Karen took a few moments to wander up and down the road either side of where the victim had been found. She peered into dusty windows but couldn't make out much from the dark interiors. Some units had artistic graffiti sprayed on to the windows. It made Karen wonder what type of people were using these units, and how often. She instructed the uniformed officers to make enquiries as to their ownership, and if they could track any down that were here last night.

"Mason, can you fire up his phone? I want to see what apps he's got on it," she asked as she walked back towards him.

Mason grabbed one of the evidence bags and pressed a few buttons through the plastic before handing the bag to Karen. She flicked through the various screens and then nodded to herself.

Without Wainwright in attendance, and other officers doing the legwork for her, there was little Karen could do as both her and Jade headed back to the car. Karen slapped the dashboard with her palm. It annoyed her that the suspect had slipped through the net. Despite all the hours of searching last night, they had looked in the wrong places.

Is this a change in the suspect's approach and strategy?

46

A rush of nervous energy flooded the room as officers gathered around the incident board within hours of the discovery of a fourth victim. Officers due in on the late shift were called in earlier as Karen felt the need to get as many eyes on this case as possible.

As Karen looked around the room, there were a few weary faces and tired bodies slumped in chairs. The strain of a multiple murder investigation was taking its toll on her officers and Karen appreciated the amount of stress they were under. She admired each one of them. She had pushed them, and they had worked tirelessly to chase up every scrap of evidence, lead and enquiry.

Jade had put up photographs of the new crime scene that included pictures of the victim and his injuries.

"Before I kick off, I want to take this opportunity to thank every one of you for your hard work so far. It's been a difficult and protracted investigation, and the discovery of a body this morning means that we've got even more work to do."

Karen stuffed her hands in her pockets and paced up and down in front of the assembled officers.

"You should all have a copy of the recent crime scene, and everything we have will be put on to the database within the next hour. But as far as we can tell, the victim is Lee Barnes aged twenty-nine. He hasn't been formally identified, but we found a wallet on him with a photo ID driving licence that appears to match the victim. For the time being we will assume that it's Lee Barnes. Jade, have you been able to find out anything as yet?"

"Nothing, ma'am. We've only got one witness statement, and unfortunately she couldn't give us any further information."

"We have little to go on. Other than some CCTV footage, DNA profile and some hair and clothing fibres, the suspect has been meticulous. The forensic report on the glass stem and broken pieces of wine glass recovered from the bar came up with nothing other than a few smudged prints."

Steve's voice cut through the room. "Ma'am, I've been waiting for a reply from the NCA, and they have confirmed that nothing matches our MO completely. But they have got cases where male victims were murdered through different means, but the one thing that tied them together was the same messaging app. One had his throat slit, another had a screwdriver driven through the side of his head, and a third victim died after being tied to a bed and having his femoral artery severed."

Steve's information shocked Karen. There was a strong likelihood that all the crimes had been committed by the same person, and secondly, the attacks had become more savage with the use of acid.

Another officer added that a search of the prisoner release and offenders log had only identified one woman who had been released eight months ago following a three-year sentence for cutting off her partner's penis. She was from Leeds and released on licence. They'd contacted her and Leeds police, who confirmed her whereabouts and eliminated her.

"Jade and I are going to visit the last known address for Lee Barnes after we've been to the PM, and in the meantime, keep searching for any available CCTV footage from last night. I'm certain we're not dealing with an ex-girlfriend, unless she really got around. It's the randomness of the attacks I find troublesome. We've been unable to pin her down. She's brazen, and happy to be seen on CCTV footage. She is dangerous and we need to get her off the streets."

AS KAREN GATHERED her bits and pieces together before leaving the office, Skelton appeared in her doorway.

"Have you seen the scrum outside?"

"No, sir. There was no one there when I came in this morning."

"That was before the news leaked of another body. They're pressing for answers."

"Who's fronting it?"

"Hinchcliff is going down to do it."

"Do you want me to join him, sir?"

"I think it would be good for you to hover in the background in case he gets stuck on questions. You know what he's like."

Detective Superintendent Hinchcliff was a short rotund man, with a booming voice. What he lacked in height he made up for in stature and presence. His words were always laser focused, biting, and confident.

As he stood on the steps, a sea of cameras and microphones surrounded him. Reporters and cameramen jostled for space, each one desperate to get the exclusive.

Karen stood at the back; her eyes wide with consternation. A tidal wave of questions assaulted her ears, and she wondered how Hinchcliff would tackle this. As the SIO, it should have been Skelton on the steps, but Hinchcliff loved the sound of his own voice, and wanted to present himself as the face of the police whenever he got the opportunity.

"Is the discovery of another body linked to the suspicious deaths that have plagued the area?"

"Do we have a serial killer on the loose?"

"Is it safe for people to go out at night?"

The questions came thick and fast, Hinchcliff doing his best to bat them off. He raised his hand to silence them. "We can confirm that the body of a male was discovered this morning in the Hoxton area. At present we cannot confirm his identity until next of kin have been informed."

"Were all these men gay? Are these homophobic attacks? Should the gay community be worried?"

Hinchcliff shook his head and furrowed his brow. "We have no information or evidence to suggest that this attack was homophobic in any way. At present we cannot give any further details because our investigations are ongoing."

"Is this killing linked to the other suspicious deaths?"

"We cannot give you any information because it's an ongoing…"

"Why has there been a wall of silence? The public have a right to know if there's a maniac on the streets."

Hinchcliff raised his voice above the wave of questions that attacked him from all sides. "Let me assure you, we are doing everything within our power to ensure that our streets are safe twenty-four hours a day. There is no immediate threat to the public, and we are drafting in more resources to provide a stronger visible presence to reassure members of the public."

"That sounds like a panic and knee-jerk reaction," a reporter shouted from the back. "What are you *exactly* doing?"

Hinchcliff shook his head. "We have over forty officers following up several lines of enquiry."

"Why are you keeping the truth hidden? The public has a right to know. Have you got a description of the suspect? The word is that the person uses disguises, can you confirm that?"

"Listen, listen. We will release further information when we have it. As I've said already, this is an ongoing investigation and we are unable to say anything further at this time. What I will say, is that I ask the public to remain vigilant, and report anything suspicious. That'll be all for now," Hinchcliff said firmly.

Hinchcliff turned and headed back followed by a barrage of questions and accusations that erupted from the crowd.

Karen followed Hinchcliff through the corridors, his heavy footsteps and breathing revealing his annoyance. He stopped outside his office and turned to Karen.

"Karen, we need answers. And we need them now. How the bloody hell did they know that our suspect uses disguises? Do we have a leak? Because if we do, I'll string them up by their fucking balls," he fumed, his tiny nostrils flaring.

"Sir, I trust our team. They were chancing their luck to get a reaction from you. They're fucked off at being kept in the dark. They've been pushing the press office for answers since our first vic."

"Homophobic attacks? Where did that come from??"

"Sir, they're chancing their luck. They were trying to hit you at all angles to provoke a response."

"Karen, we cannot afford for the press to harangue us, or influence what we do. We need to stay one step ahead of them and manage the information they receive. And now, there is a risk that they'll uncover more than we do. It's been over a week now, and we're still chasing our tails. We've thrown a ton of resources at this investigation which has got us nowhere."

"Sir, with all due respect, I don't think we are chasing our tails. We've made some solid progress. If you've got a moment, I'll give you an update right now."

Hinchcliff shook his head. "Karen, Skelton briefed me already this morning. I'm fully up to speed with how you're handling this investigation, and that's why I was trying to keep the press from our doorstep just a few moments ago."

Karen fumed inside. *Skelton would. Anything to cover his own backside.*

"Listen, Karen. A triple murder investigation is hard for any officer to handle, but you now have four on your plate. And I share Skelton's concerns about the size of the job."

Concerns?

"Anyone in your position would feel overwhelmed. I mean, Jesus Christ, the amount of information that we've got pumping into the database is mind-boggling. We spoke at length, and despite Skelton's offer to take some workload off you, you appear to prefer going solo on this."

Skelton's offer of help? Are you fucking kidding me? The lying toerag!

Hinchcliff left Karen standing in the corridor alone as he went into his office and shut the door behind him. She stood there stunned, her mind unable to comprehend what had just happened.

Skelton didn't stick up for me. He totally fucked me over.

47

Karen sat in Wainwright's office after attending the post-mortem. The examination itself had been straightforward, the cause of death being exsanguination. With such significant blood loss, the victim had little to no chance of survival. The killer had inflicted the burns on the groin after death. Wainwright had taken samples of tissue to be sent away for analysis but was confident the results would conclude that the same substance had been used on all four victims.

Scrapings had been taken from beneath his fingernails, and they had bagged his clothes to be examined later by forensic services. Wainwright confirmed the estimated time of death between ten p.m. last night and two a.m. this morning, which gave Karen a smaller window to work with.

"Chocolate bourbon?" Wainwright offered, extending a pack he retrieved from his desk drawer.

Karen shook her head and stared at her cup of coffee.

Wainwright stood up from his side of the desk and came around to join Karen on her side. Pulling a chair alongside, he sat and gently elbowed her in the ribs. "You've not been your normal self today. What's bothering you?"

"Do you mean I've not been winding you up?" She smiled.

Wainwright dropped his head to one side. "Something like that."

"I'm sorry. I've had a shitty morning. The super gave me grief after he addressed the press, and yet again the DCI was screwing me over."

"Oh. I figured it was something along those lines. Are you okay?"

"Yeah. I guess it comes with the territory. You get to a stage in the job where you don't trust anybody. Everyone is in it for themselves. Especially the higher up you go. It becomes a game of politics, and self-preservation."

"I guess so. I don't envy you. It must be hard when you're trying to do the right thing. But I've never known you to give up. You keep fighting, and always end up doing the right thing. And I admire that quality in you. It might be unpopular in the eyes of others, but… I guess you can sleep at night with a clear conscience?"

"Thanks, I appreciate it. I try to do the right thing, but it seems to bring me more trouble." Karen stood and placed her mug on Wainwright's desk. "I have to go. Jade and I need to see the next of kin for that poor sod."

Wainwright stood and placed a reassuring hand on her arm. "My door is always open, and even though it's not the most salubrious surroundings, you can pop in whenever you want to for a friendly chat, and a cuppa."

"Don't forget the biscuits…"

"It goes without saying."

A VISIT to Lee Barnes's apartment drew a blank. Neighbours either side confirmed that he lived alone. Jade brought a bunch of keys they had found on the victim's body. Letting themselves in, they had a quick look around. From what they could see, he lived alone, and the apartment was clean.

Further enquiries led them to a second address, his former marital home, a small terraced house about thirty minutes away from where his body had been discovered. Karen knocked on the door and waited a few moments before a woman answered, her eyes darting between the two women standing on the doorstep.

"Helen Barnes?"

The woman nodded. "Yes, that's me. How can I help?"

Karen and Jade held up their warrant cards. "I'm Detective Inspector Karen Heath from the Metropolitan Police, and this is my colleague DS Whiting. May we come in for a few moments please?"

Helen raised her brow, and pursed her lips before nodding, unsure what to say. She led them through to a small lounge where she offered them a seat.

It was a tastefully decorated room, perhaps a little cluttered, with a sofa and armchair that looked too big for the size of the room. A large TV sat on a cabinet with a bundled mess of cables hanging loosely beneath it. Shelves in the alcoves filled with little glass figurines only added to the busy look of the room.

"Can you confirm that you know a Lee Barnes, aged twenty-nine?"

Helen nodded in Karen's direction before rolling her eyes. "I do, he's my ex-husband."

"And this is him, is it?" Karen asked holding up a clear evidence bag which contained a driving licence photo card.

Helen narrowed her eyes to focus on the object, before nodding. "Yes. What's this about? What has he done?"

"I'm sorry to tell you that we discovered a body this morning, and personal items found suggest that it was Lee."

The woman's eyes widened, and she placed her hand over her mouth. Her eyes misted over. "My God. Oh, my God. It's not the one they were talking about on the news this morning?"

Karen nodded. "I'm afraid so. I know this must be difficult for you, but would you mind answering a few questions for us?"

The woman nodded, as a solitary tear escaped from her eye, snaking its way down her face.

"Could you tell us much about him?"

"Lee… Lee was a plumber. Self-employed. He'd been doing it for the last few years. He was in the navy in Plymouth when I met him. When he decided to leave, he did one of those resettlement kind of things where the navy teach you a trade that you can use to get a job when you leave."

"And as a person?"

"I guess a typical bloke. He played five-a-side football twice a week, enjoyed going down to the pub on a Saturday to watch the game and have a few pints with his mates."

Karen thanked her as Jade made a few notes.

"And then you split up?"

Helen nodded. "Yeah, I divorced him. He was knocking off one of his female customers. He started coming home late and blamed it on a lot of work. And, to be honest, as a self-employed plumber, his phone was ringing seven days a week, and he would often work every day."

"What happened?"

"He used to leave his phone by the door on the table," she said, pointing towards the hallway. "Then he started to keep his phone on him all the time. Sometimes when he would get together with his mates, they would bring their girl-friends and wives, and he would take me, too. And then that stopped which I found odd. He said he was going away on courses to learn all sorts of stuff to do with plumbing. I don't know, solar panels, thermal energy stuff," Helen said, waving her hand in the air.

Karen remained silent allowing the woman to continue with her story.

"The signs were there; I just ignored them. I told myself I was being paranoid. But then one day I followed him after work and found his car parked by a pub we'd been to a few times. And from a distance, I saw him in the car kissing a woman who was in the passenger seat. They drove off. After that I didn't need to know any more. I should have known better."

"What do you mean, Helen?"

"He was a sailor boy, and I met him on a road called the strip in Plymouth. It's a place just full of pubs, clubs and bars that all the navy boys go to, and where all the local girls go to. Even back then he had an eye for the girls. I tried to stay away from shitholes like that, but he would end up going into places where the unofficial door policy was service personnel only and female civilians." Helen shook her head and sighed.

Karen nodded, encouraging Helen to continue.

"That says it all, doesn't it? I just thought after we moved away to London he would quieten down, and he did to a certain extent. Things were good between us, but I guess he fell back into his old ways," Helen added playing with the nails on her fingers.

KAREN RETURNED TO THE OFFICE, leaving Jade to finish up with the last few questions.

The conversation with Helen reinforced the theory that all the victims had committed some form of infidelity. Karen opened her own phone and downloaded the app. Whilst she registered her details, she realised it was both a dating and messaging app. Once she had been accepted, she flicked through dozens of photos of women. Some appeared to be genuine people looking for love, relationships and even friendship. But there were just as many explicit images, and it didn't take a genius to figure out their intention.

Karen spent the next hour flicking through people's profiles out of curiosity more than anything else. Any of these women could be her suspect, and with over twenty thousand female members, the chances of finding her by scrolling were slim to none. Members had free access to all the features of the app for the first thirty days, and after that, a paid subscription kicked in allowing members to unlock further benefits and features, like video calling.

She saw how easy it would be for anyone looking for sex without questions being asked, and no evidence being left. *It's the perfect app if you are that way inclined*, she thought.

Karen needed the team to hit the streets again and mount a smaller surveillance operation. The case consumed her thoughts and most of her attention, and at times it felt like there was no room left in her brain for anything else.

Being so busy meant she'd hardly had time to think about her own investigation. All her leads had taken her nowhere, but a brief meeting with Barbara had triggered some suspicion in her mind. She needed to see her again and perhaps find a way of getting through to her. The woman had been hesitant and frightened. If she could ensure the woman's anonymity, perhaps that would be a way to get her to talk. The last time Karen had looked on the database, she'd found a small clip of CCTV footage from a shisha bar about a hundred yards from where the hijack had taken place. She hadn't examined it properly but made a mental note to return to it later.

For now, she needed a shower, and a change into an emergency set of clothes she kept in her bottom drawer.

48

The meeting at New Scotland Yard had dragged on. A briefing that should have lasted no more than thirty minutes had rolled on to where Skelton had almost dozed off on a few occasions. Detection rates, resource allocation and hot-desking to reduce space were discussed, but Skelton had heard the same rhetoric year in and year out. NSY, as they referred to the Yard, liked to be seen discussing these issues, but the delivery did not live up to the promises.

The smell of exhaust fumes and the drone of heavy traffic surrounded him. He stood to the side of the building and lit a cigarette as he watched an assortment of officers enter and exit the building. It was impressive both inside and out compared to its predecessor. The sense of pride he once felt being a police officer had long gone, his opinion tainted by the bureaucracy and the stranglehold that their political masters had over them. The police were nothing more than puppets in his eyes. Much of their bite had been taken away by legislation which meant crimes had menial and ineffective sentences, coupled with the lack of support from both the public and successive governments.

He could have walked away years ago, but what else could he do? He came from a long line of police officers, and if he left the force today, he wondered how much his life would spiral out of control.

Skelton smiled at the irony of his current location. They had instructed him to wait here until further instructions. Here he was, standing at the epicentre of the Metropolitan Police, the heart of the Met, with his political masters just around the corner. He looked out towards Westminster Bridge to his right, and the London Eye in front. There was far more to look at around here than in Shoreditch, including the women, as he watched two women walk by speaking in Spanish. He looked them up and down, staring at their bodies more than their faces. They exuded sex appeal as something stirred inside him.

A further text message instructed him to cross the bridge towards St Thomas' Hospital and wait around the back of the building. Twenty minutes later he sat in a black Range Rover with two of Sally's heavies in the front, herself sitting in the back.

"Where are we going?" he asked, as they sped out of town towards East London.

"We're going to a business meeting."

He digested her cryptic words as they continued their journey in silence through the Limehouse Link tunnel, and on to the A13.

All the while, Skelton watched familiar landmarks speed by his window. He recognised most of the places as they went through Leytonstone, Wanstead and on to Chigwell. Curiosity gnawed away at him as they powered down Chigwell High Road and past the Metropolitan Police sports ground he had been to on a few occasions years ago. A few moments later they turned right into Langston Road in Debden and travelled past the industrial estate until the road came to a dead end. It was somewhere he was familiar with. To the left was the Bank of England printing works.

Skelton glanced across at Sally who looked ahead and remained silent. He knew better than to ask questions, because it was unlikely that he would get much in the way of answers. They turned off into a large car park to the right and pulled up alongside two Mercedes with blacked-out windows. Sally instructed everyone to get out, with her two heavies stepping out first and checking the area before allowing her to exit.

Skelton had an uncomfortable feeling that this meeting would involve the Bank of England printing works. Cash transit left the works every week carrying millions of pounds into London. Two large blue armoured vans were escorted by three police BMW X5s each vehicle carrying four AFOs. They would often thunder down Loughton High Road on their way to the City, their presence causing bystanders to stop and watch.

Surely Sally isn't that stupid to hit the transit? It would be suicide.

A group of seven men exited the two Mercedes and made their way the short distance towards Sally. They greeted each other like adversaries in a boxing ring. Each group sizing up the other, the heavies ready to spring into action at the slightest twitch from their rivals. From Skelton's perspective, the men looked of Middle Eastern extraction,

Iranians, perhaps Turkish. They were all unshaven, dressed in jeans and jackets, with a few of them being thickset and heavy built. They eyed Skelton with suspicion, before Sally introduced them to him. Kristos Yildiz led the other group. Skelton had never heard of the man, but Sally introduced him as the head of a major Manchester crime family.

Skelton realised why he had been brought here once they started talking business. They needed his police knowledge for a job that the Connells and the Yildizs' were planning together.

"Skelton, we'll need you to help us with this job over the next few weeks. There's a big drug shipment coming by a South London crew. The exchange is going to happen here in this car park, and it's where we plan to hit them."

Skelton shook his head. "That's fucking madness. You have one of the most fortified buildings in England less than fifty yards away with enough firepower in there to cut you to shreds. You're asking for trouble, Sally. Who's bringing the gear in?"

Sally batted away his concern. "The less you know, Skelton, the better. You don't need to know names now."

Skelton went to object again, but Sally's cold stare silenced him.

"We'll be gone in a matter of minutes. And with your help, we'll have an escape route that will buy us the time. This is a South London family coming on to the Essex patch. When we hit them, they'll think the Essex lot ripped them off, and that will kick off between South London and Essex. Our Manchester friends will take the consignment away and deal with it up there, and we get half of the cash, without getting our hands dirty."

Sally didn't need to say more. Skelton read between the lines. With a major war between two crime families, she banked on both families imploding, leaving the Connells to pick up the pieces, and give her the opportunity to expand her distribution networks.

"The shipment contains a minimum of two and a half million pounds in amphet, cocaine and weed. We're just waiting on a confirmed shipment date. We've got a man inside the South London firm, so be ready, Skelton."

Skelton moved closer to Sally and whispered in her ear, "What's my cut?"

"Twenty grand."

"Sally, I'll be putting my neck on the line for you. That's not enough. My time in the force would be numbered. I need fifty K."

Sally twisted and grabbed his arm, her fingers tightening, her nails pressing into his skin. "Skelton, never think you can negotiate with me. My brothers would tear you to pieces and bury you with just a nod from me. Count yourself lucky that you're still breathing."

"Sally, that's not fair. I do loads for you."

"Life isn't fucking fair. So shut your mouth, before I shut it for you. You get twenty grand and I'll wipe your debt clean with the boys."

Skelton shrank back. Twenty grand would go a long way, and if she cleared his debt, it meant he could go back to the tables and even double that figure if the cards worked in his favour.

"When is the job, Sally?"

"We're waiting on a date. But you'll be coming with us, anyway."

A rush of panic raced through Skelton, his mind flipping somersaults as Sally's words sent him reeling. "Me? No way. There's only so much I will do and going on a job with your lot is above my pay grade." Skelton shook his head, as he stared at the men standing opposite him. Their faces showed no expression, just a swathe of faces staring back at him with menace in their eyes. "Forget it, Sally. I can't. I just can't."

Sally reached into her pocket and pulled out her phone. She opened a gallery of images and turned the phone in Skelton's direction. She swiped her thumb over the screen to reveal a series of photographs showing Skelton entering a massage parlour. "Our Albanian friends own this."

Further images showed him naked with a semi-naked woman by his side. The final few images showed him on top of her.

The colour drained from Skelton's face as bile scorched the back of his throat. He wanted to throw up and scream as his whole body became loose and limp. Sweat beaded on his forehead, and his heart raced as if plugged into the National Grid.

"By the way, Greta isn't eighteen. She's sixteen, just. And they kept the condom you used."

The final few images sent shock waves through Skelton.

"You remember these don't you, Skelton? They took these just after you kicked the shit out of her. I stopped the Albanians from coming after you. You would have been in a body bag by now. I wonder how much you'd get for being a bent copper, having sex with a minor, and assault? I don't fancy your chances in the bin, do you? I reckon they'll tear you a new arsehole."

Skelton needed every ounce of effort to stop shitting himself. He felt light-headed, his skin becoming cold and clammy. There was no turning back for him.

49

Karen slowed as she saw Steve marching towards her along the corridor, a uniformed officer by his side. At first, she thought they were about to pass her when Steve beckoned for her to stop.

Thank God she'd had time to grab a quick shower, enjoying the massaging pulses of water on her shoulders as she stood under the cascading water for fifteen minutes. It felt good to wipe away the dirt and grime clinging to her body. After her break, she'd been in dire need of some sugar to give her an energy boost, so she'd stopped at the canteen on her way back to her office to pick up a can of Coke and some biscuits.

"Everything okay, Steve?" Karen asked as she stuffed a custard cream in her mouth.

"Yes, ma'am. I thought this might be of interest. Uniform have received a report of a missing person. He's been missing for three days now."

"A misper has nothing to do with us. There are loads of

missing people reported every day. Unless a serious crime has been committed, a murder or even a kidnapping, it's something that the other teams have to deal with."

Steve agreed, but took the misper report from the officer and handed it to Karen. "This is a little different. The circumstances ring true to the situation we've been dealing with. The gentleman in question is single, divorced and hasn't been seen at work for three days. His phone is dead, too."

Nothing in the report made her feel like it applied to the investigation. But when Steve mentioned he was last seen in one of the pubs that their suspect had been in, Karen's ears perked up.

"It's a local pub that he visited after work several times a week, and on the last occasion he was seen talking to a lady with a long brown bob."

Within the hour Karen and Steve sat in the lounge of Tori King, the woman who had lodged the missing person's report.

Tori sat in an armchair opposite Steve and Karen, dressed in a white T-shirt and loose jogging bottoms, with her hair pulled back in a ponytail. A little girl sat on her lap, dozing peacefully, worn out from a day at nursery.

"Tori, thank you for sparing the time to see us. We are following up on the missing person's report that you filed this morning. We understand that your ex-husband hasn't been in touch?"

Tori whispered softly to avoid waking her daughter. "Yes,

that's right. I didn't know if it was the right thing to do or not. But today is Paul's evening with our daughter, Amber," she said gently running a hand over her daughter's head and pushing the hair off her face. She rocked back and forth as most mothers did when their child slept on them. "And he never cancels or doesn't turn up. We split up when Amber was one. Paul gets to see her twice a week. Amber is his little princess, and there is no way on earth that he would miss the opportunity of seeing her."

"And you've tried his number?" Karen asked.

"I did. Several times. And when he didn't answer, I thought I would try his work. They said he hadn't been in for a few days. No one has seen him. Even his work lot are concerned for him."

"What does Paul do?"

"He's a sales executive for a Ford dealership. That's a fancy term for selling cars," she said, rolling her eyes.

"Have you any idea what might have happened to him? I mean, could he have just gone on leave and forgotten to tell people?"

"No. Paul is meticulous with every detail. A bit OCD to be honest. If he was going away, he would have told me, his work, even the postman."

Karen nodded, whilst Steve made some notes.

"Do you have a picture of him that we could take with us?"

Tori pointed towards the mantelpiece, and told Karen to pick any photo she wanted, not wishing to get up and disturb her daughter's sleep.

Karen stood and took a few steps towards a fireplace and

an assortment of photos that sat above it. Many depicted Amber being cuddled by either her mum or dad. Karen chose one that bore the clearest image of Paul. He looked pleasant enough, Karen thought. He had a round face, warm eyes and a cheeky smile that accentuated his round cheeks.

Karen questioned Tori further to find out what Paul did in his spare time, what his friendship circle was like, and how they got on. From what she could gather, Tori and Paul were devoted parents, who doted on their daughter. Tori had kind and generous things to say about Paul in the context of their daughter and didn't appear to have anything bad to say about him.

"And when was the last time you spoke to him?"

Tori looked up towards the ceiling as she tracked back through her thoughts. "Three days ago. I was phoning to confirm that he was coming to pick up Amber."

"And there was nothing in his tone, or anything he said that concerned you in any way?"

The woman shook her head. "No, nothing. We had our normal chat, Okay, so this time it was a bit hurried because he said he was rushing out on a date, but we just laughed about it and that was it."

"So, you got on well?"

"Absolutely. I know some couples who despise each other when they split up, but I'm not the kind of person to hold a grudge. Life's too short for that. He wasn't happy in our relationship, and I think he preferred being a singleton. So, I'll not force someone to stay with me if they don't want to."

Karen pulled back to something Tori had said. "He mentioned that he was going out on a date when you spoke on the phone?"

"Yes. Someone he had met online. Isn't that how most people meet these days? It seems the in thing to do. He didn't give me details, nor did I ask. He's always dating, and it's an ongoing joke between us. If he looks after our daughter and gives her the time and attention she needs, he can do whatever he wants with his spare time." She shrugged.

Karen pressed a little harder before leaving. "Did he mention a name? Or where he was going?"

"I'm afraid not, sorry. Oh, no wait. I think he said her name was Belinda or Briony or something beginning with B."

50

I don't need a lot in life, just enough to keep me interested. My job at the charity shop gave me an opportunity to gloat over the needy. It came with its benefits because I had the opportunity to come across people who gave me *that* look.

I sit in my lounge and have my breakfast toast and coffee. It doesn't have a lot, a second-hand sofa I found on Face-book, two small tables, some cheap prints and a TV. Crea-ture comforts were never my thing, I guess it's because I never had much in my childhood. They sold anything of value to pay for Dad's booze, his betting and his women. So, it's not like I'm missing out on anything. Besides, the only thing that interests me now is exploring the realms of human pain and misery.

I look at the tacky calendar hanging on the wall and realise that it's been ten days since I started my most recent killing spree. My packed bags sit by the door, and I'll be gone from here in a few days. I set myself a deadline of two weeks and now have days to finish my work. My coach ticket is booked, and I leave Victoria coach station Glasgow bound.

He's still alive as I open the door and peer from around the corner. He's not as jumpy as he's been in recent days. Perhaps he's getting used to me and knows what to expect. The familiar smell of bodily waste seems to cling to the carpets and curtains. It looks like he's tired today, his eyes barely flickering awake, and he doesn't wince as I tear the tape from his mouth. He lets out nothing more than a gravelly groan as his eyelids remain closed. I feed him some milk laced with honey through a straw, whilst holding a knife to his neck in case he screams.

"One wrong move and I will cut your jugular," I remind him.

He sips on the straw, each one slow and drawn out, before I apply fresh tape to his mouth.

He's drunk less than a quarter of the glass, his stomach unable to hold much more. But that will be enough to keep him going for a few more hours until I check on him. Within minutes, he shits himself, a liquid mess that spills out between his legs.

I smile. "At this rate we'll have to put on a nappy."

Score marks on his chest have scabbed over, but I enjoy running my nails across them, picking them off to expose the fresh wounds beneath them. I pick up the lemon juice bottle that I brought in with me and liberally sprinkle the juice across his chest, before rubbing it in with my hand. He groans as his back arches away from the bed, a guttural moan tearing through his throat. Tears burst through his closed eyelids as the juice seeps into his raw flesh.

"You made a big mistake crossing my path. You don't remember me, do you? We met four years ago and went for a drink. But you spent most of the night watching other women. You were like all the other men, never satisfied. You let slip that your wife was pregnant with your first kid. What a wanker! Tell a lie once and all your truths become questionable. And then you were so thick as shit that you didn't recognise me when we met again this week. Admittedly I had changed my appearance, but your only interest was sex."

I slap him around the face a few times, my hand stinging as it hits his skin.

"Any fool can be happy. You weren't interested in me then, but you are now. You only have eyes for me now, don't you?"

I hold up a small tacking pin that I picked up from the charity shop. I pull his flaccid cock out of the way and cup his balls in one hand before sticking the pin into them as far as it will go. His reflex works a treat as he clamps his legs together and pulls his knees into his chest, squealing like a pig.

I gently stroke his sweaty brow and whisper soft words of comfort. "There, there, shush, shush. It will be fine, I promise. You rest now."

51

Karen yawned as she weaved her way through the corridors. It felt like she'd just left her office. The team had worked late into the night after her visit to Tori King. Certain things about Paul King's disappearance concerned her.

Having done a full risk assessment, she had escalated his case to medium/high. Karen couldn't be certain, but she believed that Paul may have become another victim of their serial killer. Though his body hadn't been found, the nature of his disappearance suggested that there was more to this than a normal misper report.

Karen had drafted available bodies to review CCTV footage from three days ago. It was a drawn-out process which went on into the early hours. Many officers had ordered in food, and the incident room filled with the smell of pizzas, Chinese takeaways and doner kebabs.

Their efforts had drawn a blank with no footage identifying their suspect or Paul King.

Karen had called Barbara and left a message for her on her way into the office. There was no guarantee that Barbara would return her call if the last visit was anything to go by, but she hoped Barbara would reconsider.

As Karen arrived the incident room buzzed with activity. There were some weary souls, and many officers had just left to go home for a shower and a change of clothes. Brad had volunteered to stay all night and was ready to brief Karen the moment she arrived.

"We did as much as we could last night, ma'am. But we found nothing. I asked some of the team to look at phone triangulation for Paul King using cell site analysis data."

"Good thinking, Brad. I know it was a shitty job last night, but we didn't have much choice. It would have been a stroke of luck, and we need all the luck we can get now."

Brad stretched his arms above his head and yawned for what felt like a minute.

Like most officers, Karen hated trawling through CCTV footage. It was a painstaking job and tiring on the eyes. It was easy to miss the smallest of details in a blink of an eye, so she knew how Brad felt. "Get yourself off home and get some sleep. If you're up to it, come back in later today. Thanks for overseeing things whilst I went home."

Karen took time to go around each member's desk getting an update in case Skelton came on another fact-finding mission. It was important for her to keep the morale of the team going, with weary minds and bodies, work would slow down if she took her eye off the ball.

"Morning, ma'am," Jade groaned cupping a big mug of

coffee that she had made as soon as she'd switched on her computer.

"How are you feeling today?" Karen asked.

"Don't ask. I am so tired that I think I could sleep for a week if I put my head down now. I'm not sure how my feet got me here."

"Yeah, I know, it feels like shit at the moment. But we've got to keep pushing through. How about I shout you some breakfast downstairs? And to be honest, I didn't have time to eat this morning. I felt too sick. But I'm bloody starving now."

KAREN AND JADE waited in line, walking along the service hatch picking the bits they wanted. Karen tried to be good and stick to a few pieces of toast, but the sight of scrambled eggs, sausages and bacon, proved irresistible as she helped herself to some generous portions. Jade had the resolve to stick to her healthy eating and settled for scrambled eggs on toast.

Just as Karen was about to head to the cashier, her phone rang. She pulled it out of her back pocket and saw Steve's name on the screen. "Hi, Steve. What's up?"

"We've got some interesting information on the cell site analysis for Paul King's phone. You need to have a look at this."

Karen relayed the information to Jade as they tipped their food into disposable containers and hurriedly paid the cashier. With styrofoam in hand, the two hurried back to the incident room where Steve waited with a piece of paper.

Steve pointed out they had found Paul King's location from the cell site analysis data, and it identified where his phone pinged last. Most of the phone usage had been in the same area as that already marked out by Craig. What drew her attention were a few data points flagged up outside of the zone, and then his phone went dead. She examined all the data as Steve talked her through the spreadsheet.

"It looks like we are focusing our attention on an area about half a square mile?" Karen suggested.

"Correct. And we also compared cell site data for the other four victims. And again, there's a lot of activity within the area that we've already highlighted as the patch our killer visits."

She thanked Steve and returned to her office to consider what she'd just learnt. The problem Karen had with this case was that it was proving impossible to predict the suspect's pattern of movement. The best she could do would be to flood the area, shops, bars, restaurants and offices with an e-fit in the hope that someone could either recognise or locate her.

But before she could do that, she visited the high-tech unit and one contact she had there, Charlie Whitworth. She had often relied on him when she needed enhanced imagery in previous cases. Charlie was as good as they got, an expert in computer analysis and facial recognition software.

She spotted Charlie poring over his screen, a serious expression on his face.

"Not you again," he said, his response tinged with sarcasm.

"Charlie, that's not nice. I thought I was your favourite person?"

"You are, when I don't hear or see you."

"I'm mortally wounded, you cheeky fucker," Karen said placing a hand to her chest. "How's tricks with you?"

"Well, you know, too much work to do, and not enough hours. I've got another course I'm going on next week about enhanced 3D facial mapping, so I'm trying to get all my work done before then."

Karen rolled her eyes and knew Charlie would geek out at the prospect of attending. "I need a better picture of our suspect. I need to flood our target area with a clear, high-quality picture. The CCTV stills aren't as clear as I'd like them to be. I hope that with your magic fingers, and whatever gizmos you use, you can come up with something better?" she said, pulling up a chair alongside him. "Please, pretty please with a cherry on top?" she added putting on her best, cheeky smile.

Karen knew some of the facial mapping software could be vital in identifying the suspect and would prove invaluable as part of the prosecution evidence. She knew in reality the quality of the picture or video footage was often so poor that a clear identification couldn't be made. This would often lead to added legal disputes and the need for further forensic evidential examination. And with enhanced imagery, it would lend the extra weight to the presentation of the case before the courts.

"Well, we can have a go, and because you are my favourite person, and you keep refusing my offers of dinner, I will continue to do whatever I can to impress you," he said, rolling his brow. "I've got three main techniques that I use with the facial mapping software. Photogrammetry, morphological and superimposition. Each one of them has a different job."

"And they do what?" Karen asked.

"Photogrammetry deals with a comparison of measurements between facial features, morphological investigates the facial features between different pieces of evidence to tie them all together. Although I hasten to add, that this technique is more subjective than the others. And lastly superimposition, which involves placing a similar photograph of the subject over any disputed evidence and using a flick or swipe technique which helps us to identify any differences or similarities. Have I made myself clear?" he finished pausing to catch his breath.

The speed of Charlie's explanations left her dumbfounded and speechless. Before he'd even mentioned morphological, he'd lost her. Her eyes widened as she shook her head in disbelief.

"Perfect," Charlie replied as he began clicking through various screens and uploaded images that Karen had provided.

Karen thought his hands moved as quickly as his mouth as she saw screens appear and disappear, the clicking of his mouse sounding more like a musical rhythm than anything else.

"The importance of this software is that it allows us to use biometric facial mapping to create a facial map. If you look at the screen, Karen, you can see the red dots in the different images. Each one of those dots represent a match and a reference point. The more of those we get, the greater clarity we have. And each point is then fine-tuned to remove as much pixilation as possible and enhance the image as best as we can."

Karen looked at several facial images on the screen which bore no resemblance to any of the stills captured from video, but looked like something out of a science magazine, with blue lines criss-crossing over the face at various angles to form shapes. She waited as Charlie went about his work in silence, his eyes darting around the screen as tables of figures and editing functions appeared.

"Sorry, Karen. What was your question? It's slipped my mind."

"Christ almighty, Charlie. You'd forget your own wedding."

"Karen, my lovely, I would never turn up late for our wedding."

"Flattery will not get you anywhere. Going back to my question, I need to be sure that we are looking for one person. I'm certain we are, but I need it confirmed before we head back out there."

Charlie sat back in his chair and looked at his final analysis. He paused for a few moments before saying, "We can be eighty-four per cent certain that the different images on screen are the same person. And in my opinion, that's pretty good. That would hold up in court."

Karen had the reassurance she needed. Beth was one person, who was adept at disguise. "Charlie, you're a genius. I would say that I love you, but I'd be lying," she said, squeezing his arm and blowing him a kiss before scooting out the door.

52

"Look at this, ma'am," Jade said handing over a few printouts. "We looked at his bank and credit card accounts, and from what we can gather, neither have been used in the last three days. His last cash withdrawal was from an ATM on Old Street between Rufus Street and Hoxton Street."

The team had pulled out all the stops to identify Paul King's last known movements through cell site analysis, CCTV and calls to his contacts list. Karen had called King's ex-wife, Tori, to find out if she had heard anything since their visit. The news wasn't encouraging as Tori had drawn a blank. Another day with no news started to worry her further. She had called around to all his friends for a second time only to be told they hadn't seen or heard from him.

Further information from the team only added to Karen's concerns for Paul King's welfare and safety.

"Any sightings of him after that?" Karen asked.

"Yes. A camera close to the cashpoint picks him up. He was alone and heading towards Curtain Road just opposite the ATM."

Karen moved across to the map pinned to the wall. She ran her finger along Paul's path. "So, he headed off south down Curtain Road and straight into the area we've been focusing on."

"To begin with, yes. Then for some reason he turned around and headed back towards Hoxton Square. He was picked up outside Troy Bar. We'll have to assume that he went inside. The venue confirmed they have no CCTV footage."

Karen narrowed her eyes and continued to stare at the map as she wondered whether he had turned around willingly or on request. To some extent she was second-guessing his movements and who he'd been talking to. Unlike the other victims, they didn't have Paul King's phone, so couldn't confirm whether he was using the same messaging app as the others.

Jade continued. "Forty minutes later, analysis confirms he was back on Old Street near to where he had begun."

"Any meeting points in the area?"

"Yep, the Redemption Bar, and before you ask, yes, they have got CCTV footage which they've sent over and we are reviewing."

Karen hated the wait. The more eyes they had reviewing footage the better it would be for them. With the amount of people walking past from day-to-day in full view of the cameras, it was easy to overlook a face in the crowd.

Karen made her way to the video room, with Jade in tow. A

detective from her team sat in a cubicle running the footage at half the speed, whilst sipping on a bottle of Ribena and looking bored.

They both pulled up chairs alongside the detective and squeezed in. It was cramped as their shoulders pressed against each other, but it allowed them to study the monitor.

"Anything?"

"Nothing yet, ma'am."

"Speed it up a little. We've got three sets of eyes on this now. One of us must be able to spot something."

It was wishful thinking on Karen's part, but the only line of enquiry they could follow in relation to King's disappearance. Whilst the team worked on the few thin slivers of information from the other four murders, Karen wanted to plough all her efforts into finding Paul King. Without a body hope remained, and at this point, Karen held on to every shred of it.

All three watched an internal camera feed that focused inside the front door of the pub. Prior to viewing the footage, Karen had checked online for images of the front of the pub. It had surprised her to see a large set of golden wings painted on the wall. They'd looked about five feet high, and customers had posed in between the wings for effect.

If that wasn't weird enough, she'd noticed artwork with unusual quotes placed at odd angles on the interior walls of the bar. Glancing down at the screen, her eyes were drawn to a few of them, "any fool can be happy", "tell a lie once and all your truths become questionable", "never argue with someone who believes their own lies". She found them both curious and dark, and not the kind of average quotes you'd find in a pub.

They continued to watch the video footage in silence, keen not to miss anything and their perseverance paid off after a short while when they saw a customer resembling Paul King. He arrived at the bar alone and ordered a drink before moving off to one side and waiting at a table. He looked nervous, alternating between sipping on a bottle of beer and checking his phone. Karen checked the timestamp; it was a further eleven minutes before his movements changed as he stared towards the front door. Karen held her breath as a woman appeared in view and made her way towards King. She had long blonde hair tied in a ponytail, wearing a white top and jeans.

The detective with Karen cropped the shot in order to take a closer look at both people. Karen double-checked the photo that Tori had given them, and she was certain the person they were looking at was Paul King. The woman, having a different hairstyle, bore a striking resemblance to the e-fit and still shots they had recovered from previous footage. Karen scrutinised the woman. She was attractive, slim, and flirty. She smiled and placed her hand on his arm as he wrapped his other hand around her waist.

The couple appeared to get on well as they enjoyed some drinks before leaving together. The detective switched to the outside footage and punched in the timestamp for when they left the pub. A few seconds later the three officers stared at the couple as they walked together hand in hand. They could trace some of their route south along Charlotte Road and then left into Mills Court before losing them after that.

"I guess we've got nothing after that?" Jade asked.

"Unfortunately, not." The detective shook his head.

Karen left the detective to continue trawling through footage on the off-chance that they might spot Paul King again, whilst she returned to the incident room and examined the map of the area. Jade and Steve gathered around as they shared their thoughts.

"The cell site statistics put him in this area, and we lose a visual on him after fifteen minutes. But the phone data continues to pick him up to just a few hundred yards before the data identifies the phone as being static," Steve added.

"So, his phone ran out of charge, he lost it or it was switched off?" Karen speculated.

The cunning changes in appearance staggered Karen. In all the images, she presented a different look which was both attractive and alluring. It wasn't hard to understand why it had been so easy for the killer to pick up men.

Whilst she looked at the map Karen froze. Her mind tracked back through the video footage and replayed it scene by scene.

"Where are you going, ma'am?" Jade asked as Karen spun round and headed at speed from the incident room.

"Back in a sec," Karen shouted as she quickened her pace.

Karen barged back into the video room much to the surprise of the detective scrolling through the footage.

"Ma'am?"

"The footage of our suspect in the bar, pull it up again," Karen demanded as she jumped back into a chair.

Within a few moments they watched the same scene play out again. Karen studied the screen, and the suspect. "Stop! Stop there." Karen tapped the screen. "Zoom in on that bit there." She pulled herself closer and could just about make out a tattoo on the top of the suspect's right arm.

Armed with a still image of it, she headed back for the forensic high-tech unit.

53

Barbara's breath switched from hard and laboured to short and raspy as quickly as her thoughts did. She had answered the door moments ago to be confronted by two men, one thin and tall, the other as wide as her doorway. Both had stubbly beards and dark hair. They stormed inside before she could close the door. They walked through the hallway into her lounge and dropped into the sofas, despite her protests.

She raced back through the hallway to her front door only to find a third man blocking her exit. He placed a finger to his lips, the sign enough to silence her as Barbara's body stiffened with fear. He stepped in and shut the front door before jostling her into the lounge where his two associates sat.

With little effort, he pushed her back into the armchair, her eyes shifting between the three men as her fingers gripped the armrests in panic. She wanted to say something, but nothing would come. Perhaps self-preservation stopped her from saying something she might regret later.

"Mrs Barbara," the thin one hissed, "you talk with wrong people. That dangers."

His stocky associate sitting by his side interrupted, "Excuse Alexander. He's Polish, and his English is fucking awful." The man sniggered at his friend. "I think what he meant to say was that you've been talking with the wrong people, and for someone in your position that can be dangerous."

Barbara's throat was as dry as a desert, she licked her lips trying to moisten them. "I… I haven't said anything. I promise."

The man clicked his tongue off the roof of his mouth. "That's not what we've heard. A little birdie told us you've been talking to the police. They paid you a visit?"

Both men stared at her as the third man positioned himself behind her on the armchair and placed his hands on her shoulders.

His physical presence was enough to make her cry. "I swear. I didn't say anything. I had a visit from the police. But I did as I was told. I said I got my facts wrong, and I couldn't remember much about it."

"That's good, that's good," the man said. "But I have a feeling they might come and see you again. The police are persistent. I don't think they'll give up until they have what they need. What do you think?"

Barbara thought about the message Karen had left this morning. She had deleted it straight away, although part of her wanted to call back. But what would she say? She was in a terrible mess, one not created by herself, and yet she found herself in the presence of three men who she thought might kill her.

"You see, Barbara, we need to make sure you keep your mouth shut because we wouldn't want anything bad happening to you, now would we? I mean, these apartments are like tinderboxes, and the tumble dryer in your kitchen tends to catch fire. I just wonder if you'd have enough time to get out of the flat if it caught fire during the night, or whether you'd die… from breathing in those fumes before you wake up."

He paused letting his words sink in. "Then there's your daughter and her family. You'd never see your little granddaughter again." The man shook his head in disbelief. "That would be so tragic, wouldn't it?" he said, turning to his associate who shrugged nonchalantly in reply.

The third man's grip on her shoulders tightened, and bolts of pain shot through her back and up her neck. She grimaced and snarled her teeth in response.

The Polish man stood up and reached for something in his pocket.

Barbara gasped, fearing the worst, expecting to spend her last minute on earth, but he produced an envelope and dropped it on the coffee table between them.

"My Polish friend is feeling generous and has just dropped five thousand pounds in front of you. You have a choice. You either take a little holiday and make yourself scarce, or you say goodbye to your granddaughter as your flat goes up in flames. It's your choice." His icy stare stalled the breath in her lungs as his dark eyes tore through her.

Barbara felt helpless, even when they used only words as weapons. She wouldn't dare move or say a word in her own defence. These men were nothing but bullies, but whoever had sent them meant business. She had never met the woman who had called several times not long after witnessing the hijack. But the woman's words had left her without any doubt that if she wanted to live, she needed to remain silent. "I have a distant cousin on the Welsh coast in Aberporth. It's in the middle of nowhere. I haven't seen her for a long time, perhaps it's a good idea if I paid her a visit."

The man smiled and winked. "I knew you would see sense. Just remember, if you decide to say anything… and I mean *anything* to the police, there will be nowhere for you to hide. Do we make ourselves clear?"

Barbara nodded; a simple yes trapped in her throat. Her eyes travelled to the brown envelope. She couldn't bear to bring herself to look at the men. At the time she thought she'd done the right thing as a dutiful citizen, and now found herself on the run and evading the police.

All three men left the lounge, leaving Barbara rooted in her armchair. She held her breath until the front door opened and closed. Only then did the crying follow. Hysterical crying, screaming sobs only interrupted by her need to draw breath. She cried as if her brain had been shredded from the inside, emotional pain flowing out of every pore. From her mouth came a cry so raw that even she doubted whether she had made it.

Only one safe action remained as a choice for Barbara.

Leave.

54

Armed with evidence from cell site data analysis, Karen and Jade visited the area. She had sent Steve and Craig to visit a second triangulation site of interest to them.

Whilst Jade studied the map, Karen whipped out her phone and redialled Barbara's number. Again, it went to voice-mail, but she couldn't leave a message as Jade was standing next to her.

Perhaps Barbara is out shopping or with friends and hasn't returned home since this morning. She would try again this evening if it wasn't too late.

The forensic imaging team had confirmed that the tattoo on their suspect was a black keyhole. Karen thought it was odd as she stared at the grainy picture. With a clearer image thanks to digital enhancement, it gave Karen an opportunity to find out where it had been done. She had dispatched other officers to over a dozen tattoo parlours within a three-mile radius of Shoreditch. It was a long shot, because the tattoo could have been done anywhere in the country, or abroad.

Karen had a hunch about the killer's movements. It was a common trait amongst serial offenders, that many would commit their robberies, rapes, killings or burglaries in an area they were comfortable with. She had spent countless hours getting into the mindset of their suspect and understanding both the reasons and next steps the killer might take.

In her experience only a few had ventured further afield, and committed their crimes either across different counties, or in different parts of the country. In her mind there were two types of killer, organised and disorganised. Karen thought this killer carried traits of both categories. Organised killers had some social grace, were charming, and often talked or seduced their victims into being captured. They were also more difficult to apprehend, something they were experiencing in this case. Their killer was going to inordinate lengths to cover their tracks and were forensically savvy and likely to follow media reports.

But their suspect also showed signs of being a disorganised killer because she used sudden and overwhelming force and left the body at the location of her attack. Disorganised killers made no attempt to hide or conceal their crime. It wasn't uncommon for a lone offender to exhibit both if they were undergoing a psychological transformation through their killing career, and Karen believed that their suspect had been honing and shaping their approach for many years.

One by one, other officers checked in with Karen. None of the parlours recalled doing a tattoo matching the picture. The heat of the afternoon sun made Karen weary as she trudged up and down the streets with Jade. They stopped at a newsagent to get another drink before continuing. The first five tattoo parlours visited had drawn a blank, and the sixth sounded too vague.

The seventh parlour they visited was the second to last one on their list. As Karen pulled the door open, hope seeped from her body. Tracking down an obscure tattoo had been another throw of the dice, chasing a small lead hoping to get the breakthrough they needed. A man greeted them with a gravelly welcome. With an overgrown beard and tattoos up his arms and around his neck, he looked more like a biker from a notorious biker gang than a tattoo artist. His leather waistcoat over a bare torso, and jeans with a heavily studded leather belt only added to the stereotype.

Karen showed her warrant card. "I'm Detective Inspector Heath and this is my colleague DS Whiting. We are conducting general enquiries in the area and visiting as many tattoo parlours as possible. We wonder if you've ever done a tattoo like this?" Karen asked, holding up a printout of the keyhole.

The man took it from Karen and held it in his chubby fingers as his teeth sunk into his bottom lip. He took a few moments to examine it. Karen noticed that the fingers on his right hand had stained yellow fingernails from years of smoking.

"Yeah, I think I remember doing that. It was a good few years ago."

Karen felt a flutter in her chest as excitement rose through her. "I don't suppose you have any details on her, do you?"

"As it happens, I probably do. Every new customer

completes a health disclaimer form. Hang on a sec and let me pop out back and see if I can find it."

"This would be a right result if we can get some details, Karen," Jade whispered as she glanced at dozens of tattoo examples pinned to the walls.

Karen walked to an opposite wall and stared at further examples. Some were basic, but others were so intricate that she wondered how many hours or days it took to get them done.

"Here ya go. Beth. I remember her now. Pretty thing. Fit if I remember, and a very sexy voice."

Karen blotted out the man's words as she grabbed the disclaimer form and pored over the details.

"Does the person in these images look familiar?"

The man examined the photos that Jade handed over. He raised a brow. "I can't be one hundred per cent certain because she's got different hair in these, but I'd say it looks like her. The face looks the same. As I said, she's a looker so it sticks in your brain."

Bethyan Calladine, aged 34. Not only could they put a name to their suspect, but an address. A shiver of anticipation crept up Karen's spine. Perhaps this lead represented the break she needed.

55

After indulging in a few hours' sleep, and not wishing to miss out on the action, Brad joined Steve and Craig as they made their way to the address that Karen had given them. They found Karen and Jade hovering towards one end of the street out of view.

The five officers gathered around in a small huddle as Karen briefed them. The location was less than fifteen minutes' walk from the area that they had been concentrating on and where the crimes had been committed. It lent credibility to the assumption that their suspect had been a local with a strong knowledge of the area.

"Right, the address we're about to visit is the last known place where Beth Calladine lived. Jade and I have taken a walk past, and from what we can see there's only one way in and out of the block. I suggest the three of you," Karen pointed to Brad, Steve and Craig, "hold back, and spread yourselves out around the block in case she slips past us. Jade and I will keep it low-key and approach the address. Any questions?"

Karen had taken extra precaution by organising uniformed officers to be in attendance. Three officers approached and joined the group, and Karen instructed them to come with her in case the situation turned volatile. Karen didn't want any drama, so the quicker they could detain the woman, the better it would be for all of them.

Satisfied that everyone knew what they had to do, Karen and her team made their way along Old Castle Street, a narrow road, where old met new. To her left modern, low-rise apartment blocks heavily influenced by architectural design, with cream brickwork, and orange stained-glass balconies, stood in marked contrast to older, angular predecessors, with their dark and weathered brickwork and sixties feel.

Karen pressed the intercom to several other apartments before one resident let them in. The corridors were dark, tight and bland as they made their way up to the second floor, the sound of their feet on the concrete stairwells echoing around them. The block had a mustiness that came with age.

Karen knocked on the apartment door several times before a small Asian man of Bengali extraction answered the door and eyed his visitors with suspicion. A woman dressed in a shawl covering her head stood behind him. His long white beard in marked contrast to his dark skin. Because of his poor English, it took Karen a while to explain the nature of their visit. It took her even longer to convince him they needed to look around the apartment. They didn't stay long, the apartment was untidy, cluttered and had an overpowering smell of Indian cooking.

"Bollocks," Karen muttered as the team gathered together outside the block. A quick search of the apartment confirmed the absence of their suspect. It transpired that it was a rental apartment, and the occupants had moved in three years ago. The current tenants were unable to provide a forwarding address for the previous occupant, but confirmed a lone female matching the picture that Karen showed them had lived there prior.

A call to the letting agents confirmed the story. Beth had given a forwarding address when she had moved out, and with that new information, the team moved off to the next location. It was a common problem in their job that intelligence didn't always result in a positive outcome. There were too many variables that influenced their course of action. Intelligence may be old and not updated, people who didn't want to be found would move once a week, and sometimes friends, associates and family hampered searches by pleading ignorance.

Just a few weeks ago Karen and four of her officers had spent two long afternoons walking around Brixton searching for a witness to a rape and murder and had drawn a blank. So, standing around second-guessing someone's movements came with the territory.

The second address given was one street away in Bell Lane, but again was another dead end. Beth had rented the apartment on a six-month short rental agreement. The current tenants and lettings agency had no information as to her whereabouts now. It was clear to Karen that the woman moved around a lot, but considering the proximity to the crime scenes, and the fact that both apartments were one street apart suggested that Beth was a creature of habit. In Karen's mind, there was a clear possibility that Beth was close by.

A local café proved an ideal spot for them to camp out

whilst they figured out their next move. Karen paid for a round of teas and cakes before getting on to the team back at the office to check social services records, bank and medical records as well as phone companies. She felt there was little point in returning to the office in case they needed to react.

56

An anxious wait followed for results as the team made their enquiries. Karen paid for three rounds of tea and a tray of sandwiches over the next hour to keep the café owner happy. He had moaned they were taking up too much space and spending too little money.

Karen tried to blag it saying they were on an operation and waiting to move any second, but the owner wasn't having any of it and continued to moan. Karen thought the man's accent was Greek or Cypriot and smiled as she remembered he bore a striking resemblance to Stavros, the kebab shop owner, and one of Harry Enfield's characters back in the eighties. At one point Karen wanted to say, "hello peeps" but doubted her attempt at humour would go down well.

She took a moment to call Skelton to update him. "Sir, we visited the two last known addresses for our prime suspect, but we've drawn a blank."

"Figures," came his dry reply.

Karen chose to ignore his typical smarminess and carry on, "Like the murders we believe she has committed, she isn't leaving much of a breadcrumb trail for us."

"Karen, she could be anywhere."

"True, or she could be right under our noses. I just have a gut feeling that we're close to tracking her down." There was an uncomfortable pause, as Karen heard Skelton's heavy breathing. "Sir?"

"Yes, yes I'm here. I'm just thinking. We're running out of time. You need to come back to the office so we can figure out what you're going to do. The chief super wants another update by the close of business and it's already late in the day."

Karen sensed the tension in Skelton's words as he rattled off his sentences without taking a pause for breath.

"We will be back, sir. But not yet. I'm giving it another hour for the team at the office to come up with anything for us. If they don't, we'll be back."

"An hour, Karen. That's all. And then I want you back here, regardless."

The line went dead. Karen took the phone away from her ear and stared at the blank screen in bewilderment. She rolled her eyes in frustration. *Why does he always do this? He talks to me like a piece of shit.*

Skelton's hour deadline came and went, and with two missed calls from the DCI, she knew her reception back at the office wouldn't be a warm one. Karen was on the verge of giving up and calling it a day when one of her officers called with another two addresses for Bethyan Calladine they had discovered from calls to HMRC and Vodafone.

Feeling vindicated for staying out, the team moved off with a sense of urgency. The two addresses were in different directions, so Karen sent Jade and Brad to one address with two uniformed officers, whilst the rest came with her to the second address.

The second location appeared to be a converted house with an entryphone system to the side of the front door and four buttons which denoted four different apartment numbers. The information indicated apartment four, so they tried the other three first. Their patience was rewarded when the tenants in the second apartment answered the intercom and let Karen in. The ground floor of the house held the first two apartments, and a central walkway led them up to the first floor which again had been divided into the other two apartments.

Karen glanced around at her team just to make sure everyone was in position and ready before she knocked on the door. There was no answer to begin with, so Karen tried again with more force, banging with the side of her closed fist. Nothing. Karen sighed in frustration, but then the door to the apartment across the landing opened, and a white woman with dreads appeared in the doorway dressed in tie-dyed T-shirt, denim shorts and flip-flops. A cat lingered around her ankles, purring and meowing for attention.

"Can I help?" the young woman asked.

The officers turned to face the woman, readying themselves.

"We're looking for Beth Calladine. Does she live in this apartment?" Karen asked, flicking her head back towards the door behind her.

"She does. But you've just missed her. She left about five

minutes ago to grab some milk from Tesco. I'm sure she'll be back soon."

"Is this Beth?" Karen asked, holding up CCTV stills.

The woman glanced at the shots and nodded. "Is Beth okay? Is she in trouble?"

"I'm not at liberty to discuss the nature of our visit, but we need to speak with Beth regarding an ongoing investigation."

Karen thanked her for the information before the woman disappeared and shut the door. She called control to send units to the any Tesco stores close by as she glanced at the other officers. "This is it," she said as a nervous energy rushed through her, her heart pounding like a drum.

57

The door shook as the uniformed officer put the full force of his boot into it. It took two further attempts before the door relented; the lock breaking away from its housing. The officer took a step back and shoulder-charged the door. It flew back crashing against the wall, wood splinters breaking away and littering the floor. The force of his shoulder charge sent the officer stumbling through the open space and nearly landing on his knees in the hallway.

He stepped to one side to allow Karen to enter, followed by the rest of the team. The smell hit Karen first, almost bringing her to her knees. That kind of putrid stench stopped your thinking, and all that remained in your brain once the smell reached you was a desire to flee, the gag reflex automatic.

Karen placed a hand over her mouth and glanced back towards Steve and Craig who contorted their faces as the smell reached them. She had faced situations like this many times in her career, especially whilst in uniform when they attended houses where the victim had remained undiscovered for a while. The overpowering smell of bodily waste attacked her from all directions.

"This is fucking gross," Karen muttered as she made her way through the darkened hallway. The officers split off in different directions, the smell becoming stronger as they moved around the apartment. Karen paused in the kitchen doorway, her eyes trained on the worktops where she noticed an array of tools and utensils. Small kitchen knives, large meat knives, hammers, pliers, and a tub of nails. She glanced around the rest of the kitchen and noticed that everything was clean. The sink was empty, cutlery and plates washed and left on the drainer to dry, and the bin wasn't overflowing.

The curtains were drawn in each room, and with the light fading, the final rays of sun cast gloomy shadows that crept through the gaps and left light and dark silhouettes on the walls. She noticed everything was immaculate. There was no clutter on the floor, no discarded cups or bottles, not even untidy heaps of clothes. From what she could see, the woman was obsessively house-proud, which contradicted the offensive smell.

"Jesus fucking Christ, over here, ma'am," Craig shouted, the heavy sound of his footsteps bounced around the walls as he recoiled back.

Karen darted out of the lounge towards the final two rooms, which she imagined were the bedrooms. Craig pressed his back against the wall in the hallway, his eyes fixed wide at the sight before him. As Karen turned the corner, she fell into step behind Steve. The smell overpowered her, causing Karen's eyes to water. Bile rose to the back of her throat as her stomach rolled as if she stood on a ship in rocky seas.

The nausea clawed at her throat, as she tried to force it down. But poor Craig succumbed, chunks of partially digested sandwich spewing out of his coughing and choking mouth. His stomach kept contracting violently, forcing everything up and out. His ashen face dripped vomit and tears. He lurched forward and sank to his knees. The pungent stench invaded his nostrils as he heaved, his empty stomach protesting with each convulsion.

The apartment smelt vile, but as she entered the bedroom, the smell worsened, and the sour scent of puke added to the already disgusting stench that lingered in the bedroom.

Karen rushed to the lifeless form tied to the bed. He was semi-conscious and stripped naked, his hands and feet tied, and his mouth gagged with tape. Steve spoke into his mobile, calling for backup and an ambulance. Karen dropped to her knees and stared at the man's chest, a pattern of random cuts and bruises peppering the flesh. Some cuts were raw, others had scabbed over. She paused, not wishing to touch him, staring at his chest, looking for any signs of movement.

A slight rise and fall.

"He's alive. Steve, tell Jade and Brad to get over here." Karen snapped on a pair of blue latex gloves before gently ripping the tape from the man's mouth. She grimaced and drew breath in through gritted teeth as it clung fast. Karen persevered, wincing to herself as she imagined how painful it would have been on her own skin. She gasped at the red and weeping raw skin beneath it. The man's lips were cracked, swollen and bleeding.

Despite his underweight battered and bruised form, Karen was certain he resembled the photo of Paul King.

Karen needed to think fast as she processed the situation. She rationalised and viewed the problem from different viewpoints, her mind racing through a number of options as she sought the agreement of different parts of her brain. Knowing that their suspect had been here just moments ago, meant that she was close by.

More importantly, Karen knew where the woman was heading.

58

With darkness falling, an urgency propelled Karen forward as she hurried along the pavement. Two thoughts crossed her mind. First, the risk they may lose Beth during the night if she returned to see the police presence outside her apartment, and secondly, was Beth really going to Tesco or was she going out to meet someone?

Using Google Maps on her phone, she located the quickest route to the Tesco Metro. It was the nearest one to Beth's apartment, so Karen had to assume she'd head towards the closest location. The sound of approaching sirens wailing in the distance reassured her that the man in Beth's flat would soon receive urgent medical care. So, for now, her focus would be on tracking down Beth.

At this time of night, the Tesco store wasn't so busy. Shoppers milled up and down the aisles picking up the essentials that they needed. Karen walked along the front of the store, glancing down each aisle. She saw a couple sharing a joke as they picked up a handful of chocolates from the confectionery aisle. Moving on to the next aisle, a solitary male pinched his chin as he stared at an array of tinned products. As each aisle passed by, her hopes of tracking down the woman faded fast as she scanned the shoppers. No one in the store matched the suspect's description.

Karen made her way to the till points and breezed past the self-service checkouts until she got to the tobacco counter. The customer in front of her was ordering twenty B&H, so she waited patiently in line. When her turn came, Karen pulled out her warrant card and several pictures of Beth, before asking the sales assistant if anyone matching her description had been in the store.

He was a small Indian man with thick-rimmed glasses and a receding hairline. His English wasn't perfect, but Karen took the gist of what he was saying. He rolled his head from side to side as he confirmed he recognised the woman in the pictures.

"She comes in a few days a week. She looked at her phone and swore before leaving her shopping on the floor there," he said, pointing at an abandoned basket near the doorway, "and rushed out of the door a few minutes ago in a hurry. She crossed over the road and went down that alleyway," he said, pointing into the darkness beyond the bright glare of the store.

Karen didn't hang around as she bolted across the road, weaving in and out of the traffic before heading down the alleyway. She barked into her radio to confirm her location before searching the doorways as she ventured further into the darkness. Her radio sprung into life as other officers confirmed that they were converging on the location. Karen's eyes searched for any sign of movement. The buildings were tight together and loomed over her like a forest of stone. When she looked up at the roofs, they were so close together that she could barely make out the darkened sky beyond. The alleyway twisted and turned back on itself, first going to the left, and then to the right. From where Karen stood, whether she looked in front or behind, she saw nothing but brickwork.

The alley became angular and straight like a drinking straw and almost as narrow. Karen dismissed the idea of waiting for reinforcements to arrive for fear that she might lose Beth altogether. She gritted her teeth and pushed on as her eyes adjusted to the blackness. A few yards further ahead the alley came to a dead end and Karen realised that she had ended up at the back of a hotel. Karen looked over her shoulder for any signs of movement. She hoped that Beth hadn't lurked in a darkened corner somewhere and slipped past her.

She walked along the back wall of the hotel and noticed one of the fire escape doors hanging open. Karen stepped up to it and glanced through the doorway at the space beyond. There was nothing there. Taking a few tentative steps inside, Karen was keen to avoid making too much noise. Metal cages full of large blue bags which contained dirty linen awaiting collection surrounded her. To her right were boxes of supplies. A row of strip lights above her cast a yellow haze above her, and red luminescent fire exit signs hung from above the doors.

"Is anyone here?" she shouted, expecting a staff member to appear from behind the cages. Silence. She continued to move through the ground floor area before arriving at an open doorway that led downstairs. The situation sent tingles spiderwebbing over her skin, but with no sign of Beth, she had to assume that the woman had followed this exact route, and for that reason needed to do the same. Taking the stairwell down to the basement, a myriad of corridors snaked left and right beneath the building. Rows of cabling and metal conduit ran the length of the walls for as far as the eye could see. These were no doubt the main service tunnels used by the maintenance team.

Karen reached for her extending baton and flicked it open with a sharp click. She balanced the tip on her shoulder ready to strike as she edged along the tunnel. The sound of generators and electrical equipment hummed in the background, and above their din, she could barely hear her own breath. She peered around corners and doorways as she moved through the space.

A searing pain hit her in the back of her neck and caused stars to explode in front of her eyes.

59

Beth didn't hold back as she attacked. She pulled out hair in handfuls, scratched, bit, kicked and headbutted Karen. A rageful scream paralysed Karen's thinking, shutting her down into the foetal position to protect her vital organs and ride out the storm.

Karen didn't have time to react when the small blade penetrated her shoulder. A searing pain erupted through her back, leaving her shocked as the assault continued. Beth screamed like a wild banshee, her lips pulled back in a snarl, spittle erupting from her mouth. She'd caught Karen unawares and exploited her vulnerability as she sat on the officer. Despite her efforts, Karen couldn't push Beth off. Panic washed through her as her body tightened, desperate to deflect the blows.

Grabbing Karen's hair again, Beth dragged her along the dimly lit corridor. Karen scratched around on the floor to steady herself, but each time she attempted to rise to her feet, Beth pulled her back down by her hair, the searing pain and heat spreading across her scalp like molten lava.

Karen took a wild sweep at Beth's feet, sending the woman crashing to the floor. But no sooner had she fallen, she sprang back on her knees clawing and grabbing at anything. Karen held on to Beth's wrist, the knife perilously close.

Beth's rage made her feral… wild… willing to do anything to win the battle. Karen tried to placate Beth whilst fighting her off, but the younger woman proved too strong and soon got the upper hand to pin Karen to the floor again. Beth made a lunge for Karen's face, Karen deflecting Beth's arm as the knife swung across her face. Karen pulled at the woman's hair to find that it came off in her hands, and once removed, revealed a bald scalp with an intricate black artwork tattoo covering most of it, which made Beth look demonic and evil. They traded blows, and as each second passed, Karen struggled to breathe. Somehow, she kicked Beth off and it was a race to see who got to their feet first. Beth had the edge, and as she attempted to flee, Karen gathered her baton from the floor and took a swing but missed.

The pain in Karen's shoulder grew, as each attempt to move felt like a hot poker in her back. As soon as all hope of being rescued faded, Beth went flying as Steve shoulder-charged her and sent her sprawling to the ground. As he scrambled over her to pin her, Beth turned on him, her fingers raking at his eyes. He screamed in pain as her nails tore down his cheeks, but he drove his elbow into the side of her face, pinning her against the floor as Karen clumsily joined in, her head spinning.

Steve wrestled the knife from her hand and threw it across the floor out of harm's way, but Beth continued her savagery as she screamed and spat at them. Karen reached for the woman's arm, and between them they flipped Beth on to her front and pinned her to the ground before placing her in handcuffs. With Karen's head pounding, and Steve's face stinging as if he had walked through a field of brambles head first, they collapsed on top of Beth, sweating and gasping for breath.

Karen composed herself before reading Beth her rights. Karen dropped on to her backside and stared at the woman's head unsure what to make of it as she heard jangling utility belts and heavy footsteps in the distance.

60

Following her arrest, they removed Beth Calladine to the nearest police station. Karen and Steve refused medical treatment to begin with, but with a small stab wound in Karen's back, Skelton ordered her to be treated in hospital where she was stitched up and released a few hours later.

With her mind buzzing, and her body charged with adrenaline, Karen found it hard to come down from the events a few hours earlier. With industrial strength painkillers, Karen returned to the office for a full debrief with her team.

Paul Banks teetered on the precipice of death, but urgent medical attention administered by paramedics and doctors at the scene had kept him alive. Suffering a multitude of injuries, dehydration and a lack of nourishment, he remained unconscious for over twenty-four hours. Once he'd opened his eyes, Karen's officers spent more than six hours getting a full statement from him. Apparently, Paul had met Beth through the online messaging and dating app, and a few weeks of exchanging dozens of messages culminated in their meeting, and his subsequent ordeal.

A detailed search of Beth's apartment revealed several mobile phones, rope and a few cans of Nitromors paint remover. A small penknife found beneath the bed and a hammer had been forensically matched to some of Paul's injuries and Beth's DNA. Officers also discovered a small motion activated CCTV camera mounted on a shelf in the bedroom. The camera had been linked to an app on Beth's phone which alerted her when the police had raided her apartment and entered the room.

The nature of the murders allowed Karen to apply for a further thirty-six-hour extension to detain Beth in custody whilst a psychiatric assessment took place to ensure her mental fitness to be interviewed. It also gave Karen the opportunity to tie in all the forensic evidence gathered. With what they had, the CPS agreed to charge Bethyan Calladine with four counts of murder and one count of false imprisonment and actual bodily harm.

At the onset of the interview, Beth remained silent, rocking back and forth. Her icy stare bored through to Karen's soul. She felt the full force of Beth's evil both during the capture and interview.

Systematically, Karen went through all the presenting evidence. A small hair fibre found on Adam Manners' bedding was a DNA match for Beth's. The short black fibres discovered on his bedding went through forensic fibre analysis. Finer than a human hair, forensic experts had used intensive microscopic methods including separation, cleaning and mounting of the fibres before undertaking a comparative analysis with clothing taken from Beth's apartment. They had carried out an analysis of the dyes and fixing agents to confirm that a black top in Beth's wardrobe was a forensic match for the fibre found on Adam's bedding.

The synthetic brown hair fibres found on Dulani Kalagho's clothing underwent the same comparative analysis and confirmed a match for a brown wig found in one drawer, the same wig she'd been wearing in the CCTV footage recovered of her with Dulani.

Karen continued to present all this information to Beth for comment, but Karen only received a grizzly, cold smile. The blonde wig that she'd worn when she'd met Harry Kruger at the Ace Hotel was discovered along with the other wigs. The knives used in the murders of Harry Kruger and Lee Barnes were discovered wrapped in some cloth and hidden inside cereal packets.

The evidence presented stared Beth in the face and couldn't be disputed or explained away. Karen felt satisfied at ending Beth's two-week trail of destruction and murder.

In the end, Beth had finally relented and explained her past and her hatred towards men. In her opinion they were nothing more than violent and cheating scum. She spoke about the mental and physical abuse that her mum had been through and what she had witnessed as a child. It became clear to Karen that the seeds of hatred were planted at a very early age, and as a defenceless child she had been unable to protect her mum from the torture she'd endured. Witnessing those childhood experiences appeared to be the turning point in Beth's life. A monster was born and her fascination with inflicting pain and death took over, consuming her.

Karen had paused the interviews to discuss the outcome of

the psychiatric evaluations. Beth displayed elements of the battered woman syndrome. And though her mother had been the victim of abuse, Beth had developed some symptoms from what she had experienced and witnessed. And as she'd grown older, the feeling of isolation, the sense of feeling embarrassed for not being stronger, and becoming emotionally withdrawn through lack of support, only reinforced her pattern of thinking.

As Beth went through life, low self-esteem and social isolation led her to use aggression to resolve the difficulties whilst her desire for power and control grew. Her views changed about gender roles. Now, she believed that men could never be in control of a relationship. And despite the psychiatrist suggesting that Beth probably had borderline personality disorder that would require further investigation, he still found her competent enough to stand trial.

61

Karen sniffed the aromatic air and let out a chuckle. Twenty-seven police officers in a curry house. It couldn't be more stereotypical even if she had invented it. With a strong case presented to the CPS, and the case file being prepared for court, Karen and the team enjoyed a celebratory meal.

Brick Lane in East London was a favoured destination for them, and the home for curries in London. The aroma of Indian spices wafted up and down the street tempting hungry diners inside. Indian restaurants sat shoulder to shoulder with vintage clothing shops, bookshops and trendy urban clothing boutiques.

As an officer in uniform, she recalled many a late night where the public order van would pull up outside the bagel bakery in Brick Lane and they would pile in to grab their famous smoked salmon and cream cheese bagels. With it being open twenty-four hours a day seven days a week, the shop bustled, but particularly at night when late-night revellers would stop off and grab a bite to eat before heading home.

The team were in full wind down mode, with loud conversations, beer and wine flowing freely, and dozens of dishes being consumed. Much to the amusement of the few other diners that had squeezed into the spare spots, the team took over the entire ground floor of the restaurant.

Karen couldn't decide whether it was the heat from the summer evening, the heat in the restaurant or the curries themselves that caused a fine sheen of sweat to break out on her forehead. But as she looked around, it appeared that most of the officers suffered as well. Never one to get drunk in front of her colleagues, Karen stuck to alternating between wine and water to pace herself. The others in the team threw caution to the wind, as empty beer bottles filled the table.

"I think we've finally found a woman that didn't fall for Steve's charms!" Brad shouted across the tables. They met his comment with a rapture of laughter.

Steve tipped his beer bottle in Brad's direction. "Thank God. I think I had a lucky escape. She was a complete psycho," he said referring to Beth. Steve tried to laugh, but winced, his face sore from the deep scratches. Once they had scabbed over, it looked as if one pissed off feral cat had scratched him instead of a deranged killer.

Karen's mind drifted back to her own struggle with Beth and resulting injury. The knife had been small and caused little damage other than a sore back and a few stitches. After the arrest she found patches of blood beneath her hair. Her scalp had been sore to touch for days after. In the hours that followed Beth's arrest, waves of emotion washed over Karen. She confessed to herself she wasn't paid enough for this bollocks but was perplexed at how someone with such extreme mental health issues had managed to go undetected by health and social services for so long.

Beth had fooled everyone. The team had tracked down her place of employment and spoken to the charity shop manager who described Beth as a quiet but a keen worker. She got on with others who volunteered and stayed friendly with most of the shop's customers. Karen wondered how Beth could have had such differing sides to her personality. A charity shop worker by day, a serial killer at night. The woman had been living in a fantasy world designed and orchestrated by herself, driven by anger, sadness and revenge.

For a change, Karen lingered at the table, in no hurry to return to the office. It approached midnight before the team fell out of the restaurant, their raucous noise turning heads. They went their separate ways before Karen caught the train back to Epping. Exhaustion slumped her shoulders, her head hurt, but the result made it worth it. The team had rallied behind her and worked their socks off. Personally, Karen knew the case had given back much of her credibility and belief in herself. It had silenced the doubters. She knew what she needed to do tomorrow morning, and her first stop before coming into the office would be paying a visit to Barbara Murphy who had avoided her calls.

But for now, her soft bed called her name.

And the rest of the world could damn well wait.

SEE NO EVIL -EXCLUSIVE EXTRACT

DI Karen Heath Crime Series Book 3

OUT NOW

If he's watching, you're already dead…

Nothing could prepare her for what she would find inside…

In the warmth of a hot summer's night, Detective Inspector Karen Heath is called to a murder scene.

In an abandoned building a woman is found murdered, bound and tortured in the most grotesque way, the victim of a twisted psychopath.

As Karen and her team set to work, they quickly realise they are on the trail of a killer who has already made their next move.

He takes Karen to the darkest places of her mind, as she delves into the killer's mind, obsessing over his twisted psychology, and finds that evil truly exists.

A day later, another victim is found dead, in exactly the same circumstances. As Karen digs deeper, she discovers a calculated serial killer – stalking their victims before choosing the right moment to strike.

As the body count rises, each victim's injuries more barbaric that the last, Karen wonders how far the killer will go to satisfy his thirst for pain.

What connects the victims?

It's now a frantic race against time to find him before he kills again.

READ AN EXCLUSIVE EXTRACT

PROLOGUE

When the warehouse loomed in front of her, the journey ended. The once proud building stood alone, dark and haunted, a crumbling shadow of its former self. A curved roof like an aircraft hangar and the brickwork, perfect beneath the dirt of years, rose upward to the sky, adding a chilling coldness to her surroundings. The building lay empty, but for a few obsolete pieces of rusted factory equipment, pieces that appeared perfectly at home within the building's vine-covered walls.

Alone in the centre, surrounded by soft shadows dancing in the candlelight like mystical ghosts, stood the woman. Her face heavily streaked with tear trails that zigzagged through her make-up. Lank, damp hair clung to her face; her eyes fixed closed but gripped in terrifying fear. Her body shivered as the cold swirled around her, beads of cold sweat glistening on her body.

She wore only white underwear, with a petite bra barely holding in her large breasts. It was one of her favourites, the one that got her the most attention, and the best tips. The bra that made her breasts look like they still belonged to a pert twenty-year-old college student, rather than a thirty-two-year-old single mother of one.

Death neared… its icy hand hovering ever so close.

Second chances didn't exist in this harsh reality. No pleas. No begging to be released.

Her fate sealed.

Barbed wire secured her to a steel column. Her hands bound behind her. The rusty metal grated against her bare back. Each movement felt like a hundred nails biting into her skin. Shock gripped her; her body unable to comprehend the pain.

"I wanted you to confess, to tell me all of the things you've done wrong. But you didn't, so now you pay the price."

More squeals of despair rattled in her throat.

He didn't care. Her captor had started and now needed to finish his task. He pulled down his hood to hide his face and began to circle her. As he disappeared behind her, she screamed, the sound lodging in her throat. The pain tore through her once again as he lashed out, the barbs cutting deeper. The dozens of cuts delivered stung beyond comprehension.

"Look at me," he whispered, his voice calm and cold.

She raised her head and looked at the hooded figure in front of her.

He held a brazing gas cylinder in one hand and a lighter in the other.

A warm trickle spread between her legs as her bladder let go. A sharp intake of breath followed as her eyes flicked between the man and what he held. Any attempt to shake her head sent further bolts of pain down her spine like surges of electricity.

The fear kicked into high gear. The primal fear all living creatures held, the fear of fire. Her mind swirled in confusion as it raced to join the dots as he lit the burner and picked up the metal rod beside him. She knew what followed and felt powerless to stop it. At first her screams had been cries for help, hoping someone would hear her. But as each minute passed, they had dissolved into unintelligible howls of torment. Adrenaline flooded her system, it thundered through her trying to escape. Her eyes remained fixed on him, wide with terror.

The candles surrounding them danced and flickered wildly as if expressing their own frenzied excitement about what the future held.

Immediate and intense, pain cascaded through her with hurricane force, like she'd never felt, like her blood simmered over an open flame. Her eyes bulged as every muscle locked rigid, her skin tearing as the barbs ripped at her flesh, blood trails snaking down her face and arms.

She tried to scream once again, but it remained trapped when it hit the obstacle in her mouth.

The smell of burning flesh lingered in the air like meat on an open fire. It sizzled and steamed as her body fell limp. In a matter of moments, it became too much for her as her body shut down, saved from witnessing the worst as she lost consciousness.

Her captor continued to circle; his soft whispers barely

audible. His face remained firmly buried in his hood as he muttered and chanted to himself, not stopping to look at the woman.

The final acts happened in silence, his work done as he watched her body slump, left hanging like a macabre work of modern abstract art.

CHAPTER 1

"In which 1986 movie starring Matthew Broderick, did the following line come from, 'Life moves pretty fast. If you don't stop and look around once in a while, you could miss it'."

"Ooh, ooh, I know this one," screamed Jade as she bounced from her seat, her arms waving frantically in the air.

Karen shook her head in disbelief as a ripple of laughter spread across the tables. She grabbed Jade's arm and yanked her back into her seat. "You really are missing the point here, Jade. It's a pub quiz, not a classroom competition. If we know the answer, we write it down on here," added Karen, waving their answer sheet in her face.

"I know, I know. I just get so bloody excited at these things."

Karen, Jade, Steve and Brad had signed up for the inter-departmental pub quiz which happened once a year. It certainly wasn't Karen's idea of fun, but it gave her and the team an opportunity to relax and have a laugh, something they didn't have much of in their jobs.

The office had pretty much taken over most of the ground floor of the pub, with a few of the regular punters propped up against the bar watching the circus being played out in front of them. Each of the small round tables dotted around them had small teams of officers gathered in mischievous huddles desperate to outdo the others.

Karen's team represented MIT. Many of the other teams included officers and staff from forensics, support services, uniform and CID. The rivalry between the teams led to slanging matches, as they deployed subversive tactics to gain the edge.

A bartender dropped off another round of drinks at Karen's table as Jade scribbled away on the answer sheet. "It's *Ferris Bueller's Day Off*."

"How did you know that?" Brad asked.

Jade's eyes widened with glee. "It's a classic. Everyone has watched *Ferris Bueller's Day Off*."

Brad sank back into his chair and pretended to occupy himself with his drink to avoid admitting he hadn't seen the film.

"Okay, pop pickers, general knowledge now," the bartender barked in the cheesiest of game show host voices. The topic met with a round of heckles and jeers. "Which Yann Martel novel won the Booker Prize in 2002?"

A sea of blank expressions filled the room as the various teams exchanged glances of consternation.

"How the fuck are we supposed to know that?" came a voice from one of the tables. "We are not literary wizards."

"Speak for yourself. You're thick as shit," shouted another officer from an adjacent table.

The banter met with roars of laughter, as loose peanuts flew through the air like tiny missiles.

"Settle down, settle down. There will be no profanity in my pub, or I kick the lot of you out," retaliated the manager with a smile.

"Anyone?" Karen asked as she scanned the faces of her team, settling on Jade.

Jade shrugged her shoulders and shook her head. "I haven't got a Scooby, and judging from the looks on the other tables, I'm not the only one."

Karen grimaced, "Bollocks."

"Next category is food," announced the bartender. "Which food product has used the slogan, 'taste the rainbow', since 1984?"

"Skittles," Steve chipped in.

"Oh, good shout."

"The final category is geography. Which river rises in the Himalayas in India and drains into the Bay of Bengal?"

Excitement bubbled in Jade as she balanced on the end of her seat and tapped her hands rapidly on the table. Karen wedged her firmly back in her seat, keen to avoid Jade blurting it out for the benefit of all who would listen to her.

"It's the Ganges," whispered Jade, getting the hint.

Karen sat back with a smile, checking her answer sheet as a waitress began to move amongst the tables to gather the responses. From the thirty questions asked this evening, they had answered twenty-seven of them, passing on only three.

"We've done well gang, thanks to Jade. You are a mine of endless knowledge," Karen said as she tapped Jade on the thigh.

One thing Karen couldn't fault in Jade was her enthusiasm, a trait she had displayed consistently in her job, and outside at events like this. Not long after working together with Jade, Karen had picked up on how clever, knowledgeable and meticulous she was. She had high hopes for Jade and without a shadow of a doubt knew her young officer would go far.

Karen had sent Steve up to the bar with twenty pounds to get another round in whilst they endured an anxious wait for fifteen minutes during the score tallying process.

"Ladies and gentlemen," the bartender wasn't letting up with his impersonations, and now sounded more like a ring-side presenter at the start of a boxing match. "The results are in. Drum roll, pleeeease."

The crowd met his delaying tactics with heckles, "Get on with it!"

"In third place are the Curry Tasters (CID), in second place are Lip Gloss United (MIT) and the comprehensive winners tonight are Stuff A Thong (Forensics)."

"Fix! Fix!" came the roar from one table which spread like a Mexican wave across all the tables.

Karen slapped her hand on the table and flopped back in

her seat. She hated losing more than anything else. And losing to their adversaries in forensics for the second year in a row, made the pill harder to swallow.

The team spent the next hour consoling themselves over their drinks and weighing up their options about leaving when the call came in about the discovery of a body in suspicious circumstances. Any thoughts of a quick exit from the pub and a quick takeaway on the way home were dashed as Karen and her team scrambled, leaving behind a cacophony of sound as the music kicked in and the poor attempts at singing began from those left behind.

SEE NO EVIL
Available now

CURRENT BOOK LIST

Hop over to my website for a current list of books:

http://jaynadal.com/current-books/

OTHER WAYS TO STAY IN TOUCH

Other ways you can connect with me:

Like my page on Facebook: Jay Nadal Author

Email jay@jaynadal.com with any questions, ideas or interesting story suggestions. Hey, even if you spot a typo that we've missed, then drop me a line!

ABOUT THE AUTHOR

I've always had a strong passion for whodunnits, crime series and books. The more I immersed myself in it, the stronger the fascination grew.

In my spare time you'll find me in the gym, reading books from authors in my genre or enjoying walks in the forest… It's amazing what you think of when you give yourself some space.

Oh, and I'm an avid people-watcher. I just love to watch the interaction between people, their mannerisms, their way of expressing their thoughts…Weird I know, but I could spend hours engrossed in it.

I hope you enjoy the stories that I craft for you.

Printed in Great Britain
by Amazon

17923171R00212